The Arrival of Fergal Flynn

The Arrival of Fergal Flynn

BRIAN KENNEDY

Hodder Headline Ireland

Copyright © 2004 Brian Kennedy

First published in 2004 by Hodder Headline Ireland
A division of Hodder Headline

The right of Brian Kennedy to be identified as the Author of the Work
has been asserted by him in accordance with the Copyright, Designs
and Patents Act 1988.

A Hodder/LIR paperback

3 5 7 9 10 8 6 4 2

A CIP catalogue record for this title is available from the British Library.

ISBN 0340 83229 0

Typeset in Plantin Light by Hodder Headline Ireland
Printed and bound in Great Britain by Clays Ltd, St Ives plc

Hodder Headline Ireland
8 Castlecourt Centre
Castleknock
Dublin 15
Ireland

A division of Hodder Headline
338 Euston Road
London NW1 3BH

1

Mr O'Connell, the permanently itchy maths teacher, normally ignored Fergal Flynn in a friendly kind of way, until that particularly hungover Monday morning in 1982. After repeated waves of nausea, dry swallows and cold sweats, the teacher realised that he'd squandered yet another weekend. A rerun of the previous few days filled his aching head on fast forward: the frantic pints of beer fuelling the Dutch courage to trawl the seediest bars in the centre of Belfast in a vain attempt to get some legless girl to sleep with him – only to be dropped like a half-finished cigarette the second he hesitated to pay for the umpteenth round of Harvey Wallbangers, while someone else poached his 'kill', as he liked to call them in the male-dominated staff room. A wave collapsed in punches at the centre of his skull like a hundred boxing gloves falling from a great height. He groaned out loud, holding the sides of his head for fear it was going to split in half.

When he finally snapped back into the reality of the fifth-year classroom, he realised he'd been staring directly at Fergal. His frustration erupted like one of the boils on his hairy back.

'For fuck's sake, Flynn. Can you not even manage to *sit* like a fella, never mind talk like one? Do you have to cross your legs like a bloody bitch in heat? Jesus, but you're some class of a sorry fucking queer handbag, so you are!'

Before Fergal had time to blink, Mr O'Connell launched the wooden-handled blackboard duster as viciously as he could and it caught its target hard across the ear. The rest of the class ducked for cover behind their filthy jotters, then exploded laughing as a little cloud of chalk dust burst on impact into the stale classroom air.

'See, even the teachers hate you, Fruity Boy Flynn,' said Frankie Burns triumphantly through tight-lipped convulsions, as factual as the schoolmaster's dull voice that tattooed Fergal's brain every day.

Home was no better. In fact, it was often worse. Fergal's reputation at school only served to cement his death sentence within his immediate family, especially his three brothers. Paddy Jr and John, the sport-obsessed twins, were seventeen – a year older than Fergal – and Ciaran was the fourteen-year-old 'baby', their da's favourite because he'd actually been planned, sort of. Conversation came to an immediate standstill if Fergal entered the tiny front parlour where the mortified twins planned their endless matches with friends. If he made the bigger mistake of hanging about the house too long, he miraculously transformed into a punching bag, and even his mother Angela turned a blind eye.

She hoped that some of her other sons' manliness might literally rub off on him if they hit him hard or long enough. Her husband always said it would.

In the Flynn household, fists were questions and bruises were answers. Fergal spent as long as he safely could away from the house, if there weren't too many riots, because he just didn't speak the language.

~

Angela had just turned nineteen when she discovered, to her horror, that her favourite skirt no longer fitted her. She was not only three months pregnant by her equally petrified twenty-two-year-old husband-to-be, Patrick Flynn, but it was twins. He was a local hurling champion and part-time barman, sinfully hand-some. When he'd asked her to come up the fields with him one Sunday afternoon she'd hardly been able to breathe, never mind refuse. She would never be allowed to forget her first time sur-rendering, deep in the damp heat of neglected grass that would one day become a housing estate, to Patrick's warm whispered reassurances that he'd pull it out in time. It was all started and over in a miracle of seconds.

When the news of her impending motherhood eventually reached Angela's father, he drank a full bottle of rum that had been in the back of the cupboard for about fifteen years and went looking for the culprit with a wrench. He found Paddy behind a tyre factory drinking bottles of stolen vodka with his mates, who ran at the sight of the old man swinging the rusty tool. The future father- and son-in-law rolled around on the waste ground trying to kill each other for the guts of an hour, with an audience of about thirty neighbours, until an army patrol unit appeared and they had to break it up. Angela married Paddy so quickly that her home-made dress was still being altered right up until the morning she left her parents' house for the wedding. Her sister Concepta stood in front of her, repeatedly pinning her hair into submission to distract her from the fact that their father couldn't look at her. They ignored the neighbours' net curtains that rippled with disapproval as they got into the car (borrowed from a friend whose daughter had been in a similar predicament). All Angela's mother Noreen would say over a tight grip on her rosary beads was, 'Youse have already laid in your bed, so youse'd better make the best of it!'

The newlyweds left the chapel under a man-made arch of hurling sticks held aloft by Patrick's team-mates. A sudden starving flock of pigeons dropped from the window ledges, diving on the uncooked rice that a few brave well-wishers threw even though the church forbade it on a huge sign in hand-painted black letters. Most of the pigeons landed on the groom, trying to get at the flecks of perfect white rice lodged in his raven hair. The shoulders and lapels of Patrick Flynn's immaculate black morning suit were instantly destroyed by squirt after panicked squirt of slimy white pigeon shit, amid disgusted groans and howls from his mates. He'd only hired the suit the day before, under pressure from his mother.

He grabbed one of the hurling sticks and swiped at the ravenous darting beaks, roaring. 'Cunting rats with wings! Nobody shites on Paddy Flynn and gets away with it! Especially not on his fucking wedding day!'

The parish priest went purple in the face and made the sign of the cross over and over again. Angela burst into tears. Her mother's oldest friend finally calmed her down. 'Shite is good luck, love – whether it's from an oul' pigeon's arse or not! Don't you be crying on your wedding day, there's time enough for tears.'

Paddy carried his ruined, rented jacket over his arm in the rain to the strained reception a few hundred yards away in the Bee-hive pub, and drank until he couldn't stand up.

~

No one had ever told Angela how a child was born. When her time came, the pain was so bad that she prayed and screamed for Jesus to forgive her sins with every unbearable contraction. She thought that maybe the babies would rip out through her belly button, but she was too scared and too embarrassed to ask the midwife a single question. The labour lasted for thirty-two agonis-ing hours. When nature did eventually take its course, she almost died from the shock of how the babies were delivered. While she lay in the city hospital with a fever, her husband was well into what would become a lifetime commitment to alcohol, hurling and hollow talk.

Soon after the birth of Paddy Jr and John, an old spinster woman died in Walker Street, not too far from Angela's parents' house, where the newly wed and the newly born had no choice but to start their family life in the confines of the postage-stamp-sized back bedroom. Angela and Paddy waited till it was dark and carried what little they had into the tiny two-bedroom house that time, but not colonies of insects, had forgotten. They changed the locks and took over the rent book after a tricky bit of negotiation with the head priest – the bishop happened to have 'inherited' the entire street. Angela's father refused to visit because he wanted to hit Paddy Flynn every time he clapped eyes on his smirking face.

Apart from the fact that they were God-fearing Catholics, Angela couldn't even spell contraception, never mind get hold of it. When the howling twins were only six months old, she broke down, behind a mountain of damp home-made nappies, when her period refused to come and the morning sickness did. She wasn't even twenty-one when every drop of blood drained from her husband's face as she nervously told him he was going to be a father again. The news was more than her own ailing father could take. Coupled with the cancer that had been sworn to secrecy in his lungs for a good few years, he was dead before he could see his namesake's head being dampened in St Bridget's baptismal font.

Now that her beloved daddy was gone and she was about to have three babies under the age of two, Angela fell into a downward spiral of depression. Her husband flew into a violent rage, calling her a 'moody oul' bitch', if his clothes weren't laundered to perfection or his dinner wasn't steaming on the table when he came in from work. It was worse if his team lost. Patrick had been spoilt rotten by his own adoring mother, who'd opposed the wedding from the start and had gone so far as to suggest that the pregnancy was not her innocent angel's doing. The moment the twins were born, though, their strong features were clearly straight out of the Flynn gene pool and that had put a lid on that argument.

The night Fergal first opened his eyes, there had been a riot at the bottom of their road. Not far away, a few Catholic families were living right beside a predominantly Protestant area. Most of the neighbours were friends, but that didn't stop gangs of masked men torching the houses of the Catholics, whether they were inside or not. Everyone was terrified they were going to be burnt to death, but the Flynns' little house was temporarily safe – an overturned bus had smouldered on the avenue for two whole days making it impossible to pass. Paddy was watching the news, with the volume down low, as Angela got the twins to settle. Every available space in the wee house was covered in miniature clothes that she was trying to dry in an endless rotation of laundry.

She was about to hand her husband a dutiful cup of tea – even though, yet again, he wasn't speaking to her – when it crashed to the tiles. He threw her a menacing look, but she grabbed her swollen belly as her waters broke all over the floor, along with the china, two full weeks before she thought they would. Paddy Flynn bolted out of the house in a panic to get her mother and Concepta, the only one of her sisters who hadn't yet escaped to England. When they arrived Angela was in the wee back room, in the throes of birthing Fergal. Anyway, the riot meant they couldn't have gone to the hospital even if there'd been time.

Angela was terrified that she would wake the twins, so as the contractions increased and the pain stabbed her repeatedly, she stretched her mouth as wide as it would go in a muted mime of agony. Noreen and Concepta screamed that she should push and shout for all she was fucking worth. They crowded into the tiny, bare-bulbed room, voices pleading, as Fergal prepared to enter the world.

'C'mon, our Angela. C'mon, love, push! You know you can do it! You did it before, love, and you can do it again. Thank God it's only one this time! Jesus, will you not cry out, Angela? God, let's hope it's a girl and not another one of them smelly lazy fucking boys.'

Secretly, Angela wanted a girl too, but the pain was so bad she felt like she was having an elephant. She just wanted it out of her, no matter what kind it was. They pleaded over and over for her to at least answer them, but the only evidence of the torturous miracle taking place was the thick stream of tears that soaked the top of her nightdress and blurred her vision. She was staring at a fixed point on the wall. Her father's younger, kinder face, smiling and proud from behind glass in a framed photograph as he held her hand on the day she'd made her First Holy Communion, before she'd disgraced the family.

The local midwife arrived just as Angela's third son was almost out. He began testing his lungs after a slap and the proclamation, 'It's a wee boy, Mrs Flynn.' Noreen and Concepta looked at each other and said 'Fuck' in disappointed unison.

As the shock began to evaporate, Angela looked at her newborn's face and then again at her framed father. Finally she spoke. 'I want to call him Fergal, after Daddy.'

She knew her husband would resent it, but she was past caring.

2

From the moment they could walk, the Flynn twins had been like little celebrities, stared at by everybody. They ran rings around anybody who dared to challenge them, on or off the football pitch. Everybody wanted to be on their team if a game started because they were scarily competitive and stopped at nothing to win. Paddy was the brains of the outfit and John, with his easily ignited temper, was definitely the brawn. Sometimes Fergal felt dizzy just looking at them. He felt like he was their exact opposite – he was tall and a bit gangly, while they were sharp-featured, naturally strong and thickset – and he couldn't help feeling outnumbered by the simple fact that there were two of them and only one of him.

The twins were brought to the hurling matches with Paddy if they were good, and they fought for their father's attention, which he loved. As soon as they were old enough, he taught them how to head-butt. Fergal was instantly afraid of his father and he cried every time Paddy went near him.

'Jesus, Angela. Are you sure he's a fucking boy? Can you not keep him from yapping? Just like that fucking no-good father of yours – he was well named after that oul' bastard.'

He knew exactly how to hurt her, and every time he said Fergal's name it sounded like he had a bad taste in his mouth. Angela was as protective of Fergal as she could be, but the twins were constantly demanding, and when Ciaran came along she began to rely more and more on the little white pills for depression that the doctor handed out like sweets, without even looking at her. She never got a chance to tell him how sad and angry and tired she felt at the same time, all the time.

Paddy went from job to job. He was hot-tempered and unemployment for Catholic men was at an all-time high. There were long periods when Angela had to quietly keep the house afloat financially. She took in washing from the wealthier areas and stitched together a variety of cheap dolls outfits by hand for a greasy one-eyed man who ran a busy stall on the market. Their tiny house looked more like a sweatshop with neatly piled stacks of little unfinished fairy costumes here and material for petite nurses uniforms there. Cyclops, as Paddy referred to him, called once a week with her cash wages and another load of miniature clothes parts for his patient, identical, plastic princesses-to-be.

Fergal grew into a soft-featured little fella with a cowlick that made him look like the front of his hair had been in a roller all night. When he was with Angela in the family-allowance queue at the post office, it wasn't uncommon for someone to ask how old her little girl was. In the morning, he often woke up crying and in a panic, thinking he'd gone blind, because his long eye-lashes had managed to glue themselves shut overnight. Angela would curse him to hell and threaten to cut them off with her sewing scissors – giving him nightmares – as she'd have to stop in the middle of twenty different things to warm the kettle, dip the corner of a flannel into the hot water and dab his eyes till the gunk was dislodged and he could see again. His chest was deli-cate too and in the days of experimental medication for asthma he was regularly off school with a chest infection, which the damp, dusty house didn't cure. Sometimes he helped his mother fold the mountains of ironing she took in.

One such morning, when the twins had gone to school, Ciaran was asleep in her bed and Fergal was wheezing on the sofa, Angela was ironing a beautiful pink nightdress for a girl about the same age as Fergal. She'd had a particularly nasty fight with her husband that morning. He wanted to go to Donegal on a weekend hurling trip and insisted he couldn't bring her or any of the kids, but she knew for a fact that some of the other wives were going. She knew she couldn't go anyway – they couldn't afford it and no one would be able to mind her brood – she'd just wanted to be asked. On top of all that, it was her twenty-eighth birthday, and he'd forgotten. She felt like an old woman.

Two Valiums later, though, things were looking up. As she smoothed the little cotton nightdress, she remembered the time when it would have fitted her own body, when she had been just somebody's daughter and nobody's wife or mother. She held it up against her own adult body, whose shape the babies had changed forever, and tried to do a little spin, but there wasn't enough room. She said to Fergal's sleepy head, 'We thought you were going to be a girl, you know. I even had a few wee bits put aside – but, sure, then I had to give them away to Mrs Carson, who ended up having five girls and no boys. Jesus, I don't know which is worse – imagine having to pay for all them weddings.'

Fergal was six years old and, although he hated not being able to breathe properly, he loved curling up on the settee in his under-wear beneath a wee blanket, away from school and his brothers and his da. He had been drifting in and out of sleep. The doctor had given him a large measure from a bottle of cough mixture which was so strong that alcoholics got it on prescription if they couldn't afford vodka that week, and lay around in the fields, comotosed from drinking too much of it. Angela looked over at the back of his head, and again at the dress. Then she remembered the picture of her with her father after her First Holy Communion.

It was as if someone else was controlling her movements. She picked up the freshly ironed nightdress and knelt down beside her sleeping son. She looked at his wavy hair and imagined it was longer. Then she sat him up and, with one movement, pulled the dress over his drowsy head. Fergal was more awake now, but even at such an early age something told him not to say any-thing. The fresh, crisp cotton felt soft and clean against his skin, and it fitted him perfectly. Angela stood him up and smoothed out the creases, then took the hairbrush from the mantelpiece. She began brushing his thick hair like a doll's, humming 'Happy Birthday' to herself, a huge smile radiating from her face.

Then, gradually, she began to cry, and the brush strokes got harder and harder until Fergal cried out and pulled away. Sud-denly embarrassed, Angela dried her eyes on her sleeve and she asked him to walk up and down the room to see if she'd ironed the nightdress right. Just at that moment, Ciaran woke up and began roaring for her upstairs. She pulled the nightdress off Fergal so roughly that it ripped under the arm. She hissed frantically that she would lose her job because of him if he couldn't stay still and that he wasn't to tell anyone what had happened.

Fergal, climbing back under the relative safety of his blanket, was confused and frightened. He had thought he was helping her, but now she was saying he could get her the sack. As he drifted back into cough-mixture sleep, his panic was slowly replaced by the comforting realisation that he and his ma had a secret. It was the first time he'd ever felt important.

Right up until he was ten, Fergal would be kept off school at a moment's notice to 'see if I've ironed this wee dress properly'. One such day, a friend of Angela's had dropped off a Confirmation dress that needed to be taken up at the hem as her youngest daughter wasn't quite as tall as the rest had been. When Angela unwrapped the treasure from its brown-paper embrace, her eyes lit up.

She took an extra pill with the end of her tea and stood Fergal on the little coffee table in his underwear. She asked him to raise his hands to heaven, pulled the snow-white satin down over his pale body in one careful movement and shook out the bottom of the dress. When she stood up to get a better look, she gasped and put her hand over her mouth.

Fergal was instantly worried. 'What, Mammy? What's wrong? I didn't tear it – I didn't...'

Angela couldn't really hear him. The Valium had begun its numbing journey in her bloodstream and she was convinced that her longed-for daughter stood in front of her, getting ready for her Confirmation. She went around behind Fergal, smoothing any crease that dared ruin the calm surface of the pearl satin fantasy, and saw that the zip was still undone. Fergal tried to stand still as she coaxed the fragile zip upwards and the table wobbled in protest, but he couldn't help fidgeting.

'Hold still, love, for fuck's sake… You want to look nice for your big day, don't you?'

'What? What big day?' Had she really called him 'love'?

Angela didn't answer him. She was busy trying to get the zip to go past Fergal's shoulders, which had broadened just enough to make it impossible. She held her breath in concentrated silence for what seemed like an eternity before finally exhaling loudly and cursing in defeat. 'Fucking, fucking… *no*! Fuck!'

She sat down on the arm of the settee, suddenly exhausted. The angry sentence escaped out of her mouth before she knew it, 'Why couldn't you have been a girl? You were meant to be a bloody girl!'

Fergal froze. He wanted to rip the dress off in a fit of anger but, when he saw his mother's face, he could only step carefully down onto the living-room floor and stand there, not knowing what to do. The words 'You were meant to be a girl' echoed in circles above his head. He caught sight of himself in the mirror above the fireplace, squeezed into the miniature wedding dress, and felt a hundred times stupider.

'Mammy, I'm taking it off now, OK? Can I? Please? I'm roasting, and I don't want to wear it any more. I'm not… I'm not a girl.'

Angela looked at the dress that would never fit her son, and crowds of tears gathered at the corners of her eyes.

'I'm sorry, Mammy – I'm sorry…' Fergal didn't know what to say, he hated to see her cry.

Suddenly she stopped. 'I'll finish the job on my own,' she said.

Angela thought their secret was intact until Ciaran announced casually at dinner one day, 'Mammy puts dresses on our Fergal, Daddy.'

All hell broke loose. Angela screamed her denial and locked herself in the bathroom, but it was too late. Paddy broke up half the kitchen. It was weeks before they were on speaking terms again.

~

Fergal tried his best to get on with his brothers, but he was useless at sport – Ciaran could kick a ball straighter than him before he could even walk properly – and his brothers and father were scathing about it. One day a few girls from the top of the street asked him to join them in a skipping game. After a few days he started to get the hang of it, but John, always the slyer of the twins, told their da. The moment Fergal came in, he was thrown against the wall in the living room. His da held him by the hair and warned him that he'd fucking kill him if he ever saw him playing with girls again.

'It's all your fucking fault, Angela. Why the fuck would any boy want to *skip*? What is he, a fucking kangaroo?'

Fergal couldn't understand. He thought the girls were brilliant. They were kind to him, and funny, and really good spellers too and he loved that. He knew he was different, but he also knew better than to answer his da back.

He passed his eleven-plus exam, which meant he could go to the grammar school up the road, but the fees were too much. So that was the end of that. When September came he dreaded the short walk to his new school. The first thing he saw in the unfamiliar playground was a whirlpool of boys swarming in a circle of charcoal-grey nylon, shouting and swearing. He got sucked into the churning current of uniforms and suddenly found himself looking under someone's bent arm at two older boys fighting on the ground. The taller boy held the other down by the hair and was kicking him repeatedly, sickening dull blows to the face from his new Oxford brogues with steel tips. Then someone shouted that a teacher was coming. The boys untangled themselves from the murdered moment and Fergal, frozen to the spot, was left staring down at a pool of thick raspberry blood on the grey concrete, like a moat surrounding three broken white teeth. The teacher took the dazed, toothless boy off to the hospital to have his jaw wired, just as the bell rang for the first assembly on the first day of Fergal's six-year sentence at St Bridget's Secondary School for Boys.

It took a while for him to recognise some of the other pupils from St Bridget's Primary School because they looked so clean in their new, freshly ironed uniforms. Within seconds everyone seemed to have chosen their own wee gang of friends. Fergal knew a few of the fellas to say hello to, but that was all. When he did eventually coast the conversations bubbling away in the playground, he hadn't a clue what or who most of them were about – it was almost always football, and they were merciless if you didn't know all of the up-to-the-minute details. Paddy Jr and John were in the year above him at St Bridget's, winning every sporting award that could be won. Fergal knew he would have been beaten up a lot more if he hadn't been related to them, so he was as grateful as he could be for that.

Fergal was bright and he listened, so at least he got on all right with most of the teachers. His favourite lesson was the music class – if it could be called that. The hard fellas all sat at the back of the class, flicking phlegm and doing homework for any teachers they were really afraid of, while he and the other geeks sat at the front because those were the only seats free. They listened as their teacher, Baldy Turner, alternated between telling them about his musical childhood – the joy of piano lessons with his granny, the way he'd practised for up to four hours a day until even his fingers felt like crying – and describing his 'wild years' at college in a desperate attempt to keep their attention and earn cool points.

As soon as puberty started knocking, Fergal had to find a way to stop doing PE. Any time he went near the changing room – or, worse yet, the showers – the increasingly unpredictable muscle between his legs began to thicken and lengthen without his permission at the slightest sight of someone else's pubes or penis or the manly beginnings of a hairy stomach or chest. He tried his best not to look too interested as his classmates nonchalantly stripped off and went after each other in the nude, flicking rolled-up towels. Fergal envied how confident and sure of their own bodies they were. He thought he would burst as they crowded the lukewarm showers and scrubbed themselves, stopping only to throw soapsuds at each other, and then dried themselves all over, talking away about this or that girl who they were on a promise with.

He wondered what it would be like to have a girlfriend and go on dates. He knew girls were great company and tried to imagine what it would be like if one of them was standing in the shower. Maybe he would fancy her if she was in the nude? But, somewhere in a little locked room in his heart, he knew the answer was written on a rolled-up piece of paper in a tiny drawer, waiting to be opened someday – and he knew it was *No*. The thought filled him with dread. He didn't want to fancy his classmates. It wasn't normal. He wanted to be normal and fancy girls, didn't he?

Fergal couldn't even stand up in the shower room until the last lad was out the door, lest his erection give him away. He wished he could stop it happening, but it was beyond his control, like his asthma. He was convinced that all his classmates knew what was going on, and he was terrified that the twins would somehow find out. So, every week, he convinced his mother to give him a note asking for him to be excused from Physical Education because of his asthma. He ended up writing the notes for her, anyway – she'd never really been able to write that well.

The PE teacher was a big burly man from the country called Mr McGann and he loathed anyone who he thought wasn't trying. When he'd first learned that Fergal was the son of the famous Patrick Flynn, and indeed the brother of Paddy Jr and John, he had got very excited about having another fledging champion under his wing but, much to his disappointment and disgust, he had soon learned that Fergal was anything but. When Fergal repeatedly showed up without his PE kit, Mr McGann made him carry all the revolting unwashed kits around the playing fields in the lashing rain or write stupid essays about being a football shoe.

In his final year, Fergal successfully argued that, because there was no exam to be done in PE, he ought to use that period to study for his O-levels. If any of his class hadn't completely hated him before, they certainly did now. While they marched off to the playing fields, he'd sit by himself in any available empty classroom either doing that night's homework or reading the growing number of notes he found in his bag, informing him of which teacher's dick he was sucking or which one was fucking him up the arse that week – or, just to contradict popular opinion, how many times a day he was breastfeeding from the ugliest mother they could think of.

The instant the half-past-three bell rang, most of the pupils bolted out of the school like junkies in search of a fix, heading home to their football-poster-encrusted bedrooms to further obsess about the details of the coming matches. Getting home wasn't so easy for Fergal. If one of the hard men had had a particularly tough time from one of the teachers, it was only a matter of time before someone lower down the food chain would end up winded by a boot in the back or hit by a handful of razor-sharp graveyard stones up the side of the head. Sometimes Fergal was lucky enough to escape with just a bog-standard punching until they got bored and tipped his schoolbag into somebody's garden, preferably one patrolled by a crazed Doberman.

Then he had to be at the ready when he walked in the front door of his house. If both parents were out, he was fair game to the twins. If both parents were in, it could be a different kind of danger. Whenever he got the chance, Fergal barricaded himself – under the excuse of studying for exams – into the upstairs front bedroom that Paddy Flynn had partitioned into two box rooms. The twins shared one and Fergal now shared the other with Ciaran – a deep sleeper from birth, who was relaxed to the point of profound laziness. Most mornings, Angela still carried him downstairs and let him lie outstretched in front of the fire for a while, before dressing him in his school uniform as he stood yawning and drooping like a scarecrow. If she'd offered to carry him to school too he would have let her. He and Fergal didn't fight, but Ciaran mainly followed other people's example. He knew he was their father's favourite and had inherited his appetite for sport, so there was no chance of him and Fergal ever being close.

Meanwhile, at the top of the street, the twins retained their imaginary world titles in every competitive sport ever invented – handball, cribby and, inevitably, football. Regardless of the political climate, the players every local boy impersonated as they scored their classic goals were usually from Manchester or Liverpool, and the top of the street, where the factory wall made a kind of cul-de-sac, was always referred to as 'Old Trafford'. Fergal knew he would be asking for trouble if he tried to find out what Old Trafford actually was. He thought it might be a horse.

Fergal's mother came to the rescue at all the wrong moments. She even went up to the school, accompanied by her impossibly bosomy sister Concepta for support, to complain about the repeated ripping of Fergal's good school blazer that was still only half paid for – not to mention the regular insertion of chewing gum into his 'lovely hair' that she'd had to perform surgery on with blunt scissors that left him looking like he'd caught his head in a lawnmower. Of course, this only increased the attacks. The twins turned on their heels if they saw Fergal coming along the corridor, usually accompanied by an angry crowd of insults ranging from 'no dick' and 'gee-head' through to 'fruity boy', 'blouse' and 'you fucking girl', as if a girl was the worst thing you could be and deserving of every conceivable punishment. On the rare occasions when the twins did actually speak to him directly, it was only to deliver a warning, through clenched teeth, that he hadn't seen them smoking on the way home.

Fergal fantasised about telling his ma lies about the twins, just to see how they would like it. But he knew it would turn out to be more trouble for him in the end, so he settled for just thinking about it. He also imagined gluing together the lips of the people who shouted insults at him – maybe while they were asleep or something… It made him smile, for a while anyway.

He wondered what his life would be like if he didn't have asthma. Would he be more like his sporty brothers? Would they all be great friends and do everything together? Would he finally understand what they were talking about when they shouted at the matches on TV? Maybe his da would even like him and talk to him… But, at the same time, the thought of spending more time with his father and brothers made him shudder. Deep down, he didn't want to be anything like any of them.

3

The hunger strikes in the Maze Prison were the scariest thing Fergal had ever witnessed. They were constantly on the news. Aerial footage of H-shaped cell blocks and then the insides of the shit-smeared cells being steam-cleaned by men in space suits while the naked, skeletal prisoners wrapped in blankets stared motionless, hopeless and vacant into the camera. Fergal thought they looked like archaeological finds, perfectly preserved famine victims from centuries before.

Paddy Flynn covered everything he ate in HP Brown Sauce. He would sit in front of the TV, staring at the images of the dirty protest and mopping up the last of the discoloured grease on his dinner plate with a bit of fried bread. Nobody seemed to notice that the HP stood for 'Houses of Parliament', or that there was a picture of the British government buildings on the front of the bottle.

Regardless of the time of day, whenever the news came that a young man had starved himself to death and drawn his final breath, everyone took to the streets. On their hands and knees, they repeatedly banged the lids of their bins, or of the biggest pots they had, off the middle of the road until it was morning. Army helicopters scraped the sky in response and then hovered as low as they could get, making the air tremble with each push of their blades. They aimed blinding spotlights over the terrified streets and for an insane second the circles of light made Fergal, shivering in the street in his old pyjama bottoms and a vest that was getting too small for him, think of an old Hollywood block-buster he'd seen on Granny Noreen's black-and-white TV.

It wasn't long before the cold night air forced him awake prop-erly. Nothing could drown out the desperate Morse Code of the bin lids, calling to the world for help. Petrified kids wailed them-selves hoarse as the older people chanted rosary after pointless rosary into the hopeless, soaking, percussive darkness. Fergal suddenly knew what Hell sounded like. He heard his da talking to other men about the Civil War and concentration camps, the more religious of the pensioners talked about the end of the world. They stayed there, waiting, until, one by one, the bin lids stopped and they could go back to bed. The lights had to be left on all night in the living room of every house and the fires were kept going.

Angela was out of her wits with fear that her husband would get arrested himself, or killed, at any second. The Flynns were far from political – it was sport that really got Paddy Sr fired up – but he agreed to join a few of the other husbands on a night watch to patrol the area. There were countless stories of soldiers and 'snatch squads' kidnapping men and boys over yard walls during the night – or, in some cases, in broad daylight – to kill them, or at the very least inflict serious damage. So every once in a while one of the local men could be seen walking the length of the yard wall behind the terraced houses with a hurling stick, to see what or who was coming. There seemed to be a funeral every week, and with it usually came more trouble, more deaths and more funerals, in an endless cycle of misery.

When the first anniversary of Bobby Sands' death came, there was the riot of all riots. It lasted for days. No one could go out, no milk was delivered. The guns and bombs and sirens sounded like they were in the next room. The Flynns heard about people they knew who'd been shot dead – one of the neighbours' sons had been brain damaged by a plastic bullet to the head. Their house was raided, along with the whole street, and the army's mucky boots ruined the stair carpet while Angela screamed at them to get the fuck out. Paddy said nothing. He knew he was a heartbeat away from being arrested and beaten to a pulp if they felt like it, and he'd just managed to get a new job with the civil service. Once the front door was locked again, no one dared go out of it. It was the first time Fergal had felt safer in the house than out.

The next morning, when the milk was unexpectedly delivered, Fergal negotiated the minefield of bricks, broken glass and tyres along the back streets of West Belfast on his way to school. It was impossible to avoid the soldiers and their *Coronation Street* barks. They'd blow 'is fucking 'ead off. Where was 'e going? When was 'e coming back? Fergal answered in Irish first, for a bit of practice, but one of them jammed his rifle right against Fergal's balls and told him it would be a pity if it went off, 'by accident, like'. That kind of accident wasn't exactly uncommon and Fergal blurted out too fast, in English, that he was on his way to mass and then to school. *Why else would I be wearing this stupid fucking uniform?* he thought.

The soldiers' camouflage made them stand out like fridges in the desert. Why they never thought to wear dirty, brick-coloured clothes, with the odd bit of badly spelled graffiti across the chest and back, was a mystery. They would have made much less prominent targets for dog shite. Discarded nappies were another great form of ammunition, if you could wrestle the prize away from the feasting mutt who'd just claimed it from the pram of a particularly well-fed child or from next door's bin – seeing as the lids were usually missing.

~

St Bridget's Parish Church was quiet just after eight o'clock every weekday morning – most of the insomniac pensioners went to the seven o'clock mass and the next one wasn't until nine. Fergal had started going to church with Angela's mother, his Granny Noreen. He'd stayed the odd weekend at Noreen's because of the rioting and had begun to accompany her to mass a few times a week on his way to school. She'd started to find it difficult to walk, so he'd link her arm and they'd move at a snail's pace. Inevitably she met about a thousand people she wanted to talk to, and Fergal would make it to school just in time. Gradually she found it harder and harder to leave the house, whether there was 'trouble' or not, and Fergal found that he missed the little ritual, so he went on his own.

He'd become fascinated with the entire building. There wasn't another one like it on the road. It was so clean for a start. The thick, graffiti-free walls were made from enormous blocks of precisely cut stone, and you had to crane your neck to see the weathered green crucifix perched at the very top of the single steeple, high above the neatly slated roof that the parishioners were still paying for. Above the entrance there was a huge, circular stained-glass window that had been perforated by the stray bullets of a riot, but the damage was too high up to show. The church had managed a strange balance of strength and fragility. Fergal thought it looked like it had dropped out of the sky, like Dorothy's house in *The Wizard of Oz*. It was surrounded by identical, tiny, red-brick terraced houses, huddled together like they were queuing up to sign on the dole. The moment he was inside and the big wooden doors shut behind him, peace fell like an invisible command. It was as if someone had unplugged the rest of the world – except for the little squad of mantilla-clad widows polishing and tidying everything in their path, stopping only to genuflect arthritically towards the altar if they had to turn away to dust a clay saint or a difficult-to-reach wooden crucifix. Fergal sat in the middle row, clamped like a limpet to an ancient radiator – on Sundays it was hogged by the quickest of the pensioners who couldn't afford to heat their own houses.

The newly lit candles gossiped amongst themselves, and there was a faint smell of incense and brass polish lingering in the cloisters. Fergal loved the wordless calm. He sat there studying each religious depiction with his hands interlocked as if he was praying, just in case he was suddenly challenged. He thought that if he sat still for long enough, he would be buffed to a spit-shine by one of the widows, who always vanished as silently as they arrived.

All too soon, the clock above the entrance sounded half past eight. It was time for Fergal to leave, for his final year of school.

4

Paddy Flynn was in training for the Silent Olympics. The only thing that broke this strict regime was whiskey, which translated itself into swift and vicious blows to any part of anybody that was in his way.

He was unusual in that he'd been the elder of only two children – most families had a minimum of four – and the sole surviving child of Ernest and Ethel Flynn. His sister had suffered a cot death within a week of coming home from the hospital. His mother had blamed herself and had never really got over it.

Ethel and Ernest had met at a dance hall when he was on leave from the army. She was seventeen and he was almost thirty – he knew she was the one before they even spoke, and she thought he looked like Clark Gable. Their romance was instant. When he went back to the war she discovered, like so many of her generation, that she was pregnant, but she was luckier than most. Ernest was old-fashioned enough to do what was considered the right thing. They were married in England within the month, just after she'd turned eighteen and she suddenly found herself an army wife, away from home, living in unfamiliar barracks in East Anglia. When their whopping ten-pound boy arrived on 17 March, toasted by copious pints of Guinness in the officers' club, what could they call him only Patrick?

The marriage went well for the first few years, but when the little one died and Ernest was away more and more, Ethel started to miss her family in Belfast. As Patrick got closer to school age, they decided it would be best if she returned home on her own to bring him up there. For the first ten or eleven years of his life, Patrick rarely saw his father and when Corporal Ernest Flynn eventually moved back to live with them, he brought with him stiff army distance and severe beatings for the smallest mistake.

Patrick tried throughout his childhood to crack the code and find the secret that would bring him the approval he so desperately craved. He threw himself into competitive sport but, no matter how many cups and medals he brought home, his father had always witnessed someone better in the army. Then he'd rant on about the front line, and anyone who dared interrupt him – including Ethel – would get a swift kick and, if they argued, a vicious beating. His attempts to assert his masculinity knocked the love and spirit right out of Ethel, and she transferred all of her hopes and dreams to her big strong son. Patrick grew taller than his father by the time he was fourteen. He developed a habit of hitting his mother, too. Though he was always sorry for it and she always forgave him, saying she'd driven him to it.

Ernest died of bowel cancer – that he'd kept hidden even from Ethel – just before Patrick turned seventeen. The other surprise was that he'd managed to gamble away all of his army pension. At the wake, some old army companion harped on about what a hero Ernest had been until Ethel leaned in and slapped her husband's dead face in front of the whole room.

~

One day, when Angela asked Fergal to put some boxes in the attic, he stumbled across an old bag that held all kinds of trophies – from big silver cups to medals hanging from little hooks on carved wooden plaques. When he had a closer look at the engraved details, he discovered that they were all his father's. When he asked his mother about them, she said they'd been there since they'd moved in – but suddenly she started talking about her husband with a completely new expression on her face. She played with her hair and told Fergal how, when she'd first seen his father at the bus stop, carrying his hurling shoes over the flat end of his stick, she'd thought he was the handsomest fella she'd ever seen. 'He was whistling and looking up at the sky, and I knew I was in trouble right then and there.'

'Why? What happened next, Mammy?'

She told him how they'd talked, in a shy kind of way, and how Paddy had invited her to see him play in the Falls Park the next week. 'He was the best player this place has ever seen, I'll tell you that for nothing. He even won a gold medal, Fergal – and he gave it to me on a chain.'

She rummaged under the neck of her jumper and pulled out the gold medal on its little chain, tangled round a tiny crucifix that her father had given her. She rubbed it to see if it would shine as she told Fergal that there had even been a few talent scouts sent to see Paddy Flynn play, but that his temper had been the undoing of him. He was sent off for fist-fighting with the referee time and time again. Even some of his team-mates called him 'Fisty Flynn'.

'Anyway,' Angela said, as she pushed the necklace and the memory back under the neck of her jumper, 'that was all a very long time ago, and he hates to talk about it, so never bring it up if you know what's good for you.'

The next time Fergal was off school with yet another chest infection and had the place to himself, he went up to the attic and hauled the bag of trophies down into the kitchen for a closer look. Most of them were so dirty that he couldn't read the engraving, so he decided to polish them with the cleanest cloth he could find. They sparkled in appreciation. Fergal was amazed that they had been relegated to a bin bag in the dusty attic. He knew only too well that his mother often exaggerated – surely, he thought, his da didn't hate being reminded of his hurling past as much as she made out. He was always bringing the twins to matches and fixing their hurling sticks.

Fergal decided that, seeing as he'd gone to the trouble of cleaning the trophies, he might as well display them. Things had been particularly tense between him and his father recently and somewhere at the back of his head, Fergal hoped that his da might appreciate his efforts and see that he was proud of him. So, one by one, he set out the medals and trophies in every available space in the tiny living room, until every last one was displayed.

As he was admiring the effect, the twins came in and stopped dead in shock. In unison they said, 'Who the fuck owns them?'

'Da does,' said Fergal.

Angela was behind them, with bags of shopping, and when she saw what Fergal had been up to she went mad. 'So this is what you've been doing while you're supposed to be fucking sick? Are you out of your mind? Your da will kill you when he sees… sees… fucking Aladdin's cave!' The twins roared laughing.

Fergal didn't know where to look. She made him take every last one down and put them back in the attic, and told him he was 'fucking in for it' when his da got home. And the twins slapped the head off him when she wasn't looking.

Angela had become just as unpredictable as Paddy. She would go up to the school to give out about some injury done to Fergal – but then, when they got back home, she would suddenly beat him till he bled, with the hose or the tongs of the twin-tub washing machine, for making her lose a morning's wages. Then she would beat him again, for hurting her hand.

The waiting was the worst part of all. When Paddy came home and found his wife hysterical, he would have no need to ask who had caused it. Fergal knew he would be kicked and punched like a stray dog, until Angela turned on her husband, shouting that she didn't want to have to take Fergal to the hospital and have those nosy fucking childless social workers coming out with their notepads, telling her how to bring up four kids with no money in the middle of a war. They'd have a fight, and Paddy would storm off to the bar like a silent hurricane.

Fergal ran out the back door. As usual, the only place he could think of to go was his Granny Noreen's. One of her neighbours was gossiping with her when he burst in the door, so he ran through the house to the outside toilet to calm down and clean away the tears that had made his face filthy. Then he reappeared and offered to make them tea.

When he and Noreen were on their own, she asked him what happened and cursed the day her Angela had met his da. Fergal knew from his mother, though, that Noreen had been vicious enough when she'd still had the energy. He hadn't forgotten how she'd belted him when he was younger. Her favourite method had been to swipe wildly with the wrought-iron poker, catching him across the backs of the legs. It wasn't lost on him that this was what he and Angela had in common: their mothers had beaten them both.

He crept home an hour or so later, to find his mother lying on the settee with her eyes glazed over. He thought she'd killed herself. It was as if a magician had hypnotised her and she'd fainted into a kind of trance from which no amount of pleading by the terrified boys, in rare unison, could wake her. Fergal tried to revive her with a wet flannel – he remembered seeing that in a soap opera – and his brothers warned him that he was going to have to make the dinner if she was dead.

All of a sudden she snapped right out of it, as if nothing had happened, and sent Fergal round to his Aunt Concepta's. He was to ask her for 'a wee message' wrapped up in silver paper, but if his uncle was the only one in he was to get an Oxo cube instead – sure, it would be a shame to waste the journey. Concepta was in. She called Fergal into the back kitchen, wrapped up six white pills in cooking foil and pushed them into his pocket, warning

33

him not to run. When he got home Angela took them into the toilet and emerged a bit later, looking very relieved.

Almost every morning, when she handed Fergal his barely buttered toast, he saw her own blood caked under what was left of her fingernails. She'd been tearing at the broken skin on her back for as long as he could remember. For years it had been one of his jobs to clean her worsening wounds and dress them with antiseptic cream and plasters, nicked by one of her mates who was a domestic in the city hospital. She was always going on about how Concepta could wear backless dresses if she was going somewhere special, and she could never borrow any of them because her back was in such a mess. This thought made her pick her wounds even more so that her nylon blouse would stick to the weeping sores and rip them open again when she undressed to go to bed, starting the septic cycle all over again.

The sores never got a proper chance to heal because she scratched them constantly. Fergal would come into the kitchen to see her stirring the stew with one hand, with the other halfway down her back, scratching and clawing. If she managed to pull a scab off in one unbroken piece, she'd exhale in near-ecstasy and then throw it into the back of the fire, where it would crackle in blue flames for a satisfying second. Then she would deny it.

At these moments Fergal felt as though he was the parent and she was his child. As much as she beat him, and as much as he hated her for it, he still felt sorry for her.

5

For as long as he could remember, Fergal had had a strangely comforting recurring dream that always seemed to arrive just when he needed it most. There he'd be, as a much younger boy, sitting on the doorstep of the house and all of a sudden a big, clean, silver car would slide up the street and out would step his real parents, beaming, with open arms. Through tears of relief, they would apologise for having taken so long to find him. Then they would bundle up their long-lost son in a brand-new blanket, kissing and hugging him, and carry him to the wheels of his new life. Everything was in slow motion, and they would drive and drive for the longest time, out to the countryside, with him safely asleep on the back seat. Then he'd wake up and wish he hadn't.

~

For his weekly ablutions, Fergal would stay in the tiny bathroom – the only room in the house that could be locked – as long as he could. The bathroom would transform into a steam room when the hot water hit the cold air. The tub would fill about a third of the way before suddenly turning cold again – the immersion heater took ages to work and Angela roared at him if he left it on too long. After making doubly sure the door was locked, Fergal would lower himself into the roasting water, ankles first. Gradually he would let the rest of his body sink into the water, until he was almost completely covered, and exhale loudly. Then he'd start to wash himself with soap from yet another hospital heist by Angela's domestic friend. He had had dandruff for a while – his head had itched like crazy, and by the end of every school week his blazer had been dusted in a thick white avalanche of flakes – but he'd started washing his hair with a shampoo that the doctor had recommended and the difference was brilliant. His hair shone and he'd stopped scratching so much.

It wouldn't be long before one of his brothers started knocking, saying they were bursting for the toilet – but the locked door gave Fergal an extra bit of courage and he'd tell them to go round to Noreen's if they were that desperate. There was no way he was letting them in while he was in the bath. He'd duck his head under the water for as long as he could bear so as not to hear their whispered threats.

Fergal had it all organised. Once out of the bath, he hand-washed his dirty underwear in the water – he always made sure he had a clean pair to put on. Their towels were all in a terrible state, but the green one, which had been sent over from England by an auntie a few years earlier, was his favourite. It was ripped and rough and hard now from all the boil washes it had been through, but he still liked to dream about the shop where it had been bought, over in London. He'd wipe the steam off the window and open it a bit to let the heat out. *One day I'm going to have nice towels. I'm going to have loads of them – and loads of knickers too.*

When he felt safe enough, he'd inspect his ever-changing body in the badly hung cabinet mirror, balancing precariously on the toilet seat to get a better view of his genitals. The damp hair on his body was suddenly darker and thicker and he marvelled at all the places it grew that he hadn't noticed before. As he untangled the coarse private nest with his fingers, he suddenly wondered what his parents looked like without their clothes on. Then he decided he didn't want to know. He wondered about his brothers too – was he very different from them? It was a minor miracle that, in such a small house, they'd never really seen each other naked – apart from one time when Paddy had tipped a scalding cup of tea into his own lap when his team had scored on the TV. He'd had to pull down his tracksuit bottoms to his ankles and hop about the room, frantically blowing on his scorched penis and finally throwing cold water on it from the kitchen sink. It was one of the only moments when the rest of the family had laughed together at him, and he'd been so mortified that he hadn't said a single word.

Fergal tried flexing his arms to see if he had any muscles yet, and was surprised at the result. He pictured the girls he knew – the ones from the street who were always practising their Irish dancing up and down the pavement and the older ones who slouched to school with greasy ponytails, looking like they hadn't gone to bed, and sometimes said hello to him. He knew he preferred the company of girls – for one thing, they never tried to beat him up. And they weren't that interested in sport, except for newspaper pictures of George Best arriving at Belfast Airport, looking every inch the movie star. Fergal had agreed that George was gorgeous, but the girls had fallen silent, before giggling and staring at him, so he hadn't said anything more.

In school he overheard the fellas all the time talking about which girls they fancied and what they were going to do to them. They had to be careful enough, though – the sexiest girls always happened to be the kid sisters of local boxing-champion hard men. It was much safer to fantasise about the girls on television. When the first episodes of *Wonder Woman* had aired, there had been pandemonium. 'Did you see Wonder Woman's tits last night? She can fucking save me any time!' They'd gone on and on, swapping details of what they would do to her if she ever turned up in their bedrooms on the way to save somebody's life. If anyone actually went out with a real girl, there would be a steward's inquiry – 'Did you buck her? Did ye?' – until the chanting started, 'Mickey got the diddy last night!' This seemed to be on a par with discovering the cure for cancer.

Fergal wanted to fit in, but this was yet another subject from which he felt desparately disconnected. He watched in mild amazement, laughing along nervously, as one particularly animated boy mimed 'sticking it up' So-and-so, thrusting his crotch wildly back and forth. Fergal pictured himself kissing a girl he sometimes saw walking to mass – surely it couldn't be too difficult? – but the image quickly evaporated into nothing. He orbited the conversation from a safe distance, trying to appear interested and wondering whether he was the only one amongst all these fellas who thought about – well, about other fellas.

Fergal had developed a crush on a lad in school, Stevie Barry. The first time he saw him, he thought maybe his mother had slipped one of her tablets into his tea that morning. Everything seemed to move into slow motion. Stevie Barry was a sports star and, inevitably and unfortunately, was friends with the twins. Fergal found himself following him around just to watch the way he walked. If he was playing hurling, Fergal would try to catch a glimpse of him in his shorts from the relative safety of the crowd. He thought Stevie had the most incredible legs, like tree trunks. Sometimes, at the end of a match, the fellas would take their jerseys off and as Stevie walked past, with his sweat-soaked jersey tied around his waist, Fergal saw up close the beginnings of what would be a very hairy and muscular chest. It was enough to make him break out in a sweat, his heart beating so hard it felt like it was wearing Doc Marten boots. It wasn't long before the guilt would kick in, though, and Fergal would force himself to think about a girl with her top off – but somehow it just didn't have the same effect. Late at night, when he couldn't sleep, Fergal allowed himself to think that Stevie felt the same way about him – that they would secretly meet under the cover of night, and kiss in the moonlight near the deserted school pitches. But Fergal knew this would never, ever happen.

Far too many thoughts jostled for position in his mind. *Maybe I'm a freak. Why can't I just like girls? Why do I want to… to kiss him, every time I see him? What the fuck is wrong with me?* He thought that maybe he should talk to a priest about it – confession boxes were supposed to be confidential after all. He constantly worried about what these thoughts meant. There were all kinds of names for it – but there was no way he thought they could apply to him.

Now that they were in their final year, the headmaster had set up a series of mortifying sex-education classes, in an effort to give the boys a sense of maturity. The teacher – an anorexic priest from the South called Father Clancy – ended up sending half the class into the corridor for disruption within the first ten minutes. He ranted about the sins of the flesh, with his eyes nervously shut, and informed the class that 'pleasuring the self' was an active waste of God's seed, which should only be spilled within marriage. He ended each lesson by getting everyone to chant, 'God can see everything! God can see everything! Especially in the dark!' Fergal prayed it wasn't true. He'd had two dreams in a row that made him blush if he saw Stevie in school.

A few days before, he'd been trying to get home the back way – someone in his year had issued him with yet another death threat – and had unexpectedly discovered Stevie pissing against a telegraph pole behind the school. Fergal had felt like a rabbit caught in headlights. Try as he might, he couldn't stop staring at the way Stevie confidently held his penis in one hand as he nonchalantly drained himself. His trousers were completely undone at the waist and pulled down so he could cup his hairy balls with his other hand, eyes shut, whistling, with a big, broad smile of relief. Fergal's heart hammered his throat. He tried his best not even to blink as Stevie finally shook himself dry, did up his trousers and wandered off. Fergal was erect and uncomfortable all the way home and, to his horror, had developed a large wet patch in the front of his trousers – he pulled his shirt out to hide it and hurried straight to the bathroom that was, miraculously, free.

Now, safe behind the locked door, he rinsed his face and

looked at his own eyes, bright green and sparkling from the cold water, in the foggy mirror of the wee bathroom. He thought back to the showers at school, picturing Stevie's thick, hairy legs. He was instantly hard again. He knew he had to be quick. He ran the cold water to drown out the sound, and pulled at himself as fast as he could. He replayed the dream he'd had: him and Stevie in the locked changing rooms after the school was closed for the day, rolling around naked on a pile of fresh football kits, kissing and touching each other... He ejaculated quickly, into the scum of the sink. Then he bleached the white porcelain twice. The sink had never looked so clean.

As he left the bathroom and passed the closed parlour door, he heard his brother Paddy Jr explaining defiantly to his hurling mates – including Stevie – that Fergal was in fact adopted. 'Sure, who else in our family has big cow eyes and curly fucking hair?' The fact that Fergal was so shite at sport, he added, was the final proof. 'We reckon he's a cross between a girl and a boy, anyway,' John put in. There was a chorus of what sounded like vomiting.

Fergal went into the yard and sat on top of the newly delivered coal, crying soundlessly, not caring how dirty his school trousers got.

~

Early the next morning, not far from the Flynns' house in Walker Street, Mrs Mooney, the priest's housekeeper, brought old Father Bradley his usual cup of tea to help him wake up. She found him frozen to the spot, kneeling in a prayerful position by his undisturbed bed, wearing only pyjama bottoms. Father

Bradley's asthma had plagued him since childhood, like the ghost of a drunken accordion. Recently he only ever ventured out of the house in emergencies and to take the early mass. He had tried in vain to give up smoking his treasured untipped Sweet Afton cigarettes but they were the only thing that gave him any genuine pleasure, so he'd ignored the doctor's advice and continued rasping his paper lungs until they could take no more. The old man of the cloth had been lifeless a full eight hours before Mrs Mooney reluctantly attempted to disturb his arctic, freckled shoulders with her warm, worn hand. Then she screamed the alarm.

For the first time in Fergal's life, a borrowed primary-school blackboard at the top of the steps of St Bridget's announced the cancellation of that morning's early mass. It wasn't long before the news of Father Bradley's demise reached every house, and everyone started asking the same question: who was going to replace him?

6

The same bishop who, five years earlier, had sent Father Dermot MacManus to West Africa dispatched a decree and, one week later, Father Mac found himself careering through an unfamiliar one-way system in his old hometown on the back seat of his sister's Toyota Starlet, sandwiched between their parents. He had changed so much that, if it hadn't been for his collar, they wouldn't have given him a second glance as he came through the Arrivals gate. His da had rewarded his broadened shoulders with endless slaps on the back, while his sister and mother kissed him and commented on how healthy he looked.

Father Mac was amazed to think that so much time had passed since he'd been posted to the missions. He had been ordained only a few weeks before receiving the bishop's message that God's work was needed more urgently on the other side of the earth. He had been glad to escape the claustrophobia of the seminary. Out of the thirty young men with whom he'd shared his initial vocational studies, only eight had completed the full course. At his ordination his mother had wept uncontrollably with pride and menopause, while his father mumbled something about 'answering the call' and 'sure didn't your brother make me a grandfather'. Only his sister Dympna had come close to understanding his reasons for joining the priesthood, even though they never spoke about it properly. He had pictured a message written in the sky in smoke by one of those advertising planes: 'Think You Might Be Different? Join The Priesthood Today. You Know It Makes Sense!'

They reached the back entrance of St Bridget's just as the heavens opened, and they had to sit in the car while someone found an umbrella. The first thing Father Mac noticed was that the huge white marble sculpture of Christ on the cross had taken the full impact of a blue paint-bomb right in the middle of its loincloth.

The housekeeper, Mrs Mooney, widened her eyes when she saw the new priest for the first time. He was at least six feet tall and the African sun had deepened his complexion to the extent that she thought the statue of St Martin de Porres himself had come to life, after all the rubbing by the cleaners. She blessed herself nervously at this blasphemous thought and silently asked for forgiveness before guiding them in through the side door, out of the wet.

She settled the family in the front parlour, with enough tea and sandwiches to feed the entire village that Father Mac had just left. He had forgotten just how much food people ate in Ireland. His mother clucked approvingly at the obvious effort that went into maintaining the house while his da had gone predictably quiet. Dympna asked about the friends he'd mentioned in some of his letters home, and Father Mac rummaged in his bag for photos of a hurling team that he had started with some of the local fishermen. He described his new congregation's amazement when the hurling sticks had arrived from Ireland. 'They just couldn't believe what they were for. One day loads of the sticks went missing and I eventually found them in the boats, doubling as oars.' His parents looked shocked, but Dympna thought it was funny.

Finally Mr MacManus said, 'So did you manage to convert many of them niggers?'

A cold silence dropped into the room and closed around the word that Father Mac hadn't heard for years. '*What* did you say, Da?'

Mrs MacManus saw the look on her son's face and started to say something to cover for her husband, but the past five years had had quite an effect on their son's confidence. 'Da, I know you don't mean it, but that word is… You know, it's beyond offensive.'

His father looked blankly at him for a second, then at his wife, who usually explained things he didn't understand.

'Look, Da, you might think I'm making a mountain out of a molehill, and I know we grew up with that word, but I met some of the most beautiful human beings I've ever known over there in Africa. I mean, we think we know about poverty here… let me tell you, we don't know the half of it. I never saw such bad conditions in my life – and yet I've never been more welcomed and made to feel at home.'

'Ah, Jesus, son. Don't be getting into a state over nothing. I don't mean it like that. Sure, you know—'

'I know, Da, I know, but you're talking about my friends. I don't ever want to hear it again.'

After an uncomfortable lunch, they said their goodbyes. Dympna gave him a very long hug and rubbed the side of his shiny brown face. Mrs MacManus said she hoped it wouldn't be another five years before she saw him again, and that next time he would have to come to their house. Mr MacManus mumbled something and pretended to look for the car keys, even though he knew they were in his pocket. Father Mac went back inside and waved from the parlour window, guiltily relieved they were gone and wondering how Dympna put up with them.

As their car drove off into the Belfast morning, he thought about how one word had brought the last five years of his life into such sharp focus. He knew he could never make his father, who had never experienced life outside Ireland, understand his point of view. He also knew his father hadn't really meant anything by it, and he regretted that their first meeting in five years had turned sour. It had also made him think about the reality of living in his hometown again – would his parishioners be better or worse?

As he picked up his travelling bag, he stopped at the upright piano and ran his hand along the locked lid, saying aloud, 'I'll introduce myself to you properly later.' Mrs Mooney appeared in the doorway and nearly fainted, thinking that he'd been checking for dust. She stuttered something about how, since the demise of dear Father Bradley, no one played it any more, but she kept it as clean as she could.

Father Mac put her at ease immediately. 'Mrs Mooney, for the last five years or so I've lived in a wooden hut with insects the size of my fist. And I can tell you I've never seen a house as clean and well cared for as this one. I'm looking forward to getting used to it, and I hope I don't upset you by playing the piano. I know you looked after Father Bradley for a lot of his life, and I want to take on this position as respectfully as I can – with your help, of course.'

Mrs Mooney's face relaxed for the first time since the new priest had arrived. 'I'll show you to your room now, Father. Sure, you must be worn out,' she replied in a hushed murmur. She pointed him to the stairs that generations of beeswax polish and female elbow grease had left looking like dark, sculpted molasses.

Father Mac's room was right at the top of the house and when he opened the newly painted door he gasped at how pristine it was, with a welcome scent of lavender in the careful air. He put down his luggage. Mrs Mooney had tried to insist on carrying it for him, but he had been too quick for her protestations and was gone, up two flights, with her relieved voice trailing after him – she had stooped enough under the weight of the tea tray. He closed the door behind him, wondering if it might be a good idea to have a wee lie down. He touched the perfect white cotton on the high bed. When he sat into its softness he smiled, and unexpectedly his eyes filled up. His room looked out over the Falls Road and he could just see the Royal Victoria Hospital where he'd been born, nearly twenty-eight years before.

When he opened the sash window he was reminded of the first time he'd seen the view from his African room. For a split second he was transported back: red dirt roads, cloudless blue skies, the permanent soundtrack of fat crickets singing in rhythm with the distant drummers who seemed to play all night, whether there was anybody with enough energy left to dance or not. He laughed to himself, remembering. At first he had thought the constant drumming would drive him mad, but within a week he had found it actually helped him to sleep. When he'd first arrived, he hadn't been prepared for the culture shock, the flies, the heat or the open sewers. It was a completely different kind of poverty from any he'd ever known, and he'd been humbled by how quickly the local people had offered to share what little they had with him. All of a sudden he had experienced what it was like to be a minority – he was one of only a few white people living and working at the mission. He hadn't been able to help staring at some of the darkest skin he'd ever seen, it was so beautiful. Late at night, when he lay thinking in bed, it had astounded him that, after all that Westerners had done to devastate their country, the people had only the biggest smiles for him, no matter how far he wandered off the beaten track.

The daydream faded as the handmade djembe drums, honed from single trunks of wood, were echoed in the unmistakable city clacking of black taxis' diesel engines. They always moved off from the side of the road a little shakily at first, sounding almost unsure, but then the accelerator would push confidence into the engine and they would roll off along the Falls Road.

Father Mac slowly unpacked for his new life. It felt good but strange to be back in the place where he'd been baptised, confirmed and then ordained by the dead man whose job and house he'd just inherited. He knew only too well that there would be pressure not to make too many changes – at least, not immediately – but his mind was racing with ideas to create positive energy and hope. Sitting on the side on the bed, he pulled off his shoes, and a sudden wave of tiredness took him by surprise. Just as he was about to stretch out on top of the duvet, an ambulance panicked its way out of the side gates of the hospital, bullied its way along the main road and turned down the side street that ran under Father Mac's window. He got up to see where it was going, but it continued at breakneck speed away around another corner.

The siren was beginning to fade and he was turning back to the bed when he heard another note join it, in perfect harmony. He wondered if the jet lag was making him hear things. But, in fact, the harmony was getting louder than the original siren. He put his weary head out the window and looked back towards the hospital. The last thing he had expected to see was a young lad, weighed down with shopping bags, singing a perfect third above the original siren. He watched as the young fella scrunched up his face, trying to match the tone of the ambulance as closely as he could. Father Mac burst out laughing in disbelief, he'd never heard anything like it. Just as he was wondering whether he should shout out to the boy or not, the phone rang.

He went downstairs and took the call. His first official duty was a request to administer the last rites to the reason the ambulance had been in such a hurry. As he wrote the address in his new notepad, he told Mrs Mooney what he had heard from his bedroom window but she just tutted, 'It was probably some drunk, Father.'

'No – no, he couldn't have been. He only looked about seventeen or eighteen, I think.' She looked at him and realised he really had been away for a long time.

Father Mac pulled on his coat, double-checked the directions and hurried out into the street. He wondered if he could catch up to the young fella, but it was too late. Fergal Flynn was already out of sight and halfway home.

7

The Flynns had outgrown their tiny house before they'd even moved in, and it was even more cramped now that all of the boys were bigger than their father. This, of course, only made the fighting worse. Everything came to a head one night when Fergal decided to challenge the man of the house.

Yet again, there wasn't a single clean dish to eat off, and Angela refused to cook the tea. Fergal couldn't understand why, after spending all day cleaning and cooking for other people, his mother came home to no help from anyone but him. He brought it up with his brothers, but they looked so confused that he might as well have asked them to recite the Our Father in German.

Finally John told him, 'She's a woman. Women clear up after men.'

Fergal looked at his exhausted mother, propped up against the sink, and then at his father, who was sitting on the sofa with his feet up on a stool, completely oblivious and reading a paper. He took a deep breath and went and stood in front of him. 'I'm sick of doing the dishes, Da. It's always either me or Mammy, and it's not fair.'

The whole house was silent. Paddy slowly turned over a page.

Fergal continued, 'We all eat off the same plates. Why don't you ever do them? Can you not tell Paddy or John or Ciaran to do them? Mammy's not a slave and she's exhausted.' He sounded exhausted too when he got the last nervous word out.

Paddy folded his sports paper perfectly in half and threw his hot cup of tea in his third son's face. 'I won't have your whiny fucking voice telling me how my house should be run!' Then he turned to Angela. 'Did you put the nancy boy up to this? Did you? Right – I'll do the fucking dishes for youse. I'll give them a right fucking doing.'

For one second, Fergal thought he'd made a breakthrough. His brothers looked even more confused. The next thing they knew, though, Paddy had got his hammer from the yard and begun smashing the dishes in the sink. Angela screamed at him to stop, whilst the twins and Ciaran fled.

'It's all your fault, Fergal Flynn,' Angela said bitterly. Paddy had hit the stainless-steel sink so hard that he'd dented it, then he'd thrown the hammer into the carnaged crockery before storming out the back door to the pub. 'Why did you have to open your big fucking mouth?'

'What? Mammy, I was only trying to help! I—'

'Ah, shut up, for fuck's sake. My head is bursting.' She took a little plastic bottle out of her apron pocket and dry-swallowed two pills, then pushed past him and went up the stairs.

Fergal ran out of the house and around to Granny Noreen's. He stood by her back door and wondered what he was going to do. The rain fell, and he looked up at the sky and whispered, 'It's not fair. Why can I never do anything right?'

~

As Noreen's health began to fail, Angela became her official carer. The government had introduced a scheme where an appointed member of the family could get an allowance to look after an ailing parent. Fergal often accompanied his mother and watched her start the fire without firelighters – Angela was an expert in rolling newspapers so tightly that they burned like twigs – before she delivered Noreen's tea and toast, and he left for school.

The unspoken deal was that he got to sleep at Noreen's every weekend, thus avoiding his father and brothers as much as possible. He did all sorts of wee jobs for his granny. She gave him his taxi fare to town and back because he had to go to the other side of Belfast to pay certain debts. Various monthly instalments could only be paid in person at the corresponding head offices dotted about the city centre – and sure, Angela said, he might as well do some of the Flynns' bills as well, while he was in town. It never occurred to her to ask any of her other sons – she knew they'd only lose the envelopes containing the little amounts of money that never really seemed to reduce the debts before another loan was needed. Noreen had been paying off rent arrears for years, but the amount she could afford to repay each week was so small that she would never catch up in her lifetime. On his way home, Fergal would do the most important job of all. He would pick up her pension – the people at the local post office knew him by this time – then he would to to the off-licence for her weekly supply of the cheapest gin available. His final stop was an old tobacconist near Broadway to buy her half an ounce of Gallagher's special snuff, which she adored. It was kept in an enormous glass jar and Fergal thought it looked like the contents of an emptied vacuum-cleaner bag. The shopkeeper would carefully measure it onto old tin scales with a bent spoon, then wrap it expertly in a little brown paper bag. When he got home, Noreen's eyes gained extra wattage as she transferred the contents into her special tin and hoovered up a good knuckleful into her flared nostrils.

In his O-level year, at the guilt-ridden but convenient request of his mother, Fergal moved in permanently with his Granny Noreen. She'd become prone to falling out of bed at night, trapping herself in twisted layers of her nylon nightdress and bedclothes where she would lie until Angela found her, freezing and disorientated, the next morning. Fergal was secretly delighted with the decision, but he played it down in case his mother changed her mind.

Even though Noreen's house had two tiny spare bedrooms – admittedly crammed full of dust and broken things – Fergal had to sleep in her room, in case he didn't hear her tumble onto the threadbare rug. His bed was opposite hers, separated by a single window that was permanently shut from decades of lazy painting. There was a commode, so she wouldn't have to brave the outdoor toilet, which was often frozen solid in winter. It took her forever to use the commode every morning. Sometimes Fergal would wake up to the sound of her old bowels straining to empty. When she was finished, he'd count to three, leap out of his bed, grab the portable toilet and run – holding his breath until he got down the stairs – to empty it down the proper toilet in the yard. Then he would light the fire and make Noreen's toast, which she rarely finished – she said the wholemeal bread that the doctor insisted upon was 'pure shite' compared to the gorgeous white loaves of her day.

On top of her gin, Noreen had a huge brown handbag stocked with tablets and pills of every description, prescription and sell-by date. Her reasons to come down the stairs disintegrated with every useless visit from her pissed doctor, who just pumped her full of more pills and told her to stop drinking so much. He might as well have asked her to stop breathing. After one particularly lethal cocktail she sat bolt upright in her bed in the middle of the night and started rapping the air as though it were the window of a taxi, shouting, 'Let me out here, love, will you? I can't miss my stop!' Fergal woke up thinking he was still dreaming and just managed to get to her before she tried to struggle out from under the three million blankets she insisted on having. Her tears came as she gradually realised where she was not, and he stroked what was left of her perm-ravaged silver hair until she was unconscious again.

It seemed that not a week went by without Noreen – propped up in the bed, with umpteen layers of cardigans on and the paper spread out in front of her – finding an old school friend in the obituary column of the paper, holding her national health glasses at arm's length like a private detective, magnifying the details. Then the news came that one of her distant sons in England had died of the same cancer that had taken her husband. By the time they heard, he was already buried, somewhere in the north of England. Noreen was too fragile to travel anyway, even if she'd known.

A few days later Fergal decided to clean the house from top to bottom, just to do something. When he prised open one of the living-room cupboards, which had been painted shut by the housing executive, he found a handwritten list of names and numbers on the inside of the door.

Our Margaret, 15 Packington Road, Tottenham, 1948
Our Frances, 22 Warpendale Crescent, Stamford Hill, 1946
Our Peter, 66 Kensal High Road, Flat 2, 1950
Our Joseph, 135 Brick Lane, East London…

They were the addresses – long deserted by the time her grandson read them – to which most of her nine children had fled. Fergal knew he had aunts and uncles in England, but knew nothing about them. He tried to ask Noreen, but she either ignored his questions, wept uncontrollably or shouted 'Cunts!' depending on which of the names he asked about. When he asked Angela, she said she'd never known them. They'd left home when she was young. 'Sure, your granny and my eldest sister Briege were in the same maternity unit having kids at the one time. It wasn't that unusual then, and it still happens now.'

The new living arrangements suited almost everybody. Paddy, the elder of the twins by a crucial few minutes, now had his own room. John was grudgingly sharing with Ciaran. As John didn't want anything to do with anything Fergal had even touched, never mind slept in, he'd insisted on unscrewing his bunk bed from Paddy's and dragging it into his new room. With Fergal gone, the downstairs parlour began to look more and more like a locker room, with hurling sticks in various states of disrepair stacked against the walls, and muddy waterlogged boots and kit drying everywhere. Sometimes Angela felt she'd spent her entire life surrounded by her children's clothes.

For all the moments of madness, Fergal loved living with Noreen. It was just the two of them, and he didn't have to keep dodging his brothers. Each night he would bring her a final cup of tea, and if she had the energy she'd get him to sit on the edge of her bed while she gave him her opinions on just about everything. He laughed when she pointed out that, even though they were all supposed to hate the Brits so much, there wasn't one person she knew who hadn't made damn sure they watched every single bit of footage of Prince Charles and Lady Diana's wedding. The dress was all the neighbours and the papers had talked about for weeks. Fergal thought he'd die laughing when he heard Noreen say to a visiting neighbour one afternoon, 'Imagine that fella bearing down on you! Jesus and his holy mother, I hope it's as big as them bloody ears!'

She loved to hear him talk, too. There was a lilt in his voice that reminded her of her departed husband. In Walker Street Fergal had learned to keep his mouth shut as much as possible but Noreen was bored with being housebound and lapped up details about the outside world. She devoured any scrap of conversation that went beyond the weather or the price of potatoes, or any stories of what had happened to Fergal in school that day – the more detailed the better. Her old eyes stood out on stalks when he told her that a massive rat had made the fatal decision to appear in the schoolyard one break time. It was instantly squashed with a schoolbag and became a football for several hundred blood-thirsty boys, but the game came to an abrupt end when the mashed rodent was booted into the air just as someone yelled, 'Mr O'Connell!' The maths teacher was deep in conversation, holding a mug of weak tea and a much-envied cigarette. As he turned around to see who'd dared interrupt him, the rat's pulpy remains slapped him full in the mouth. After the yelling, the vomiting and a fruitless investigation that lasted a full week, Mr O'Connell took a holiday, in the vain hope that the incident would be forgotten by the time he returned. Unfortunately for him, *Midnight Cowboy* was on TV while he was away and so, for ever after, St Bridget's Secondary School had its very own Ratso.

Fergal left none of the story to Noreen's imagination, and she was shocked and gripped at the same time. When he finished the story, she told him that it summed up the difference between boys and girls, 'Only a boy could do something so disgusting! Jesus in heaven, young people don't know how to behave any more…' But then, being shocked and lecturing were – apart from drinking – her two favourite things.

She looked forward to hearing Fergal's key in the door every day – she hadn't realised how lonely she'd become over the years. Talking to him, she allowed herself to think that she was back in the old days, with the other Fergal, her husband. The fact that she could say his name again as he listened intently to her stories brought her more comfort than Fergal could know. And it was a two-way street. She told him he was growing up into a big, handsome, smart fella, destined for good things – and Fergal didn't know where to look as he reddened and backed out of the room.

Once she was settled for the night, Fergal had the added luxury of the living room and the black-and-white TV all to himself. He looked forward to these moments, when the front door was locked against the world and he felt truly safe and relaxed.

~

Fergal was walking home from the city centre – he'd spent his taxi money on a sandwich and two cups of tea in a little café – after paying all the various debt instalments. The queues in each place had been slow, smoke-filled and tense, and when he was finished he'd sat down outside City Hall for a rest. He loved watching the punk rockers gather, with their leather jackets, eyeliner and blue or pink or bleached hair and wondered what he'd look like if he dyed his hair blonde.

Just as he got near the corner of the Falls Road and St Bridget's Chapel, the heavens opened. He made a break for the chapel, but was drenched in seconds. His chest immediately sounded like it needed oiling. People wedged themselves into doorways, cursing the black-and-white sky and the weatherman who'd sworn it would be a dry day and made them leave their umbrellas at home.

It was Saturday, and St Bridget's Chapel was busy with a wedding. Fergal sneaked in at the back and watched the pregnant teenager kiss her terrified new husband while their respective families fumed silently in their seats. Fergal imagined how awful the reception would be, when the drink kicked in and the truth leaked out. As soon as the registry book was signed, the congregation practically ran out the doors, to a soundtrack provided by Baldy Turner at the organ up in the balcony. He was grinning away to himself: he had a bird's-eye view of the parade of ample cleavages on offer in the rear-view mirror he'd attached to the organ so he could watch the priest for cues. At least that was the official explanation.

Fergal considered going to confession. He didn't really believe in the whole performance, but there was something about the experience of being enclosed in the dark box that he found hard to resist. It was almost like being invisible for a few minutes. He got the same feeling when he went to Noreen's lightless outside toilet during the night, or when he'd been really young and used to hide under the bed for hours, until he was dying to have a shite. He could stop being the Fergal Flynn who was spat at and hit and hated. He thought he could also forget for a while that he was the Fergal Flynn who couldn't get the vision of Stevie Barry out of his wet dreams, though he wasn't sure he wanted to.

At previous confessions he had found himself repeating the same sins over and over again: how he swore inwardly at his mother, and out loud at Ciaran if no one was in earshot; how all the suffering in the world made him doubt God's existence; how he sometimes wished his immediate family would all die from food poisoning or something.

What he couldn't bring himself to reveal was how he regularly fantasised about phoning the confidential telephone number stencilled on the side of the army jeeps and informing them, in a disguised voice, that Patrick Flynn of Walker Street and his twin sons (not his third, innocent son Fergal) were active members of an offshoot of the IRA and were planning to blow up the nearby barracks. He also wanted to confess about 'pleasuring himself', of course, but he couldn't think of any way to say it that sounded less mortifying than 'wanking'. And, anyway, it was his own fucking business.

The new priest came back in the vestry, went to the centre of the glittering altar and bowed to the marble floor, kissing the enormous crucifix that hung around his neck. When he turned round, Fergal was shocked. After the usual clutch of chain-smoking, bog-breathed old badgers, he had not expected to see such a handsome young man wearing the vestments of a priest.

On his way down the recently abandoned aisles towards the confession boxes, the priest stopped to ask Fergal if he was wait-ing for confession. Fergal, startled again by the contrast between the soft Belfast accent and the dark skin that he'd assumed was foreign, heard himself reply, 'Yes, Father.'

They entered their respective mahogany wardrobes and, as soon as the dark was ready, the priest slid open the cover of the wire mesh that framed him in the half-light. Fergal stared at his soft features and started to panic slightly. His asthma sounded all the more awful in such a confined, hollow space, and he began talking far too fast.

'Bless me, Father, for I have sinned,' he wheezed. 'It has been at least six months – no, seven months' – wheeze – 'or maybe it is six months – since my last confession.'

'That's all right, young man. Take your time. There's no need to be nervous. Your chest sounds bad. Are you all right? Do you need anything?'

'I need to take my inhaler, Father – it's here somewhere.'

'Well, do that. There's no hurry.'

Fergal fumbled in his coat pocket. After two puffs, the storm in his lungs began to subside.

'That sounds better,' the priest said. 'Now, listen – take your time and tell me what's bothering you.'

Fergal was surprised at how friendly he sounded. He thought of Father Bradley, who was in denial about going deaf and would shout, 'You did what? You dirty pup! There aren't enough Hail Marys or Our Fathers for that disease of humankind! Were you reared by wolves? Get out and beg forgiveness on your knees from Our Lord!' Of course there'd always be an enormous queue right outside the box, listening to every mortifying word.

'Well, Father… I've taken the Lord's name in vain a lot. I've had bad thoughts about my family, especially my father, and my mother – well, and my brothers Paddy and John… well, all of them, really. And… and I've had thoughts about…' His voice slowed down.

'Yes?'

Stevie Barry floated uninvited into Fergal's mind, waving his erect penis in the air with one hand and blowing kisses with the other. Fergal shut his eyes as tight as they would go and said, 'I've had impure thoughts, Father, about – about…'

The sentence hung in the air longer than Fergal would have liked, and his breathing picked up a little. At last the priest said, 'Impure thoughts about…?'

'Ah, ones about – you know… below the waist, Father.'

'Impure thoughts about girls?'

Fergal hadn't been expecting that, and the words were out of his mouth before he could catch them. 'God, no! I mean, no – sorry, Father—'

'It's all right, don't panic, you're only human. Take your time.'

'Well, not about girls as such.'

There was a long silence. Then the priest's hushed voice said, astounding Fergal, 'Have you been having impure thoughts about other fellas, then?'

Fergal held his breath as though he were about to dive underwater in search of the pearl of wisdom that would explain everything, make everything all right. Finally he exhaled, emptyhanded. 'Yes, Father, I have. How did you know? I mean – you won't tell anybody, will you?'

The priest laughed a little, in a friendly way. 'What's said in confession is between you, me and the Lord above. I admire your honesty, young man.'

Fergal had never said it out loud to himself before, never mind to anybody else. His head was spinning.

At that moment they heard the box's other door opening – someone else was waiting for confession on the other side of the priest.

The priest said quietly, 'Look, young man, you've probably got enough to be thinking about for one day. Say three Hail Marys, and remember you can come and talk to me any time, in the strictest confidence. Don't be worrying yourself too much. I absolve you of your sins in the name of the Father, the Son and the Holy Spirit. Amen.'

Fergal abandoned the darkness to sit in front of the altar, where he lit a tremulous single candle and said his three Hail Marys in slow motion. Then he stayed kneeling for a long time, looking at the crucifixion scene carved in marble and trying to calm down. He asked God to help him make sense of everything. He couldn't believe what had happened.

Just as he was leaving, Father Mac opened the door of the

confession box to see if there was anyone else waiting but there were only a few pensioners at the other side of the chapel, lost in prayer. He caught sight of Fergal exiting the front doors and went after him.

When the priest caught up with him outside, Fergal dropped his eyes to the ground. The priest put his hand on his arm and said, 'I know this might sound a bit strange, but have you ever harmonised with an ambulance?'

Fergal looked up at Father Mac, shielding his eyes from the sudden sunlight, and laughed. In the broad daylight, he could see just how handsome the priest really was. His eyes shone and his teeth were the whitest Fergal had ever seen.

'Well, I suppose I do sometimes, Father. Why? How did you know that?'

The priest began to say something, but at that moment his housekeeper appeared and took him by the arm, telling him he had an urgent phone call. The rain started up again, so Fergal shouted goodbye and ran off before the priest could even ask him his name.

8

A whole week went by before Fergal got a chance to go back to St Bridget's. Granny Noreen had become more needy – she rarely left the house – and his mock exams weren't too far away. He stayed up late most nights, studying and watching TV, and found it harder and harder to get out of bed in the morning. Noreen was wide awake long before the sparrows that had built their nest in one of her broken gutters. When she looked over at the unconscious pile of blankets and legs on the other side of the tiny room she wondered aloud, 'Why is it that, when you're young, people are always telling you to get up when you need to sleep, and when you're old they tell you should sleep when you want to get up but can't?'

When Fergal did finally shake himself, after she'd blown her nose till it bled, he realised that he'd slept in his school uniform again. Noreen shouted at him for it, threatening to tell Angela. But the house was freezing, even with the fire on, and Fergal knew he shouldn't use too much coal, so he'd stay up watching the TV with his duffel coat on, drinking black tea and watching his breath match the steam from his teacup. He'd crawled out of a strange dream about the new priest, but the moment Noreen started yelling he forgot the details, which he thought was probably just as well.

When he brought Noreen her breakfast, she'd calmed down, and she asked him to do her a favour. Fergal grinned. She always changed her tune if she wanted something and it usually meant a bit of spending money for him. She fished in her suitcase-sized handbag for a little hollow plastic statue of Our Lady that she'd bought in Knock a few years previously. She screwed off its head, which doubled as the lid, and said, 'Son, will you go over to St Bridget's and dip Our Lady into the font and fill her up for me? I've run out of holy water for my prayers. I'd do it myself, only the legs would buckle under me. Your oul' granny's not able any more.' She handed him fifty pence 'to put in the collection box', but he had already decided what he was going to buy with it when he got the chance to go to the shop.

Fergal looked at the clock and he knew he'd be late for school if he went down to St Bridget's and back, so he promised her he'd do it straight after school and bring Our Lady round with her dinner that night. He still had dinner in Walker Street most nights – his final job of the day was to deliver Noreen's supper, which Angela would keep warm in the oven covered with tin foil. At least three dogs usually followed him all the way to Noreen's, just in case he dropped any. It had only happened once.

He'd dropped to the ground when he'd got caught in a sudden crossfire between the army and two masked gunmen, sending the gravy-mashed potatoes and pork chops into the air and the mutts into a frenzy. The guns, accompanied by the sudden rain of bricks and bottles, were deafening. A back door had opened behind Fergal and his saviour, in the shape of an old woman, had whispered that he could take cover in her house. Fergal had managed to crawl, shaking, past the three dogs, who were still killing one another over the pork chops. The whole thing had ended as suddenly as it had begun, and Fergal's biggest worry had been telling his mother that he'd broken one of her good plates.

Sometimes, if his mother was feeling more exhausted than usual, she'd give him money to go to the chip shop for Noreen and himself. He'd go back to Noreen's, make a full pot of tea, butter too much bread and eat slowly and happily, stretched out on the sofa with his shoes off, watching the TV in peace and quiet and complete freedom.

As he was pulling the front door closed behind him, he heard his Granny Noreen yell, 'Don't you let anything happen to Our Lady!'

When Fergal got to school, he discovered that someone disliked the English teacher so much that they'd rigged a homemade bomb to the classroom door. It had blown a hole big enough for a pregnant cow to pass through. Only in Belfast.

During the last class of the day, Fergal was looking for a red pen in his bag and, without thinking, took out the empty statue of Mary and put it on top of his desk. Two seconds later, Petrol Paul McGinley reached over and grabbed her. McGinley was famed for secretly draining teachers' cars of their fuel with a length of garden hose and impressive sucking action. Word would spread, and he'd wait behind the woodwork building for anyone stupid enough to watch him hold a lit match near his bulging mouth and spit the ignited petrol straight up towards the sky. He regularly burned the face off himself as gravity explained, in concrete terms, that what went up had to come down, all over him if the wind changed its mind. Once someone had nudged him, and he'd swallowed the entire mouthful and ended up in the emergency room for the second time in a week.

Fergal hadn't seen him kidnap Noreen's Mother of God, but he noticed she was missing. He searched frantically, until he got a pen shoved into his back and turned to see Petrol Paul grinning and waving the statue. It was, appropriately, a religion class. Mrs Diamond was busy explaining transubstantiation to Declan Feelan, who was a bit slow at the best of times. She put her hand to her head when he asked in all seriousness if it was 'something to do with Dracula, Miss?'

Petrol Paul was an amateur boxer, so Fergal knew he had to tread carefully. Throughout the rest of the class, he pretended he didn't want the Virgin bottle back – and, miraculously, this was enough to deflate the situation. As the last bell rang, Our Lady was flung back at him, with two Biro stab wounds for breasts and a big hairy vagina drawn on the front of her robe. 'The Vagina Mary' was written on her back in permanent marker. Fergal thought about going to the toilets to try and repair some of the damage, but he knew that part of the building was a whole other assault course waiting to happen. So he hid her in his bag. He thought that maybe he could clean her in the font and then Sellotape the holes.

He sprinted to the front gates and headed for St Bridget's Chapel, stopping only to see if anyone was following. It was raining hard and when he finally reached the newly painted gates of the chapel, he was soaked to the skin and trying to catch his breath. As he stood in the entry of the chapel, dripping and searching for his inhaler, he felt a hand on his shoulder. He turned, automatically expecting it to be someone from his class, and jumped back to avoid an imaginary swipe.

'Oh, goodness, I've startled you. I'm sorry,' said the new priest.

Fergal went bright red. 'Oh, sorry, Father…'

'Was someone chasing you?'

Fergal didn't know where to look and he shook his head. The priest continued, 'Look, I never got a chance to introduce myself properly. I'm Father MacManus – call me Father Mac. And I can see that a good cup of tea and a warm towel wouldn't go amiss. You're like a drowned rat, so you are.'

Fergal took a deep breath. 'Hello, Father MacManus. I'm sorry – I'm Fergal Flynn from Walker Street.'

Father Mac smiled the warmest smile Fergal had ever seen and said, 'Don't be sorry. It looks more like Fergal Flynn from Water Street to me. You're drenched. Look, you'd be welcome to come over to the house and dry off before you catch your death of cold. You're not in a hurry, are you?'

Fergal had his hand in his schoolbag, gripping the little empty statue. 'Well, no… I was supposed to fill up my granny's Our Lady bottle with holy water, but I think I lost it and she won't be happy.'

'Ah, I think I might be able to help you there. Look, your chest sounds awful. You need to be careful. I suffer from asthma too, so I know how it is. Do you have your inhaler with you?'

'No, I think I left it at my granny's.'

'Well, my asthma's been playing up ever since I got back from

Africa, and I have a few spare ones. Hopefully you don't smoke, do you? You're not as stupid as me.'

'Oh God, no, Father, I don't smoke. Air is difficult enough sometimes. You lived in Africa? That must've been amazing.'

'Oh, it was… Look, mass doesn't start for a while yet. Why don't you come over to the house and dry off?'

Fergal was astounded. All he could do was say, 'OK', and follow the holy footfalls to the main house. In the sixteen years and nine months that he had been coming to St Bridget's Chapel, he'd never once been in the priest's house. When he was much smaller his mother used to threaten to drag him in to see the priest if he didn't stop getting into trouble at school but now here he was, walking through the front door at the new priest's invitation. Fergal felt very privileged.

The first thing he noticed was how clean everything was. It smelled wonderful, too – like roses and toast or something. The reason the house was so immaculate was hovering in the hallway. Father Mac asked her for a pot of tea for two – 'Oh, and some of whatever is making that gorgeous aroma, please, Mrs Mooney.'

After depositing his damp guest in the warmth of the front parlour, Father Mac ran up the stairs and returned with a snow-white bath towel. Fergal thought it looked too good to use, but Father Mac opened it out, instructed him to take his sopping coat off and helped him dry his hair. Fergal was trembling from the sudden warmth, but Father Mac took this as a sign that he was still cold. He moved him closer to the roaring fire and realised how wet Fergal's back and shoulders were.

'Take off that jumper and that shirt,' he said. 'I'll fetch you something of mine to wear till they're dry.' Before Fergal could argue, Father Mac was off up the two flights of stairs again. He returned with a clean sweatshirt, motioned for Fergal to lift his arms and pulled off the sopping layers that made a sucking sound as they tried to stay stuck to his skin. Fergal was glad of the shelter of the enormous towel – he'd wrapped himself in it shyly, making sure his bare torso was completely covered. His skin was tingling. Father Mac saw his embarrassment and left the room, 'to see if Mrs Mooney needs a hand', and Fergal pulled on the borrowed sweatshirt as fast as he could.

Mrs Mooney came back on Father Mac's heels, carrying an overfilled tray, and Father Mac asked her to tumble dry his guest's shirt and jumper. She timed her tut of disapproval to the exact moment the door closed behind her; she'd had years of practice.

There was a big pot of tea, cups, saucers, milk, sugar, biscuits, toasted Veda bread, butter, slices of cheese and a jar of some kind of chutney that Fergal thought looked disgusting – he thought he'd better not try it, in case he had to spit it out. He waited for Father Mac to start eating and then followed his every move. They devoured two sandwiches each before laying into the biscuits.

Father Mac noticed him glancing over at the piano and the pile of sheet music. 'Do you play?'

'Me? Are you kidding? No – I've just never seen one in somebody's house before, that's all. And there's no carpet.'

Father Mac burst out laughing, then stopped as he realised the sudden sunset in Fergal's face was not coming from his proximity to the fire. 'It's better for the asthma to have no carpets. Luckily these floorboards were stripped and polished years before I got here.'

A fire engine sounded its alarm somewhere. 'Do you harmonise with them too, or is it strictly ambulances?' Father Mac asked. 'Your voice sounds quite high. Have you been training for long?'

'What, Father?'

'You know – when I heard you on the street. Do you always gravitate to the descant – above the melody?'

Fergal didn't know what to say, except that he'd never had any lessons apart from the classes with Baldy Turner.

'So you're a natural, then. Listen, do you fancy a sing sometime? I love playing the piano, but I have no one to accompany.'

'Do you not sing yourself, Father?'

'Fergal, even when I didn't smoke my voice would've stopped traffic – and not in a good way!'

Fergal laughed. He was finding it hard not to stare. Father Mac wanted to know more about this strange young lad but sensed his shyness – he didn't push him to sing, there was no hurry. He kept the conversation light and asked Fergal how he was getting on in school.

They realised that, even though they'd gone to school only a petrol-bomb's throw from each other, their experiences couldn't have been further apart. Father Mac told Fergal about the Christian Brothers' College that he'd attended and how much he'd loved his years there. The Brothers had been strict but he'd excelled at most of the subjects, and when he'd announced his interest in the priesthood it had nourished his popularity. He told him how he had decided to enter the seminary in a place called Maynooth. It had been wonderful. It was so different from Belfast in every way, and he'd been able to put serious effort into his other passion of playing the piano but the vocational commitments were stricter than anything he'd known before. 'We were only allowed to leave the grounds once a week, to go into the village.'

'Once a week? That must've been hard, Father.'

'You should've seen us, Fergal! We were like a pack of wild animals, after spending all that time cooped up studying. We'd scramble to the pub like we'd been trapped underground in a coal mine for years, and order spirits because pints took too long to drink and we only had a few hours. I didn't drink or smoke before I went there, but that changed fast.'

Fergal laughed. With each story about his past, Father Mac seemed younger to him. 'When did you know you were different?'

Father Mac suddenly looked uneasy. 'What do you mean, different?'

'I mean, when did you know you wanted to become a priest?'

'Oh, right – that... It wasn't really a conscious decision. There've been priests in my family for generations, here and there, and my mother always said it would make her so proud to have one in her brood. She used to say it to me when she put me to bed, when I was a wee boy. The priesthood chose me, really, not the other way around. Does that make sense?'

An hour and a half passed unnoticed, as the black blazer steamed on the radiator and the little fragments of their lives were unearthed in between mouthfuls of tea and biscuits. Father Mac hardly realised that he was talking about himself in a more personal way than he had done in years.

Fergal asked him about Africa and Father Mac told him how the local people had humbled him with their unwavering trust and generosity. 'If you ever get the chance, Fergal, you should spend time there. What a beautiful place it is – and the people… some of the warmest I've ever met in my life.'

Mrs Mooney knocked on the door, carrying Fergal's dry clothes in a neatly ironed pile, and reminded Father Mac that there was confession before the evening mass and Fergal wasn't the only one who needed to change his clothes. They couldn't believe how much time had evaporated. Fergal went to the bathroom to get changed. When he came back, Father Mac was holding out a bottle of holy water – much bigger than Noreen's – in the shape of Jesus' ma.

'Here you are, Fergal. I hope this will do.'

'Father, are you sure? Can I give you some money?' He nervously fingered the illicit fifty pence in his pocket.

'No, Fergal Flynn, you cannot. You can, however, promise me that you'll come back for another chat sometime. I have an idea that I want to run by you. Are you free this Sunday?'

'I think so. What time?'

'Well, what about after lunch – or will your family be upset that you're not at home?'

Fergal's puzzled face said more than any words. He agreed to come at about three o'clock, after he'd had lunch with his granny. Then he went home, humming to himself all the way. Even though they'd eaten so much, Fergal somehow felt lighter than he ever had in his life.

9

Father Mac spent the rest of the week acquainting himself with his regular parishioners. Word had spread quickly about the handsome new addition to St Bridget's. The contrast between his local accent and his exotic tan heightened the curiosity: one set of rumours said he was a well-to-do local boy, another claimed that his father had been an African, and Fergal overheard his mother and their next-door neighbour saying Father Mac had been an orphan brought up by nuns. One by one, the ladies of the parish began calling at the priest's house, with gifts of food and jumpers that were far too big for him. The bemused priest accepted gracefully and listened intently to their woes, while Mrs Mooney gritted her teeth and made pot after pot of tea, grumbling to the tray that she'd never get her cleaning done if this kept up.

~

In the early, shy light of Sunday morning, Fergal dreamt he was in the confessional and Father Mac was preparing to hear his sins. The wire mesh was only a mist-soaked silver cobweb, and before he could stop himself Fergal leaned forward on his knees, pulled the spider's hard work away and kissed the priest full on the mouth.

Fergal woke up suddenly, with a hard-on, in his tangled bed-clothes. His grandmother was snoring, and he realised he'd been disturbed by the familiar sound of his mother letting herself in the front door – she usually came round on Sundays, to have a cup of tea with Noreen before she headed to the graveyard to visit her father. The paper-thin ceiling allowed him to hear her fart loudly, giggle like a schoolgirl and then apologise to the dull, grey morning. 'Oh, Jesus Christ, I'm rotten, so I am. God forgive me on his holy day, and forgive them curry chips I had last night, too!'

Three o'clock couldn't come quickly enough.

Sunday lunch was called Sunday dinner in the Flynn house-hold. It consisted of the boys pretending to Angela that they'd gone to mass and settling down to deafening sport on the TV, while their father shouted at the 'fucking cunting useless ref' and Angela served the 'growing men' endless amounts of roast pota-toes and pints of milk. Fergal washed every dish in sight. He was in such a good mood that he forgot himself and started hum-ming, but he stopped when he caught sight of his brothers' sus-picious expressions. He left quickly, out the back door, mumbling that he was going for a walk. John usually mimicked every word he said in a high, girly voice, but Fergal closed the door just before he had to hear it.

Even the soldiers' pointless interrogation on the way to St Bridget's didn't bother him as it usually did, though they made him take off his shoes and socks to search for God knows what. Fergal wondered what their families were doing as their sons were searching him. He wanted to ask them what they were thinking. Were they dreaming of Sunday dinners somewhere in Leicester or Manchester or Norfolk?

~

Father Mac paced the room like he was expecting the bishop. He caught himself in the mirror fixing his hair for the third time, and got annoyed. What on earth was he doing?

At last the doorbell rang. Mrs Mooney ushered Fergal into the front parlour, and Father Mac gave him a delighted smile and a nervous handshake. The merest touch from him was enough to make Fergal's heart go up a gear.

'I'm so glad you could make it. What did your parents say? Oh, forgive me, Fergal – I assume your parents are still with us?'

'What? Oh – yeah, Father. Sunday dinner isn't a big thing in our house, really. It's more of a sports day – well, it is for my three brothers and my da. The house could be burning down around them and they wouldn't notice, as long as the TV stayed on.'

'Three brothers? My goodness, that must be a busy house… How does your mother cope? Any sisters?'

'No, no sisters.'

Father Mac had struck the match before he remembered. 'Your asthma – do you mind me having a cigarette?

'Ah, no, Father. You go ahead – sure, it's your house.'

Father Mac inhaled. 'And what's it like where you live, Fergal?'

'Well, I stay with my granny most of the time.'

'You do? Which one?'

At first Fergal didn't understand the question as he'd never really known his father's mother that well. 'Oh, I see… My mother's mother – Noreen, she's called. She's not very well and she spends a lot of time in bed. Our house is very small for the six of us, so I sleep there and do stuff around the house and keep her company, I suppose. It's great.'

'And what about your father's mother? Is she still with us?'

'Granny Flynn died years ago, Father.'

The cigarette smoke reminded Fergal of her. Ethel Flynn had rarely come to see them in his early childhood. She hated Angela and Walker Street – she said the broken glass ruined her high heels. Every once in a while, though, her nosiness would get the better of her and she would clack up the street unannounced, in a cloud of perfume and menthol cigarette smoke, claiming that she was just passing on her way into town and would love a cup of tea.

They were banned from calling her Granny, because she bluntly refused to be that old. Her favourite was Paddy Jr, for reasons known only to herself, and only he was allowed onto her throne-like lap. John, who hated kissing her over-made-up face, was a close second while Ciaran stayed as near to Angela as he could, with one eye on Ethel's bag for possible sweets. Since Fergal was born, Ethel had referred to him as 'that one'. She said his piercing green eyes looked evil and that his curly hair was wasted on a boy – she had to pay a small fortune to her hairdresser to perm any conviction into her lank, straight hair and force it to the desired bossy height.

Gradually her dislike of Angela had defrosted into lofty pity, but never enough for her to offer to mind the kids while her exhausted daughter-in-law went for a walk to clear her head. The other boys were interested in the possible calorific contents of her handbag, but Fergal didn't trust her. He stayed behind the sofa, listening, until they forgot he was there. On one of her visits he thought he heard her call him a 'mystic', in between dramatic drags on her permanent cigarette. It was a few moments before he realised that her voice, clogged with smoke and most of a box of plain chocolates, had actually said that he was some kind of 'mistake'. Angela had said nothing. She was looking at the clock, repeating that she would have to start her husband's dinner soon, praying that the oul' bitch wouldn't misinterpret that as an invitation to stay, and hoping that she'd leave some money for the kids. Fergal had crawled out into the hallway and broken every spoke in his grandmother's expensive umbrella, as the wind and rain tried to clean the little panels of neglected glass above the front door that no one else but the weather could be bothered to reach.

As far as Fergal knew, Ethel Flynn had ended up in some nursing home and had died suddenly. They'd been too young to go to her funeral, according to Angela.

Father Mac knew from the look on Fergal's face that he was somewhere else.

'Are you all right there, Fergal? You're miles away, aren't you?'

'What? Yeah – sorry, Father, I was just thinking about something. It's the smoke. It reminds me of her – my father's mother.'

Father Mac had noticed that, any time the conversation

strayed to Fergal's family, he would look away and skim over the surface of the answer. He tried, gently, to find out more.

'So tell me about your brothers, Fergal. Are you like them? I only have one brother and one sister, and we're not alike at all.'

He knew he'd hit some kind of nerve when Fergal almost shouted, 'I'm nothing like them, Father – nothing!' He caught himself and lowered his voice. 'I know nothing about sport, I like reading and walking, and… and, well, we're not that close.'

Father Mac knew he'd gone too far. To change the subject, he went over to the piano and opened the lid. 'Come here, Fergal, have a go.'

'Ah, no, Father – sure, I haven't a clue and—'

'Never mind the excuses. Look, just come and sit here and I'll play then.'

So Fergal did as he was bid and sank into an old reading chair, while the young priest played a Mozart selection that made his audience of one want to cry. Fergal felt transported. The sound engulfed him, and a calmness began to creep into his bones. He watched Father Mac's fingers dance on the keys like cartoon mice, and noticed how the soft down of dark hair travelled along the backs of his hands before disappearing out of sight under the shelter of his cuffs. A dim flicker of desire made him stare in the opposite direction, out the window into the cold street, where the rain had started again.

When he had finished the Mozart, Father Mac asked Fergal, as casually as he could, if he knew any songs. Fergal dropped his gaze and said, 'Not really, Father', but Father Mac instinctively started an old hymn called 'Be Thou My Vision' and kept looking at Fergal, nodding encouragement, until he slowly joined in.

When they came to the second verse, Father Mac slyly faded

out, pretending not to remember the words, and Fergal closed his eyes as he gradually found the confidence to continue alone. His voice, shy but crystal clear, was made all the warmer by the wooden floor of the room. Father Mac was astonished at how effortlessly high it was, and how moving.

As the last verse came to an end, he turned around on the piano seat and looked at Fergal with his mouth open. 'Fergal Flynn, you have a truly beautiful singing voice.'

Fergal didn't know what to say. There was no sound from either of them for a while, just the better-late-than-never app- lause of the young wood crackling in the hearth as the flames found it. A distant ambulance, muffled by the closed doors, made them bless themselves automatically before they turned again to the piano and the sheets of old music.

'Do you know a lot of other songs?' Father Mac asked. 'Have you ever been a member of a school choir?'

Fergal couldn't help laughing and telling him that Baldy Turn- er liked talking better than teaching. 'But I picked up a few in mass. I think there used to be a choir years ago, in the chapel, but they were all old then, so I think they're dead now.'

Finally Father Mac asked him to sing again. Fergal was reluc- tant, but the priest stood up and took him by the shoulders and looked straight into his eyes. 'Please? Just a few more?'

No one had ever said that to him before.

After a quick gulp of tea, they had a go at a few more hymns. Fergal was a bit nervous for the first few bars but, as the priest closed his eyes and arched his back, he began to feel calmer. He sang with such expression that he felt light-headed when he stopped.

'Fergal, where have you been hiding that voice? I mean, it's astonishing. Tell me, what have ambulances got that I don't?'

They laughed, and Father Mac started to play again. He was a natural harmoniser. Fergal, for the first time in his life, forgot where he was and who he was for the best part of half an hour.

The hall clock called time, and Father Mac looked at his watch and sighed. 'Fergal, I'm so sorry to have to stop, but I promised I'd call in on a few of the pensioners. Look, I cannot believe your voice. Do you even know what a voice you have?'

Fergal's eyes widened.

'I think it's the best I've ever heard – I'm serious. Look, we have to meet again soon, as soon as you can. There's so much more to talk about, and so much more music for your voice to sing... Look, basically, I want to put a choir together, and I want you to help me. Say you will – will you?'

Fergal was completely robbed of words. All he could do was nod his dizzy head.

They went out the front door together and then went their separate ways. Fergal was out of breath with excitement before he even reached the top of the road. Father Mac's voice played over and over again in his head: *I want to put a choir together, and I want you to help me.* As he neared home, Fergal wondered if Father Mac's body was hairy all over, like the little glimpse he'd had of his wrists.

When he got back to Noreen's, he brought her up a cup of tea. She took one look at him and said, 'What has you smiling like a big Cheshire cat? Did you find money or something?'

'Ah, no, Granny. I'm just... happy.'

'Happy? Jesus, it's well for you, love – and you deserve it, too. You're good to your oul' granny.' She pulled him down to her by his jumper and kissed him on the forehead.

Fergal was touched and mortified all at once. 'I'm away down-stairs to watch TV, if you don't need me, Granny.' Noreen stared after him, thinking that he must have met a girl.

He jumped down the stairs, three at a time, into the sanctuary of the little living room. He looked into the circular mirror on the wall. *A choir – he wants me to be in his choir! I'll be able to spend loads of time with him and learn loads of songs… Oh, God, it'll be brilliant!*

10

Fergal and Father Mac met every other day and drank India dry.

After a few informal rehearsals, Father Mac set about finding suitable music for Fergal to sing. There were loads of songbooks crammed into the cupboards, and he went into the town to buy some new ones with traditional Irish ballads. Fergal had a natural ear and learned quickly.

After a few weeks, Father Mac told him his idea. He wanted to start a small choir that would gradually build up a repertoire of songs, with a view to performing them at mass and on feast days and celebrations – maybe even at weddings as well.

'We're off to a flying start now I've found St Bridget's soloist in the shape of you, Fergal Flynn!'

'Me? Oh, Father Mac – thank you. I don't know what to say...'

'Don't say anything. Just sing and look after your voice. We've got a lot of work to do.'

Fergal was buzzing with excitement as they hatched a plan of action. They set about distributing little posters around the chapel and school noticeboards announcing auditions for St Bridget's Choir. Father Mac called on Baldy Turner for help, but Baldy informed him that, although no one could be keener than himself to encourage music in the school, he didn't think anyone would take it remotely seriously. He had tried to set up a similar choir once, but they'd turned out to be a bunch of 'no-good remedials who couldn't be relied upon to attend school, never mind rehearsals!' – he practically shouted it, in remembered frustration at many a wasted evening. But Father Mac's enthusiasm remained intact.

The auditions attracted a fair amount of interest initially. It was something different. Most of the boys were secretly still a bit afraid of the priests and, sure, it might be a way to skip a few classes. The voice tests were held in Baldy Turner's classroom during a lunch break, with Father Mac and Fergal in attendance. Two of the choir hopefuls – the big, ginger-haired, freckled Stephenson brothers – weren't bad at repeating a note struck on the piano, and Baldy Turner was in danger of looking enthusiastic. Once it was clear that the successful applicants would have to sing a song on their own, though, most of the others fled. Father Mac was still undeterred. He said they would make up the numbers themselves until replacements could be found.

So, twice a week, the fledgling choir of Father Mac, Mr Turner, Fergal and the ginger Stephensons would gather around the piano in Father Mac's house. Sometimes Baldy Turner couldn't come, so Fergal had to sing his part. He had to really concentrate on the more difficult lower harmonies, as he naturally gravitated to the higher register. Even though it was ridiculous, Fergal felt a bit jealous if Father Mac complimented the Stephensons when they got a harmony right. Very slowly, their sound started to take shape. Sometimes, if the chapel was free, they would rehearse up in the balcony with the pipe organ.

Unfortunately, that was the final nail in the coffin for the freckled twosome, who had only joined the choir under threat – their mother had a conviction, not altogether unrealistic, that they'd get to jump the queue on the never-ending waiting list for a bigger council house if her sons were in the choir. Fergal was on his way to rehearsal one evening after school when the Stephensons shouted to him from the roof of the bakery, 'Tell Father Mac to stick his fucking choir up his hairy jam roll – we're not singing in no chapel in front of nobody!' Then they flashed their bare red arses.

The feeling Fergal got when his solo voice carried into the rafters of the old church was scary and exciting all at the same time. It was his only relief from the endless routine of looking after Noreen and the mounting stress of trying to study for the upcoming exams. Only he and a few other 'geeks' were taking their O-levels seriously – even some of the teachers made it clear that they didn't care if the students all threw away their futures – they got paid either way. A few of his classmates had already dropped out of school to work with their fathers.

Fergal constantly wondered what he was going to do with himself. All of a sudden he had to think about a life outside school that was fast approaching, and it made him shiver. He hadn't a clue what kind of job he wanted, or even what he would be good at. He brought it up at the end of a rehearsal one day, after Baldy Turner had left, and Father Mac encouraged him to work as hard as he could for the exams, and maybe think about university in England or Dublin or somewhere. This possibility hadn't even occurred to Fergal – it would make him the first one in his family even to think about university – but, he thought, he'd happily go anywhere as long as it wasn't Belfast.

By the end of spring, they had ten songs learned properly: 'Be Thou My Vision'; 'Our Father'; 'Lamb of God'; 'He Is Lord'; 'Go Tell It on the Mountain'; 'For That He Gave His Only Son'; 'Blessed Be the Lord'; 'Praise Him on High'; 'O Holy Night' and 'Follow Me'.

Then, out of the bluey-grey, Father Mac had some good news that would change everything.

~

Brother Vincent McFarland was a monk in Sligo Abbey, near the coast in the west of Ireland. Every morning and every evening, he and the rest of the ancient order chanted together in spectacular harmony, in Latin and Irish, for an hour. A few recordings had been made over the years, in an effort to preserve the tradition and to acknowledge the twentieth-century way of chronicling these otherworldly compositions. In their ceaseless quest for perfection, the monks needed a young, clear, high tenor voice to act as a shaft of brilliant melodic light complementing their deep, resonant bass in the chants that had been written so many centuries before electricity almost put candles and imagination out of a job.

Father Mac had known Brother Vincent since they were in their late teens. They had met at classical-music evenings in

Belfast, had hit it off immediately and managed to stay in touch even during the years Father Mac had spent in Africa. Since the choir had started, Brother Vincent had been kept up to speed on Fergal's progress, and had grown more and more curious to hear the young man's voice. When Sligo Abbey needed a guest tenor, it was the perfect opportunity. Brother Vincent phoned St Bridget's, offering Fergal the chance to attend auditions, which could only take place at the Abbey. The monks were forbidden to leave unless it was in a brown box, and even then they were buried in the ancient graveyard that was still part of the grounds.

The day Father Mac got the call, Fergal was late for rehearsal. He often was. Usually it was because Granny Noreen had taken another turn for the worse and begged him not to leave her alone, until the latest concoction of pills and alcohol knocked her out or made her forget who he was. This time, though, he was late because an army foot patrol had insisted that he waited until they got radio confirmation of how old he was – they thought he was older than he said. Then they searched him at a snail's pace, asking him relentless questions. One of the soldiers was an enormous black man with hands the size of shovels, making his rifle look like a toy. He ran them right over Fergal's backside and then around to his groin, where the back of his hand rested against Fergal's balls. Try as he might, Fergal couldn't stop himself beginning to get hard. Thankfully, they let him go before it was noticeable. Out of nowhere, he suddenly thought he shouldn't be fancying anyone else – it felt almost as if he was betraying Father Mac somehow. He knew it was ridiculous, but he couldn't stop thinking it.

When Father Mac announced Brother Vincent's invitation,

Fergal looked like someone who'd been robbed. His mind was suddenly crawling with every negative thought imaginable. Surely there was no way he'd be able to go? His parents would see to that. And what about Noreen? She depended on him so much… How much money would it cost? Where would he stay? Would he need better clothes? Would he be good enough? He didn't want to let anybody down…

'What is it, Fergal? This is good news. Why do you look so upset about it?'

Fergal's floodgates opened, and he nearly choked on years of tears. He told Father Mac about how awful school was, about the way his brothers treated him and about his father. He told him how being beaten was sometimes better than being ignored – at least it meant his father was singling him out, paying some attention to him. He told him how his mother sometimes left bite marks on his hands, how he wanted her to stop hurting herself. He told him about the time he'd been drying himself after a bath and turned around to discover her holding a kitchen knife, threatening to stab him to death if she ever found out he was a dirty queer and how ten minutes later she'd been a different person, saying that he was the only one she could depend on. He told him about Noreen – how she needed him, how sad he was for her, how he couldn't help her.

Father Mac tentatively put his arm around him, slowly squeezing him closer as he heaved with tears. Fergal, resting his head against the priest's shoulder with sheer exhaustion, was suddenly intoxicated by the experience of being so close to this man. He had only ever seen men touch each other in fights, at funerals or when a match was going well. At that moment Fergal felt something that he couldn't articulate at first – a kind of peace. He began to realise that Father Mac was the only person who, albeit briefly, made him feel safe.

Father Mac hadn't expected the well of feeling that was gathering in his own gut. As Fergal's head pressed against him, he felt his heart hurry, and he closed his eyes to try and keep the moment under control. They sat motionless, as if on a deserted island with no other sign of life. Fergal didn't want to let go, ever.

Father Mac was the first to come to his senses and initiate their careful, reluctant parting. They found it hard to meet each other's eyes.

'I'll do everything in my power to make this trip happen,' Father Mac said gently. 'You won't be paid for the audition or the recording, but I'll make sure you're looked after, and it won't cost you or your parents a penny – the monastery will be putting us up. At most, all it'll mean is a few nights in Sligo.'

Fergal left feeling much calmer, but remained unconvinced that he would be able to go.

~

That night, as Father Mac lay in bed, he couldn't get to sleep. He tried reading, but couldn't concentrate. The vision of Fergal's face kept appearing in his mind's eye. Frustrated with himself, he took out his rosary beads and looked at the tiny crucifix. Then he began to pray. 'Dear Almighty Father, grant me the strength to remain pure in word and in deed. I know you have sent Fergal to me for a reason. He needs my help, and I must not… I must not abuse his trust… I must protect him. I must protect his gift, given by you.'

As he finally began to fall asleep he thought of Africa, and the last time his heart had been hijacked without his permission.

He'd been at the mission for about a year when, early one evening, he'd decided to explore a nearby beach. Even at night, the heat was relentless. He took off his collar and opened his shirt, letting what little breeze there was from the water cool his chest. Sitting on the beach was a fisherman. He looked like he had been expertly carved from ebony – his skin was so smooth it could have been liquid, and it was all Father Mac could do to not reach out and touch him. The fisherman's smile spread right across his face as he introduced himself as 'Basile, like the man from *Fawlty Towers*'. Then he reached into a bucket and offered Father Mac a fish from his evening catch.

Their friendship developed quickly. They both loved to talk, and Basile's command of English was almost better than Father Mac's. They met on the same beach once a week. Father Mac would bring along Irish newspapers sent from Belfast, and they would sit in the shade, smoking, reading, swapping questions and telling stories. Basile had his own boat and sometimes they went up the river, where kingfishers built their nests in the roasting sun and barracudas patrolled the deeper, darker water. When Basile caught one and wrestled it into their boat, Father Mac thought it was a shark and nearly ended up in the water in his panicked attempt to get away from it. Basile never asked what he did, and Father Mac never told him.

He knew it wasn't just the unforgiving heat that made him sweat when Basile stripped off, completely naturally, and invited him into the water to wash off the day. Father Mac protested that he wasn't really a swimmer, but Basile insisted on giving him lessons, so he shyly undressed to his underwear and waded into the sea. Basile supported him around the waist and made him kick his legs.

The tide pulled them out further, and they stood shoulder-deep in the sea. Father Mac couldn't help staring at Basile's full lips. The last thing he expected Basile to do was suddenly lean in and kiss him. There, in the orange light of the African sky, under a blanket of dark-green sea water, they explored every inch of each other, and Father Mac did what he had wanted to do all his life.

When they waded back to the shore, they parted as if they had never met. Father Mac watched as Basile moved off quickly to be swallowed by the dark. Thoughts crowded his walk back to his hut. It troubled him greatly that he'd broken his solemn vow of celibacy and that he'd sinned before God – but he couldn't see how something that had felt so good and so tender could be wrong. What harm had they done? Surely, he thought, surely God could see that?

He returned to the beach many times, but their paths never crossed there again. Not long before he got the call to come home to Ireland, he was on a bus travelling to a remote village, and he could have sworn he saw Basile driving by in a beaten-up car full of children, with a woman by his side.

~

The corrugated curtains of St Bridget's parlour offered a refuge that Fergal had never known before. When he had a rehearsal to look forward to he could think of little else. The usual barbed comments from his brothers, which normally would have torn at the core of him, didn't seem to penetrate as deeply any more. His heart was insulated in the knowledge that Father Mac was his friend.

Gradually, as they rehearsed the pieces of chant that Brother Vincent had sent, he began to stay later and later. Looking at the music written on the manuscript paper, Fergal was both impressed and intimidated by the way Father Mac translated it so easily onto the waiting keys of the piano. He loved watching him wrinkle his brow in concentration as he tried to work out the best way to play the harmonies of the ancient pieces so Fergal could imagine how it would ultimately sound.

Sometimes Father Mac could see that, although Fergal was beside him in the room, his mind was somewhere else. As much as Fergal loved being in the company of the kindest man he knew, he also felt guilty about his Granny Noreen. At the end of the evening, during their well-earned cups of tea and biscuits, he would start imagining all the bad things that could happen to her while he was away enjoying himself. He'd swallow the food far too quickly, say his goodbyes to the startled priest and run out the door, burping the whole way back to her house. Father Mac knew it was going to be tricky getting Fergal's parents to agree to let him attend the auditions in Sligo, but trickiest of all would be getting him time away from Granny Noreen.

There were other times, though, when Fergal felt free. Sometimes when their rehearsals ran over, Father Mac would share with Fergal the cold supper that Mrs Mooney left out before stacking the fire for the evening. Mr Mooney picked his wife up every evening at seven o'clock on the button. This became Fergal's favourite time of all. He allowed himself the fantasy that he and Father Mac were a secret couple. They would put away the scattered sheets of music together, as neatly as possible, and then

Father Mac would go off into the kitchen and bring back a feast of food. Fergal would sit at the coffee table and Father Mac would settle into one of the big soft chairs, and they would eat their supper off their laps, talking about music and the summer holidays that weren't far away.

'Fergal, do you have any ideas about what you might want to do with your life – you know, when you get older? You're going to be seventeen this summer, right?'

'Yeah… I really don't know, Father.'

'Well, what if you could do anything? You must have dreams. What do you dream about?'

Fergal suddenly remembered that he'd dreamt about Father Mac that very morning – he'd forgotten until that second. He'd dreamt that they were at Noreen's, rehearsing as quietly as they could because she was asleep upstairs. The tiny living room was empty except for an enormous grand piano. When they got tired, Fergal said there was nowhere for them to sleep, but Father Mac had said, 'Don't be silly, we can sleep in the piano.' Then he undressed and climbed in on top of the golden strings, and Fergal followed. The lid was like a soft brown duvet that they pulled up around themselves for warmth. Just as they put their arms around each other and began kissing, his mother put her key in the front door, calling his name. Then he'd woken to Noreen asking him to get a drink of water.

He said, 'I want to sing, Father Mac. I want to see the world, I want to learn to play the piano, and I want Noreen to get better and see me sing. I think that's it.'

'That's a good start. I think you were put on the earth to sing. Forgive me – I've not met Noreen yet – but one thing is for certain and that is that old people eventually die. That's the natural law. I never knew my grandparents, because they died before I was born. Sometimes that's the way it's meant to be. She sounds very, very fragile to me, but she's not your responsibility.'

'But she's my granny, Father.'

'Fergal, I know that – I don't mean to sound unkind. But you have a fairly big family. You also have your own life to live, and you've been living far too many other people's lives, as far as I can tell.'

Fergal sat still and let Father Mac's words encircle his head. One by one, they landed, as he began to understand what he meant.

Father Mac was tackling a huge lump of coal that proved far too big to break up. In the end, he sat it gingerly on top of the hungry flames in the hearth, and stared as they competed to devour the dark mass. The heat of the fire proved too much for the constraint of his white collar and he loosened it, just enough to afford a glimpse of his thick black forest of chest hair. Before he could stop himself, Fergal realised that he had the beginnings of an erection.

He pulled his jumper down to hide it and tried to think about disgusting things, but it was no good. Try as he might, he could still feel the familiar slippery wetness in the front of his trousers. There was only one thing to do. He said goodnight to Father Mac, being careful not to brush against him when they hugged each other, and practically ran out the door.

He didn't want to go back to Granny Noreen's cold house just yet. Without thinking, he went around the back of the house and stood in the shadows, looking up. He knew which room was

Father Mac's, and he watched the night sky reflected on the glass. Suddenly a light snapped on and Father Mac appeared, framed for a split second in the window as if it were the grille of a giant confessional, before he closed the curtains.

Fergal's thickness struggled in his trousers for freedom. He looked around. It was so dark that no one would be able to see him. Nervously he undid his zipper and let his hardness stand out in the cold air. He kept looking around, ready to do himself up again at the first sign of life, but even the buildings held their breath.

He had pissed in the yard of Walker Street before, when someone was having a bath and, if anyone caught him, Fergal decided he could always say that was what he was doing. His heart felt like it was beating in the middle of his cock as he took hold of it.

He looked back up at Father Mac's window. The light went off again. Fergal reckoned he must have undressed and gotten into bed. This thought made him even harder, and he undid his trousers so that they fell and gathered around his knees. He'd forgotten that his underpants had a bit of neatly folded toilet roll stuck to the gusset, to keep them cleaner for longer – one of his bastard brothers always stole the last clean pair.

He imagined Father Mac taking off his shirt slowly, undoing one button at a time to show his strong, hairy chest. Then walking towards him with a tender smile, kissing him lightly on his chapped lips whilst undoing his own black leather belt. The dark trousers would fall to the ground and through his gleaming white underwear Fergal would be able to see his growing erection. They would embrace and kiss, slowly at first, before becoming more confident and passionate. He would push Father Mac's underwear halfway down his thighs and take his hardness in his grip, still kissing him… Fergal was breathing harder. Without making a sound, he emptied himself in silent, mini explosions against the wall.

The guilt wasted no time in arriving, of course. As he fixed himself up in a panic, he wondered if God really did see everything, especially in the dark.

~

Father Mac had gone to bed early as a rare treat, even though he knew a ring of the phone or a knock at the front door could change his plans at any moment. Try as he might to distract himself by reading letters, he couldn't get Fergal Flynn out of his head. He knew, in his heart of hearts, that it wasn't just the crystal-clear singing voice that moved him so much. There was something else about Fergal – he was like no one Father Mac had ever met. It felt as though they'd known each other for much longer than a mere handful of months.

He placed his hand on his Bible and knelt below the wooden crucifix on the wall.

'Holy Father, I beseech you again for guidance. I've just spent some of the happiest hours of my life with Fergal Flynn. He's an extraordinary person – so raw and so trusting… How can a young man like him have such a profound effect on me? I'm a priest, I have made solemn vows that I intend to honour, but… but there are moments when he looks at me in a way that fills me with thoughts I haven't had since Africa. I need your guidance. He's not yet seventeen, I'm ten years older. He's so very vulnerable and the last thing I want is to take advantage of that in any way, but I also want to stay close to him. I want to be honest. Lord, protect and guide me. In the name of the Father, the Son and the Holy Spirit. Amen.'

He was completely drained when he finally managed to climb under the crisp, white, forgiving bedcovers.

11

'Is that you, son?' Noreen yelled when Fergal opened the front door. He went up and explained that the rehearsal with Father Mac had gone on longer than expected.

'Do you think that priest would come over and give me Communion, now that you seem to be such good friends?'

'I don't know,' Fergal said, not looking at her. 'He's always really busy.'

Fergal knew Noreen and Father Mac would have to meet eventually, but he dreaded letting Father Mac see where he lived. The priest continually offered him lifts home in his new black Rover, but Fergal always refused, 'Sure, there'd be no point, I'm not going straight there...'

Ever since he'd first visited St Bridget's House, he'd started to notice the cracks in Noreen's ceiling, the cobwebs in the corners, the decay that had set in everywhere. Every bit of carpet was as thin as paper. In some of the rooms there were big patches missing and he could see the old floorboards on which his mother had learned to walk. No matter how much he tidied it up, Fergal realised his granny's place was a tip compared to the priest's house. Everything was long worn out, like her, and there was still the unmistakable smell of the cats she used to have after his granda had died. When her drinking got out of control, she'd let them soil everywhere.

Inevitably, Noreen's faith had been eroded by the constant dull pain that she felt every day when she looked around at her crumbling life. Any time she saw the news, it confirmed her hopelessness. She told Fergal that she was convinced she'd never see peace again in her lifetime. Every once in a while, though, she'd give him little threads of stories about the old Belfast that she'd known.

One night she pointed out the filthy window and said, 'Do you see that telegraph pole, our Fergal? Well, that used to be an oul' gas street light.' Fergal thought it was a funny idea that lights could have been gas. Then she told him how young men used to gather on corners under the lamps, singing, on late summer evenings. She told him how his own grandfather used to stand there with a bunch of his friends, singing till the lamplighter came round and snuffed out the lights.

Fergal suddenly realised he'd never asked her how she and his granda had met. When he did, she threw her eyes up to the flaking ceiling as if to ask her dead husband in the heavens whether she should tell him. Then she reached for her glasses, cleaned them on her nightdress and sat up in bed, looking more alert than she had for a long time. 'There's an oul' hatbox under the bed. Get it out for me will you, son?'

He crouched down and fought his way past empty gin bottles, old fur-lined boots and two suitcases to the dirty, dusty hatbox right at the back. He handed it to Noreen and she untied the pale pink ribbon with her tiny fingers. She brought out a prayer book and a stained brown envelope, 'Oh good, these are the things that were in your granda's pockets when he died in the hospital.' Fergal saw tears in her eyes.

'Oh, Granny, I'm sorry – I didn't mean to upset you.'

She pulled herself together and unearthed a little bundle of photos. 'I haven't seen these in years, never mind shown them to anyone.'

There, in black and white, were Fergal's granda and granny as he'd never seen them before. Her hair was shiny and blonde, and she was tiny beside her husband's strong, athletic frame. There was even a wedding photo – Fergal recognised the big wooden doors of St Bridget's Chapel – they looked so young and healthy and unhurried, and Noreen was laughing confidently into the lens. They looked like a Hollywood movie couple stepping into the waiting car that would take them to their bright, new, technicolored future together.

Noreen brought the picture close to her glasses and looked at her husband's face, then stroked her grandson's cheek. 'Oh, Fergal, the only thing your parents ever did right by you was name you after your granda. Look, sure, you have his eyes and his hairline and his smile too. Oh, but he had a beautiful smile – and all his own teeth, you know!'

'When was this one taken?' Fergal said, picking out a worn snapshot of a boy and a girl out for a walk in the city centre.

'That was the week before we got married, son.' She stroked the soft black-and-white memory with her wrinkled hands. 'Do you really want to know how I met your granda?'

'Of course I do, Granny! Please, tell me.'

'Well, son, get your granny a wee glass from the kitchen cabinet and I'll tell you.'

Fergal ran down the stairs, washed out her favourite tumbler under the tap and dried it as best he could. When they were settled on her bed and she had poured herself a large helping of gin, she began, 'When I was your age, Fergal – how old are you again?'

'I'm nearly seventeen.'

'Jesus, son, is that right? You're a big lad, like your granda. Well, when I turned eighteen, I tortured my own mother Betty – God rest her soul, even though she was a wicked oul' bitch, God forgive me – to let me go to the big dance. It was a few miles out in the country and a group of us girls were going, with the priest and a couple of nuns to chaperone us. When I think of what young people have now… Jesus, sure, it was only a wee parochial hall with a band and a few bottles of lemonade, but we thought it was the dance to end all dances. You have to remember, son, there were no housing estates then. Oh, no, there was nothing but fields and country lanes for miles and miles, and the fellas arrived on their bikes from farms and all. Anyway, I spent weeks saving up for the material to make my dress and in the end my mother said I could go.

'Well, we couldn't get there quick enough. We got on the wee bus – the girls sat at the front with the nuns, and the men sat at the back, with the priest in the middle. The roads were awful, full of potholes, and we bumped along for what felt like hours. Poor wee Mary Harper from Hawthorn Street had to get the man to stop so she could get off and boke into a hedge, with all and sundry watching. Jesus, I'll never forget it – there was no way any of the men were going to try and kiss her after that!'

Fergal giggled and Noreen refilled her glass right up to the top.

'Anyway, I had a few dances all right, even though the nuns and the priest kept patrolling with their oul' rulers.' Fergal looked confused. 'Ah, Fergal, youse young ones wouldn't know what it was like. If you were seen dancing too close to a fella, you could be sent home, and the priest would give out about it at mass – and if you ended up with a bad reputation, it was the end of you. And my ma would've killed me. So they brought rulers, like the ones youse use in school, to the dance. As long as you kept the length of a ruler between you and your dancing partner, then things were OK.'

Fergal couldn't believe what he was hearing.

'Well, the band was great, and someone had hung coloured lights all around the hall… ah, Fergal, it was like something out of a film. I had a few dances with some of the girls, and a big farmer fella called… oh, now, what was he called? Give me a second… Johnny – that's it. Johnny Quinn, I think. He asked me to dance twice, which meant he really liked me and I quite liked him, even though he stood on my feet that many times they looked like they were punctured flat. He was a big brute of a man with lovely big eyes, and a bigger farm by all accounts, but I wasn't that interested. His oul' breath would've put years on you. Well, I'd seen your granda on the Falls Road there a few times, but I'd never talked to him. I thought he'd smiled at me when he saw me getting on the bus that night, but even then my eyesight was shocking, so

I couldn't be sure. Even when I was dancing with Johnny, though, I had an eye on your granda. He was dancing with this one and that one, but he kept looking over at me. And at the last dance, just when I was about to give up, he appeared and took me right out into the middle of the floor, bold as you like. We danced a perfect ruler apart to "When You Were Sweet Sixteen", and he looked at me and sang the whole song, word for word. He was so tall and handsome, Fergal… sure, I was smitten from the word go. He never said much, though, except to thank me and say he hoped I'd be at the next dance.'

'And were you, Granny?' Fergal was glued to the side of her bed.

'Well, son, that's when Fate – or whatever you want to call it – stepped in.'

'What do you mean?'

'On the way home, our bus broke down. Like I was telling you, son, it was in the middle of the country – there were no phones, no street lamps anywhere, and it was too far to walk. They tried and tried to get the thing to start – a few of the men were mechanics if I remember rightly – but the engine had had it. So do you know what the oul' priest decided?'

'No, Granny. What?'

'There was no way we were going to be allowed to spend the night on the same bus together, so they found a cowshed not far away, and the men were all herded off to that. Us girls had to sleep in our seats. It was freezing, Fergal – I'm shivering even thinking about it. I was never so cold. All we had were our frocks and our wee shawls.' Noreen gulped another mouthful of gin.

'And then? What then?'

'As soon as it was light, we left the bus behind and walked the five miles home in our dancing shoes. Our feet were bleeding. Now, we thought the worst of it was over when we got home. I thought your great-granny would be glad to see me alive, but oh, no! She was waiting behind the door with one of her boots, and she beat the head off me before I could get a word in about the useless bus!'

Fergal had twisted one of her blankets around his wrist, so tightly it had stopped the blood flow. 'And then what happened, Granny?'

'All hell broke loose, that's what happened. The priest called meetings with us, all the girls that had gone to the dance from our area, and our parents. The priests and the nuns and the parents had hatched a holy plan that was going to save us all from hell. You see, it was a scandal and a sin before God for us to have been out all night – even though the poor young men had been in a cowshed, without so much as an innocent handshake from us. And it made the church look bad, because they'd organised the bus. So my mother sat me down in the front room with the priest. They had a big piece of paper with loads of names on it. First of all they asked me which man I'd had the last dance with. I said Fergal Clooney from Bombay Street, of course. Then they asked which man I'd sat nearest to on the way home, before the bus broke down, and I said Fergal Clooney again – which was a white lie, but I'd been staring at him the whole time. So they ticked his name and my mother started crying.

'When the priest left the house, my mother dried her eyes and with her back to me told me I was to marry Fergal Clooney – your grandfather, God rest him – before the month was out. It had all been arranged. And, sure enough, exactly a month after that dance, we were all married. Everybody who'd been on the bus.'

Fergal sat on the edge of her bed with his mouth open, and saw a tear leak out of Noreen's eye. He was about to lean over and hug her, but she held up a tiny arm to stop him and said, 'Fergal, your granda was a decent man. I was a lucky girl, really. I grew to love him, and he loved me. Sure, Jesus, we had nine children.'

She dried her eyes on the sleeve of her cardigan and blew her nose hard. 'He could sing, you know. He was shy about it with his mates out at the lamppost, but when we were newly married and I was feeling low, he would sing, "I'll Take You Home Again, Noreen" – instead of "Kathleen", you know. He'd learned the whole bloody song, and it would cheer me up. But then we had all the children – and, give him his due, he worked all the hours God sent. But there was no time for singing, except maybe on birthdays. And time went so fast, and he got so tired and sick… oh, Sacred Heart of Jesus, he got so sick.'

She stared at the wedding picture. Fergal thought she was going to cry again, so he moved in to put his arm around her, but suddenly she said, 'Oh, do you remember I was telling you about Mary Harper?'

'The one that boked into the hedge?'

'Exactly. I'm glad you were paying attention, son. Well, she had to marry a man called Seamus Duggan, who was so ugly it had to be seen to be believed. Wild dogs were afraid of that man. He had the worst skin you'd ever see, with terrible boils and car-buncles from head to toe – any time he opened his mouth to speak, something would burst on his face! Oh, Jesus, how she could ever kiss that fella... Anyway, he ended up winning a fortune on the pools, and they bought a farm somewhere in America and we never saw them again. Jesus, I'd say she did the best out of all of us. Look at me – stuck here till the end of my days, with no man, no money, most of my children fucked off as quick as they could, no decent company—'

'Granny, you have me, and Mammy still comes round!'

'Jesus help us, but your mother would put years on a dead cat. I don't know how you stick her. The temper on her would fry an egg – and that wasn't the way she was reared. Your da's to blame for that. And you're nearly seventeen. You'll be gone too, before you know it. Sure, there's nothing here but heartache – nothing but heartache and more to come. If I had my time again, Fergal, do you know what I'd do?'

'What, Granny?'

'I'd travel to every corner of the world, so I would. And that's what you should do, Fergal. Get out of this hole – sure, what is there to keep you hanging around waiting to get shot or blown up? Don't end up like me, son, too old and too sick to even get out of your fucking bed. Don't waste your time, love.'

Fergal tried to find the right words, but he couldn't argue with that.

When he brought her up a cup of tea, Noreen had fallen asleep again. He fixed the blankets around her chin and moved the silver fringe of hair out of her eyes to kiss her lightly on the forehead. Then he rewrapped the old photos, closed the lid on her past and put it back under her bed.

12

Angela knew about the choir and approved of it. It kept Fergal out of harm's way, and she even allowed herself the fantasy that maybe he would become a priest – that way they would all definitely get into heaven. It always paid to be associated with Church activities.

She wasn't as pleased when Fergal told her Father Mac wanted to meet her and Paddy.

'Are you in trouble again, Fergal Flynn?' she said angrily, raising a ring-clad fist.

He dodged. 'No, Mammy! I think it's something to do with the choir,' he lied. 'He wants you and Da to come round for a cup of tea after mass this Sunday – that's all, for God's sake!'

'That's *all*, for God's *sake*!' mimicked John as effeminately as his impressionistic skills would allow, bending his wrist.

Angela spun on her heel. 'Shut your smart fucking mouth, you.' Then she turned back to Fergal, smoothed the creases in her skirt and said, 'Right, then. I'll talk to your da, but you know what he's like.'

~

That Sunday morning Fergal woke far too early, but he got up anyway. The one advantage was that Noreen had yet to use her commode, so it was safe to breathe normally on the way downstairs to start the fire. The coal was dumped in the corner of the tiny, limed yard on top of an upside-down dog kennel that had been hammered together from bits of wooden bread crates. It had once housed a wee mongrel pup that one of Noreen's vanished children had bought her on a surprise visit home, but one day the wee thing had run out the front door, chasing the postman, and ended up under the wheels of an army Saracen speeding up the street in hot pursuit of a joyrider. The bin man had had to scrape the wee thing off the road with her coal shovel. She hadn't bothered getting another one.

After making toast and milky tea for Noreen, Fergal boiled several pots of water, filled an aluminium basin and washed himself with a worn pebble of carbolic soap and a flannel made from the corner of an old towel. As he splashed water on his face, he could feel that he really needed to start shaving more regularly. He didn't own a razor and he knew he couldn't ask his da for one. Not long before, Paddy had discovered that someone had been using his razor. No one would own up, so he'd exploded at all four of them – 'I'm your da! You'll shave when I decide you can, and not before!' Fergal had ended up stealing a disposable one from a shop – he didn't have enough money to buy a packet – but it had quickly become so blunt you could have let a child play with it. After repeatedly ripping the face off himself, he'd eventually had to throw it out.

As always, everybody had made an effort for Sunday mass. Local women were virtually unrecognisable without their usual flat shoes and hair hidden under scarves, pinned around tight rollers. Some of the younger mothers wore bright lipstick and mascara, their squads of children had been scrubbed within an inch of their lives. Even the sky, after a night of rioting, had gone to the bother of laying out freshly laundered clouds. They float-ed high above the city, perfectly scattered, as a single airplane left a cotton vapour trail against the pale-blue yonder. Fergal remem-bered Noreen's advice – *Get out of this hole, sure, what is there to keep you hanging around?* – and wondered what kind of people were on the plane and where in the world they were going. As he watched it getting smaller and smaller, he suddenly felt a rush of excitement. Maybe, one day, he might be one of those very peo-ple.

The mass seemed longer than usual. Fergal had to sing a hymn. He had only ever sung in the chapel when it was empty and now, as he stood looking at the little sea of people, his nerves started to get the better of him and his heart turned up its vol-ume. He was glad of the relative safety of being up in the balcony with Baldy Turner and the organ. He couldn't help scanning the congregation for his family. There they were, all together. His father and brothers had ties and damped-down hair, and his mother was wearing some class of a hat that looked a like a duck was asleep on her head. At least they were far away, up near the front, but he wished they weren't there at all.

Communion was Fergal's cue. 'Lamb of God…' he sang, as the pipe organ swelled and his shy voice rose to keep its appointment with the chords in the cloisters. He kept his eyes closed until the last verse, because he was so nervous, but he held the music right in front of his face anyway – he couldn't risk getting the words wrong. He needn't have worried. Once the first three holy words were past his lips, his nerves vanished as quickly as they had arrived. The congregation looked around to see where the beautiful voice was coming from and Father Mac smiled contentedly.

Afterwards, Fergal thanked Baldy and ran down the narrow stairs to wait outside the church as his parents made their way through the departing throng. An old neighbour of Noreen's saw him descending the stone staircase and came up to him, saying, 'Was that you singing up there, love? Aren't you Angela Flynn's son? God, but it was beautiful.'

Over her shoulder, Fergal noticed with discomfort that his brothers showed no signs of fucking off home, and that they didn't share Noreen's neighbour's opinion of his singing. John, predictably, was mimicking him, pushing his tongue out to one side and flapping his arms like an angel who'd suffered some kind of stroke. As Father Mac escaped the monotone moaning of one of his oldest and deafest parishioners and made his way over to the Flynns, Paddy Sr stamped his foot on the holy ground and shooed the twins and Ciaran away. He also muttered something under his breath about hoping this wasn't going to take too long as he'd a match to get to.

Father Mac complimented Mrs Flynn on her choice of hat and

ushered them towards his house, in the full glare of the Flynns' neighbours, ravenous for details. Mrs Mooney (at Father Mac's request) received them with all the ceremony reserved for extra-special visitors and enquired how they liked their tea. For the first time, Fergal noticed how vulnerable and small his parents looked inside someone else's world. It made him wonder if he looked the same way. Father Mac picked up on their discomfort and started talking to Paddy about hurling, describing how he'd formed a team with some of the local fellas in Africa. But Paddy looked incredulous, and not in a good way, so Father Mac dropped the subject.

When the tea, biscuits and cake arrived, Father Mac said, 'I'll get straight to the point. I have a friend who's a member of a strict order of monks in an abbey in Sligo.'

Angela gulped. 'Does our Fergal want to be a monk, Father? Is that why we're here? I think he'd make a much better priest.'

Father Mac laughed a little, but went on, without looking at the mortified Fergal, 'No, no, Mrs Flynn. Let me explain.'

He told them that, as well as manufacturing honey and running an exclusive boarding school, the monks were highly regarded for their dedication to chanting Latin and ancient Irish hymns from as far back as the tenth century. 'And from time to time they make a recording,' he said. 'These are sold all over the world, even in the Vatican itself.'

'Really, Father?' Angela piped up, in a much posher voice than Fergal had ever heard from her before.

'So, Mr and Mrs Flynn, I've asked you both here today because my good friend Brother Vincent is holding selective auditions to find the right voice to complete their ensemble. They plan to record a small selection of rare pieces for a new album, and I would very much like your wonderful son Fergal here to represent St Bridget's parish. I believe he can do it.'

There was a moment when Fergal thought he would pass out if his heart beat any faster. Paddy Flynn looked into his tea for what seemed like an eternity. Finally he asked the rim of the cup, 'How much is it going to cost?'

Father Mac looked confused for a second. 'Oh, I see – St Bridget's will cover any travel and accommodation costs. It won't be much. I'll drive him to Sligo myself and the abbey will put us up. You don't need to pay anything.'

Angela looked up at Fergal. 'How long would he have to stay?'

'If he's successful – and I believe he will be – it will only mean a few days at most. They'll be recording the day after the auditions. If he isn't successful, then we'll be back first thing the following morning – I have my parish to think of.'

The Flynns looked at each other blankly. Angela said, 'Fergal's granny – my mother – depends on him. I can't see how he could be away for any length of time at all.'

Fergal's heart sank, but Father Mac played his trump card. 'Mr and Mrs Flynn, I realise Noreen is very attached to Fergal and it would be no good asking one of his brothers to step into his shoes. I thought perhaps this problem might be solved by enlisting my housekeeper, Mrs Mooney, as a replacement?'

Fergal hadn't seen that coming and neither had his unnerved parents.

Father Mac continued, 'I took the liberty of sounding her out about it. She says that, seeing as I won't be here anyway, she would be only too glad to help out a needy member of her own community – with your permission, of course. I understand she and your mother attended the same school as children, so I'm sure they'd have lots to catch up on.'

There was another uncomfortable silence. This time Paddy broke it. 'Father MacManus, there'll be no need to trouble Mrs... your housekeeper. Our family will make sure Noreen's looked after. Sure, it's only a couple of days, for fuck's sake – oh, excuse me, Father, but you know what I mean.'

Fergal managed a smile. The phone bleated from the hall and Father Mac excused himself, leaving them in the spotless room together.

Angela stood up, fixing her skirt. 'I won't have some nosy oul' bitch poking round my ma's house and upsetting her,' she whispered. 'Come on, Paddy, we'll go after he gets off that bloody phone. I'm fucking roasted in here.'

She swept the remaining chocolate biscuits and slices of cake into a hanky and shoved them into her bag. 'I'll bring them round to Mammy's later, to soften her up.'

Father Mac re-entered the parlour offering his apologies, and looked at the empty plates in surprise. Fergal looked away, embarrassed.

Father Mac thanked the Flynns repeatedly, assured them that they were assisting in God's plan for St Bridget's, offered them a lift home – which they refused – and walked them to the front door. Then he came back to the parlour.

'Thank you. Oh, Father Mac, thank you!' Fergal gasped. 'I can't believe you got them to agree!'

Father Mac gave him a satisfied smile. 'Fergal, there are ways and means to do things. You shouldn't miss this chance and I was always going to do everything in my power to make sure it would happen for you. You want Noreen to hear your voice on a record, don't you?'

'Of course I do, Father. You know I do.'

'Well, funnily enough, that was Brother Vincent on the phone. He wanted to know if we could come in a month's time when most of the pupils will have gone home for their summer break. I'll have to get Father Morgan to cover for me, but I don't think it'll be a problem, seeing as this is going to be great for St Bridget's community. Also, I'm due a little bit of leave, so I thought I'd combine this trip with a visit to my parents' house, it's on our way. I hope you won't mind coming along?'

'Father, after you convincing my parents to let me go, I'd do anything!' Fergal hadn't meant it to come out that way, but it was too late.

Father Mac looked away. 'They've retired to a wee place called Derrygonnelly, just outside Enniskillen. It's a far cry from where my mother grew up.'

'What do you mean?'

'Well, she's from the Markets originally – you know, real salt-of-the-earth working-class people – and my father's from farming people near Randallstown. He ended up with his own building company and it did really well – that's the business to be in, with all the houses and roads and hotels that get destroyed in this city every day by bombs or bullets or stones. We moved around Belfast a fair bit, then they settled on a house near the Malone Road and that's where we went to school.'

Fergal smiled. 'So youse are a bit posh, then, Father?'

'What? Posh? Not really. Well, my mother wouldn't thank you for saying it – but I suppose it's true to a degree. We ended up middle-class... Look, I promise we won't stay too long in their house, but I haven't seen them or my lovely sister since they collected me from the airport. Sure, it'll break up the journey.'

13

The weeks that followed felt like an eternity to Fergal. From the moment Noreen had heard about his audition, she had been especially restless during the night. She would yell out names that he'd never heard before or wail and cry like a hungry baby before she'd sink into anger, howling a stream of insults about him leaving her just like her bastard children. Fergal was confused. Only a few weeks earlier, she had encouraged him to get out of Belfast as soon as he could. He was smart enough to know, though, that her contradictory moods were heavily fuelled by the booze and chemicals fighting for control of her senses. All he could do to calm her was sit in their room in the half-light of the street lamp, and sing quietly:

I'll take you home again, Noreen,
Across the ocean wild and wide,
To where your heart has ever been,
Since you were first his bonny bride.
The roses all have left your cheek,
I've watched them fade away and die;
Your voice is sad whene'er you speak,
And tears bedim your loving eyes.

Oh, I will take you back, Noreen,
To where your heart will feel no pain,
And when the fields are fresh and green,
I'll take you to your home again.

Eventually she would drift into her broken self again, but not for long.

Fergal tried to concentrate as hard as he could on his exams. He had completed a good chunk of them and many subjects had coursework that was evaluated throughout the term, so there weren't too many written ones left – only English, Irish, religion and a baffling metalwork theory exam. Outside the metalwork exam room, someone offered Fergal a swig of vodka from a filthy bottle. Thinking that it was bound to be piss, he refused – luckily because the headmaster suddenly appeared and dragged the half-cut culprit to his office for a lashing with his leather strap. As if the exams weren't hard enough…

He noticed a difference in school, though. Some of the teachers stopped him and asked in a friendly way how the singing was going. Now that it was well known that Fergal and Father Mac were working together, lads who normally wouldn't have thought twice about covering him in phlegm and insults were more cautious; they stared at him, not sure what to do. Every now and then Fergal heard someone say, 'Here comes Priesty Hole' or 'Holy Joe!' but little by little they found smaller boys to pick on and began to ignore him altogether.

Fergal thought it was like Father Mac was his guardian angel. There wasn't a day that went by when he didn't think about him. Late at night, Father Mac was the only cast member in the little film that started up in his mind. He imagined what it would be like for the priest to hold him in his strong arms and kiss him gently around his neck. It was like a drug, helping him fall into a deep sleep even though Noreen had developed a snore like a whistling kettle.

He and Father Mac met as often as they could and went over the abbey's music with a fine-toothed comb. Although the re-hearsals seemed to be going well, Fergal felt a definite change in the temperature between them. Any time he sat too close on the piano stool to check a bit of the melody, Father Mac would visi-bly flinch and shift to the edge. And when they were finished rehearsing for the night, Father Mac would say he was sorry he couldn't offer Fergal supper but he had an urgent house call.

One night, when Fergal attempted to hug him to say thanks, Father Mac backed away in obvious panic and offered him a handshake. He might as well have kicked him in the stomach. Fergal couldn't have hidden his hurt even if he'd wanted to.

As he walked down the Falls Road, Fergal was miserable. He wondered what it was about him that made people reject him. The window of a furniture shop proudly displayed an enormous mirror that had been rescued from an old house. Fergal stared into the glass and asked his reflection, *What is it? Am I that ugly?*

Is that what it is? Am I really a freak of nature, like my brothers say? Was Father Mac just taking pity on me or something?

Fergal's eyes filled up as he walked on, not waiting for the mirror to answer. He thought about every member of his family, and how they couldn't wait to be rid of him. He knew the Flynn house was happier since he'd moved to Noreen's. John took every opportunity to tell him how, now that he was gone, the funny smell was too. And that very morning, Noreen had yelled at him to fuck off and never come back.

He slipped down a side street to avoid a load of skinheads and their equally scary girlfriends, drinking their carry-out on the steps of the funeral parlour. *I'm not the only reason Ma works so hard and Da is so bad-tempered,* he thought to the burnt-out house at the corner of Iris Street. *Jesus, I can't help it if I'm no good at hurling. Surely there's more to life than chasing a ball around a field with sticks… I just wish… I wish I wasn't here.*

An ambulance raced past him, and he threw it a dirty look. *You can go and fuck yourself if you think I'm going to harmonise with you.*

Fergal knew he didn't want to go straight back to Noreen's, but where else could he go? Definitely not Walker Street, but where? He turned back and walked in the opposite direction, even though he knew it was dangerous at night. He kept off the main Falls Road as much as he could, passing wall after graffiti-covered wall: 'The IRA Have Had Their Weetabix!' 'Maggie Thatcher, Job Snatcher!' 'Only Our Rivers Run Free!'

Fergal reached Castle Street and the beginning of the city centre. He felt terrified and excited all at once, and his heart beat in time with every step. He was amazed at how empty the town was now that all the shops were shut and dark – it was like someone had dropped an atom bomb and wiped out everybody except him. Several bars had been bombed out the week before, so Belfast's social life had taken another serious beating and no one ventured far from their area after dark. He'd forgotten there was an army barracks at the corner, but no one challenged him from the lookout box high above the barbed wire. When he saw a poster advertising a gig, he remembered hearing about late-night clashes between skinhead and mod gangs near the back of City Hall. He was more and more scared, but he was drawn towards the docks and the fresher air. He remembered how his mother sometimes cursed her sisters for escaping to London and meeting rich men and becoming 'fucking snobby whores'.

Fergal decided that that was what he was going to do. Fuck his exams, fuck his audition, fuck everybody! He was going to go to the docks and get a lorry driver to let him come to England with him. Maybe he could look up one of his aunts or get a job or… something.

~

After Fergal left, Father Mac took his supper out of the fridge and pushed it around the plate, far too consumed with guilt to manage more than a few half-hearted bites. He felt awful.

He looked over at the piano stool where they had spent the evening rehearsing, and he closed his eyes as he remembered the look on Fergal's face when he had recoiled from his attempt to hug him. Father Mac looked at the crucifix as if it might tell him what to do, but it just hung there, hogging all the pain as usual.

He decided to take a bath, to try and relax. But no sooner had he undressed and immersed himself in the hot water than his thoughts were once again hijacked by Fergal. He wondered what Fergal was doing at that very moment, and then – before he could stop himself – what he might look like completely naked. He inhaled wearily and ducked under the water for as long as he could hold his breath, just to leave the world behind for a few seconds. At last he sat up again, his hair flat and perfectly parted in the middle.

Even in the bathroom there were holy pictures hanging on the white walls above the towels. Father Mac settled on the one of Christ being taken by the guards in the Garden of Gethsemane. Knowing the house was long free of Mrs Mooney's ears, he talked aloud to the framed Son of God, 'Heavenly Father, here I lie – in the bath of all places – trying my best to be clean in spirit as well as in body. I feel like I'm trapped in the clutches of something unbearable. Did you see poor Fergal's face when he left this evening? It took all my strength not to go after him. I really thought that setting a clearer boundary would make me feel better, but I feel worse. Why? It's not like anything has happened. For the first time in my life I feel lonely – I mean, really lonely. I look forward to Fergal arriving like a child waiting for the summer holidays or Santa or something. I know it's stupid and it's wrong, but I can't… I just don't seem able to stop thinking about him – his voice, his eyes, the way he trusts me… or, at least, the way he used to trust me. I'm sure he's guessed I've been lying to him. He's not stupid. Oh, dear God and his Holy Mother, why is this so hard?'

He let the last word hang in the steam-filled bathroom. As he turned away from the holy pictures, he realised he was getting bigger under the water. He couldn't help putting a hand on his erection. He tried to think of anyone except Fergal. But, no matter who entered his head, the image always changed into Fergal within seconds.

Then he had a thought. Maybe if... no, he couldn't. But maybe if he had sex with someone else, it would take his mind off Fergal? But who? And where was he going to meet him? Then he remembered hearing a man's confession, a few weeks before – a man who wasn't from St Bridget's parish. He'd confessed that he sometimes visited the ancient public toilets near the ferry car park, down by the old docks – a place where all sorts of men, including married ones, met in secret for sex.

Father Mac got out of the bath and dried his body roughly with the worst towel he could find, as a kind of punishment for such ridiculous thoughts. He definitely wasn't going to sink that low.

But, no matter which way he lay in bed, there was no chance he was going to be able to sleep, and he knew it. He got up and poured himself a large whiskey in the parlour, but could only manage a few sips before he got angry with himself. *Oh, so now you're going to become an alcoholic? That's just brilliant!*

He smoked cigarette after cigarette and flicked on the TV, but there was nothing on that could hold his concentration. Just as he was about to go back to bed, the phone rang and he was called out to give the last rites to a pensioner. For the first time ever, he was glad of the distraction.

~

The Albert Clock, Belfast's answer to the Leaning Tower of Pisa, told Fergal it wasn't far from midnight. He'd thought it was later.

There were three women huddled at the base of the clock,

sharing a cigarette. When they saw him coming, they started straightening their mini-skirts and fixing their hair with their fingers. One of them even took a fork out of her bag and combed her hair, puffing it as big as she could get the over-bleached wisps to go. They had so much make-up on that they looked like pantomime dames. When Fergal got close enough, they asked him for a cigarette.

'Sorry, I don't smoke.'

'You look lonely, love – are you lonely? Would you not like a bit of company, a big handsome fella like yourself? Jesus, your eyes are gorgeous, love, but you look awful sad. Would you like a bit of cheering up?'

'No, no, I'm fine – it's just… Can I ask youse something?'

'Aye, why not? Sure, we're not exactly run off our stilettos, are we, love? What is it?'

'Um… which way is it to where the lorries are parked?'

'What? What the fuck do you want to know that for? Here, are you trying to steal our trade? Do you hear that, girls? Mr fucking Faggot is trying to move in on our trade.'

Fergal nearly passed out as he realised why the women were standing around reapplying their lipstick at this time of night. 'No – Jesus, no! Youse don't understand. I'm just trying to get to England, that's all. Jesus, I'm sorry I bothered youse.'

He moved off as fast as he could. The women forgot all about him as a posh car pulled up beside them, pretending to be lost, and picked up the youngest one.

Fergal kept going until, completely by accident, he saw a sign for the ferry, and then spotted the lorry park. There was a wee chip van parked near the entrance and a few drivers were eating burgers and chip sandwiches and getting their flasks filled with soup. He watched them from across the road with his heart almost flying out of him.

The Albert Clock sounded midnight and Noreen's face floated in front of him in the night sky. *Sure, there's nothing here but heartache, son, and more to come…* He thought about his grandfather, his namesake, and he pushed his hands deeper into his pockets as he asked the man he'd never met what to do. The only reply was the distant cry of seagulls fighting to get at the fish that the ferry, turning in the harbour, brought closer to the surface. He wondered if his grandfather had ever stood where he was standing at that moment. What had he been like at seventeen? According to Noreen, Belfast had been a very different place then, friendlier and safer.

He felt some coins that had fallen into the lining of his coat. He decided to go over to the chip van, buy a cup of tea and maybe try and get talking to one of the drivers.

The lorry drivers were like no one Fergal had ever seen. They were either hugely tall, as wide as buses, or both, and four out of the five of them were wearing the dirtiest jumpers he'd ever seen – and that was saying something. The biggest man suddenly introduced himself as 'Derek from Doncaster' and bit into a double fried-egg sandwich. The yolks burst out of the bread like giant pimples, all down the front of his red pullover, but he didn't seem to care.

Still chewing on the fatty mush, Derek asked, 'You going on the ferry?'

Fergal stammered a bit and then lied. 'I – well, I was supposed to, but… but I've lost my ticket. I can't afford to buy another one.'

The other drivers had moved off for a smoke. 'What you going to do?' Derek asked.

'Well, I was hoping, maybe… ah… maybe somebody could give me a lift?'

'What, for free? You get nowt for free in this life, lad.'

'But I don't have any money, and I need to get to England to visit my… my sick uncle.'

'Your sick uncle, eh?'

'Yeah. Please – I've been walking around for ages. Maybe I could help you with the lorry – you know, help you clean it or something? Please, Mister. I'll… I'll do anything…'

Derek looked him up and down. 'Anything? You sure about that, lad?'

'Yeah, I'm sure. Like I said, I have to get there.'

'How old are you, lad?'

'I'm twenty-one. Why?'

'Oh, no reason – just wondering… So you'd be up for a bit of, you know, fun – in the lorry, like?'

Fergal realised fully what he meant by 'fun' and panicked inwardly. *Fergal Flynn, what are you* doing? *He could be a killer – people get murdered all the time – once you get into the lorry you won't be able to get out… What if he has a knife? Oh, God, he's so disgusting, and the state of his jumper – if his clothes are that dirty, what must his body be like? He's waiting on an answer… Maybe it won't be that bad. Oh, Jesus, I'm going to have to do it or I'll never get out of here.*

Fergal dropped his eyes. 'Well – maybe… yeah…'

'How big are you?'

'I don't know – about five foot eleven, maybe?'

Derek laughed and dropped his gaze to Fergal's crotch. 'No, lad, I mean how big are you – you know, downstairs?'

Fergal went bright red. 'I – I don't know – never measured it…'

'Well, I'd want a look at the goods before I agree to carry them.'

'What? Where? If you think I'm getting it out here, then—'

'Calm down, lad, calm down. There's a public toilet, just down the road there, where I've had a bit of fun from time to time. Meet me there in five minutes.'

'Ah, I'm not sure – I've never—'

'Well, looks like I'll be travelling back to England by myself, then.'

'No! Look... OK... you're sure it's safe?'

'Oh, aye, lad. There's hardly anyone about at this time, and if they are, they're there for the same reason as us. You can always say you were having a piss.'

'Right.'

Fergal's heart felt like it was beating on the outside of his body. The lorry driver moved off, and he waited until he saw him slip into the public toilet. Then he took a deep breath and followed him.

~

Administering the last rites always made Father Mac feel sad, but that night he was especially unnerved. The pensioner he was visiting had no family left. He'd lived alone for years and he'd finally become housebound, reliant on the thrice-weekly visits from his home help and the occasional kindness of a neighbour. Father Mac did the best that he could, but the old man was adamant that, with so much evil in the world, there could be no such thing as God, and that the priest was wasting his breath with his 'empty oul' prayers'.

When the ambulance came to relieve the house of its occupant for the final time, Father Mac got back into his car, loosened his white collar, then took it off altogether and threw it into the glove compartment. He felt depressed as he wondered how he would end his own days. When he reached St Bridget's, he slowed down to turn, but something made him change his mind. He drove on, out to the Falls Road and turned left towards the town centre. Asleep, the city looked as innocent as any child tucked up in bed.

Signposts pointed every which way until the one that announced 'Docks' appeared. His mind changed the *D* in 'Docks' to a *C*, and he looked at himself in the rear-view mirror and said aloud, 'My good God, you really are sad, aren't you?'

He passed the lorry park and the little chip van, and pulled over when he saw the public toilets. He had begun to sweat with fear. Without turning off the engine, he lit a cigarette and cracked his window open slightly. He made sure his car doors were locked. Images crowded his mind: himself being dragged off by policemen; the nine o'clock news announcing to every household in Northern Ireland that a local priest had been caught 'cottaging', going to public toilets to have silent sex with a stranger of the same sex... A sodomite! Father Mac was light-headed with stress, and he hadn't even got out of the car.

If he had arrived only a minute earlier, he would have seen a familiar figure step through the doors of the public toilet and into the uncertain darkness. The smell of stale piss was enough to make Fergal want to leave, but then one of the cubicle doors opened and Doncaster Derek stepped over to the urinal. Fergal nervously followed, listening all the time for the slightest sound. He heard Derek undoing his zipper, and he did the same. The street lamp was right outside the window, and when their eyes slowly adjusted, there was just enough light to see by.

Derek waved his penis and looked over his shoulder. Then he dropped his hand between Fergal's legs and whispered, 'You're a big lad, aren't you? I bet you know what to do with it too, eh?'

Fergal didn't know what to say.

'What do you think of mine, eh? It might not be as long as yours, but it's fat. Do you want to… you know?'

Fergal nodded, glad of the half-light. Derek went back into the filthy cubicle, motioning him to follow with a jerk of his head.

Suddenly, the sound of a car door shutting made Fergal panic. All he could think about was the police and Father Mac. He knew he couldn't bring himself to do it. He spun round and lost his footing on the slippery urinal steps. His hand, breaking his fall, went into a pool of urine on the uneven floor. 'Fuck!' Derek forced himself back out of the cubicle with his trousers undone, and Fergal managed to squeeze out an apology as he hurried out the door and back into the night. Everything seemed brighter all of a sudden. Derek shouted from inside, 'Don't you want that lift to England, then?'

'Ah, no, sorry – I've changed my—'

The last thing Fergal had expected to see was Father Mac, standing by his car only a few feet from the entrance to the toilets.

After a stunned second, he took off down the road. Behind him he heard Father Mac shouting 'Fergal! Wait!', and then the sound of the car starting, gaining on him. He kept going, not knowing where. Blurred images of Noreen and Father Mac melted into each other, and Fergal started to cry.

Father Mac wound the passenger window down with one hand and steered badly with the other, pleading frantically. 'Fergal, please, stop – get in! Come on! What are you doing? England? Who was that man? What did he mean about England?'

Finally Fergal ran out of breath. He stopped, leaning against a set of railings that looked out over the docks.

Father Mac pulled up beside him and opened the passenger door. 'Fergal, get in right now. There'll be police along soon. This is a dangerous place to be. Do you know what time it is?'

'Leave me alone.'

A gang of skinheads turned the corner chanting some football anthem, and broke into a sprint as they saw their potential human football. Fergal just made it inside Father Mac's car in time. Father Mac pressed his foot to the pedal and sped out of range of the skinheads' missiles.

Fergal covered his face with his hands and hyperventilated. 'I'm… I'm… sorry…'

'It's OK, Fergal, we're safe – we're safe… Just breathe. Breathe.'

They drove back to St Bridget's House in complete silence. When they parked, Father Mac turned in his seat and said, in the kindest voice he could find, 'Fergal, come in and I'll make some tea or something. I don't know what's going on, but you can't go back to Noreen's like this. Can't you tell me what it is? Is this something to do with me?'

All Fergal could do was burst into tears again.

Father Mac left Fergal in the front room while he went to put on the kettle and gather his thoughts. He looked into the little mirror above the sink, and the voice inside his head accused him, *It's all your fault. You drove him to it, you know you did. After all he told you about the way his family have treated him, you go and reject him too. Well done, you bloody idiot.*

He threw a little bit of cold water on his face and carried in a tray piled with anything he could find. He sat on the sofa and offered his arm around Fergal's shoulders.

'Fergal, my dear Fergal, you're safe now. In your own time... what happened?'

Fergal had finally stopped shaking, but he couldn't look at Father Mac just yet. He stared into the fire. 'I don't know, I just... everything just got on top of me... I had nowhere to go. Even Granny told me to fuck off and not come back this morning. I mean, I know she was drunk and on tablets and all, but... Oh, I don't know.'

'But England, Fergal? What about everything we've been doing? All your hard work? Your exams? Were you just going to vanish?'

'I don't know, Father. I didn't plan it. I felt so bad when I left here earlier, and... I walked around for the longest time and then I ended up at the docks. My mother has sisters in England, and... oh, Father, I don't know what I was thinking.'

'Did I upset you, Fergal? Be honest, now.'

'Well, you seemed so... different.'

'How do you mean? You can be honest with me, this goes no further than these walls.'

'Well, any time I've been near you recently, you seemed to – I don't know – you seemed to... Do I smell bad? Is that why you don't want to be near me?'

'Fergal, it's not that I don't want to be near you! It's... Oh, how do I put this? I'm a priest, I'm older than you... I feel responsible for you. I don't want you to get the wrong idea – or anyone else for that matter.'

There was a long silence as Fergal's heart sank further and further into the bottomless depths of himself. Finally Father Mac asked, 'And what about the… the toilet business?'

Fergal went bright red again, and his voice was barely audible. 'I met him in the lorry park. He said he'd give me a lift to England if I – you know… But I didn't, Father. I changed my mind. At the last minute, I couldn't go through with it, so I ran out. I'd never gone there before in my life and I never will again. It was disgusting in there. The smell would've knocked you down. Oh, God, I feel so… so stupid and dirty.'

'Ah, Fergal… come here.' Father Mac hugged him with all his strength, and Fergal surrendered for a moment.

As they moved apart, Fergal had a thought. He looked the priest in the eyes this time. 'Father, why were you there?'

It was Father Mac's turn to panic. 'Ah – well… Fergal, I… I…'

His voice trailed off. Much as he wanted to employ a brilliant lie, he knew he could not. 'OK – seeing as you've been so honest with me, I owe you the same. I'm trusting you wholeheartedly. This is between you and me?'

'Of course. Who am I going to tell – Granny Noreen? I don't think so.'

'Right. Well… I had a terrible time after you left earlier. An old man in the parish died tonight. Death always reminds me of my own mortality but this one upset me more than usual. He was all alone in the world, Fergal, never married. His new neighbour found him and I got there just in time to offer him the last rites, but he refused, saying God had done nothing for him. He pushed my prayers away. We were the last people he saw before he died. I don't know, it just made me feel… lonelier than I ever have in my life. I couldn't sleep. I drove around and ended up in town. I had heard about that public toilet, and I found myself stopping there – for... for... reasons similar to yours. I'd changed my mind too, though. I was about to get back into my car when you appeared in front of me. I just couldn't believe it. I thought I was hallucinating or something.'

They laughed in uncomfortable unison.

'You were right to think that I've been more distant recently. I didn't mean to be so cold – I just wanted to... set boundaries. I didn't realise you'd take it to heart so much that you thought your only option was to run away! I'd never have forgiven myself. I'd have been worried out of my mind, don't you realise that? You're an extraordinary fella. I think the world of you, I really do – but we can't...'

'Can't what?'

'Fergal, we can't... be anything other than friends. It just wouldn't be right. I'm sorry if I—'

'Father... I think about you all the time. I'm nearly seventeen – I'm not a kid. I know what I'm saying. Is it because I'm too ugly? Is that why you went to that place – to meet somebody else? Somebody better looking?'

'No, Fergal! Stop! For goodness' sake – you have no idea how beautiful you are, do you? That's one of the things that makes you so beautiful – your eyes, your smile...' Father Mac took a deep breath. 'Look, I mustn't say these things to you. It's not right. I'm a priest, I'm older than you... I wouldn't want anyone to think I would take advantage of you. I just couldn't bear to see anyone hurt you, ever...'

'Father, you wouldn't be taking advantage of me! I want to be near you, to be with you. I think about me and you all the time. I've never been so sure of anything in my life. It's like when I'm singing, you know, it feels right. It just does. How can that be wrong?'

'Oh, Fergal… I don't need to tell you, of all people, about the world outside these four walls, do I? Think about what it is you're saying. This is West Belfast, we're in one of the most turbulent times in history—'

'Don't you think that's all the more reason to live while you can? You think I don't know what it's like to be lonely? When I lived in Walker Street with my parents and my brothers – that's five other people – I was the loneliest I've ever been. When I moved to Noreen's and then met you, I didn't feel lonely any more. You don't have to be lonely, Father. You… you have me… if you want me.'

'Fergal, stop. Don't say these things. If anyone found out… do you realise what would happen? Do you? People have been killed for less!'

'I don't care – I really don't! I want to be with you. There – I've said it.'

Father Mac stood and walked up and down the room. 'Look, Fergal, I think you should go home to Noreen's now. And I'm giving you a lift, it's way too late to be walking around this area alone.'

'OK,' Fergal said, even though he wasn't entirely sure what all this meant.

'Now listen, I want you to promise me that what's been said between us will stay between us, and that you will never try to run away again. The next time you feel bad about anything, please know that you have me to turn to. I'm so sorry I under-estimated the pressure you were under. You do know I care for you deeply, don't you – very, very deeply? But… we just can't…'

'But, Father—'

'Fergal, promise me you'll never do anything like this again?'

'OK, I promise. I'm sorry.' Fergal yawned loudly with sheer exhaustion.

'Look, let me get you back to Noreen's. We've said more than enough for tonight. I take it you still want to continue working towards the audition?'

'Oh, Father, I do! More than anything! I feel a lot better just being here. Thanks for saving me.'

'I didn't save you, Fergal, not really. There seems to be an angel watching over you. Did you see the size of those skin-heads?'

Father Mac dropped Fergal outside his granny's house, and waited till he found the key and was safely inside. Fergal needn't have worried about waking Noreen, he could hear her snoring from the bottom of the stairs. He got a drink of water, climbed under the freezing covers and was asleep in seconds.

As Father Mac drove back to St Bridget's, he replayed the entire evening in his mind and thought about the coincidence of it all. He felt a sudden chill across his back as he realised what could have happened if his timing had been different even by only a few minutes.

He climbed into his waiting bed, said a prayer for Fergal and once again asked God for forgiveness and guidance.

'I know you're testing me, Lord, but did you hear Fergal tonight? He said he didn't care, he wanted to be with me… What were the chances of us meeting like that tonight? One thing is for certain, Lord, I've never met anyone like him, and something tells me I never will. In the name of the Father, the Son and the Holy Spirit. Amen.'

~

When they met again, two days later, things between them were a lot better. Fergal felt like more of an equal somehow and he felt much less alone, now that he knew for sure that Father Mac fancied men too. It was all he needed to know.

Father Mac thought Fergal was singing better than ever. He did his best to tread a careful, calm line with him. As they were having tea, he asked lightly, 'Is everything OK, Fergal?'

'Yeah – yeah, Father. Noreen's not great, but I feel like… like I know you better and you know me better. I mean – well, after what happened I thought you'd never speak to me again.'

'Fergal, I can't imagine that day ever coming. To err is human, to forgive divine. Isn't that what I'm trying to preach every day of my life? I actually think you're incredibly brave. I mean, at your age, I don't think I would have coped as well as you have.'

'But I tried to run away, and to—'

'Well, yes, but you didn't go through with it in the end. You made the right decision in the middle of a lot of wrong ones. I'm glad you decided to finish your exams, it would've been a shame to throw away five years in five angry minutes. You're a brave one, Fergal Flynn, there's no doubting that.'

As a proper smile spread over Fergal's face for the first time in a while, Father Mac thought that Fergal looked less haunted, somehow. He was amazed at the way Fergal seemed to take things in his stride and bounce back. And he knew music was the glue that helped Fergal put things carefully back together, piece by fragile piece.

Over the next few weeks, they worked harder than ever for the audition, until one night Father Mac said, 'You know what, Fergal Flynn?'

'What, Father Mac?'

'I think you're ready.'

14

On the morning after his last exam, Fergal was at his parents' house in Walker Street doing some last-minute laundry for his auditions later the same day. The twins were prowling around, bored and curious, trying to wreck his ironing any time Angela left the room. He'd found an old suitcase in one of Noreen's junk-yard bedrooms that had belonged to his late grandfather, and Angela had come over all tearful when she saw her father's handwriting on the faded label.

When Father Mac parked his car outside the Flynns' house and rapped on their front door, it was like a carefully rehearsed cue for the neighbours to appear, pretending to clean their windows or front steps. Angela came to the door, beaming, and said in her loudest voice, 'Father MacManus, how nice of you to come! How are you since the last time we had tea and all at your house?'

He stepped back slightly. 'I'm fine, Mrs Flynn. And you?'

'Our Fergal is ready to go with you to make that record for the *Pope*!' She practically shouted the last word, for fear they might not hear her in the next street. 'Won't you come in for a wee cup of tea?'

Father Mac had purposely left the engine running. He told her he was sorry that he couldn't stay, but time was of the essence and they were expected at the monastery in the early afternoon.

As Fergal was getting into the car, Angela came running over with John's prized deep-blue velvet jacket, which she'd ordered from a catalogue for a formal he was taking some girl to. 'Here, our Fergal – you nearly forgot your good coat!' As the car pulled away slowly, to accommodate the fact that she was pushing the cheap velvet coat through the back window, Fergal saw John at the front-room window miming as only John could. He was pretending to hang himself with a thick rope and then pointing at Fergal.

They drove up the Falls Road in silence, past the park where the winos punched one another in slow motion, making some meaningless drunken point. They moved on towards the turning for the M1 motorway, which would carry them west to Enniskillen and eventually to County Sligo. They passed Milltown Cemetery, and Fergal thought about his Granda Flynn, lying there under six feet of clay.

Once they were safely out of Belfast, Father Mac turned to Fergal and said, 'See, fella – I told you not to worry! Everything will be great. Now just sit back and try and relax.'

'Do you know I've never been out the west before?'

'What?'

'No, never. We went on holiday to Butlins a couple of times, though, not too far from Dublin. That was mad.'

'Why?'

'The six of us and one of Paddy's mates were booked into a one-bedroom chalet. We were sleeping all over the place in sleeping bags and blankets, and Ma was always warning us not to make too much noise or we'd get found out. John nearly got caught shoplifting.'

'Well, you've certainly earned this wee trip, especially after the exams – which I want to hear all about, if you're ready to tell me.'

So, as they glided further and further away from their hometown, Fergal talked about the exams and began to feel calmer. 'I wouldn't have been able to do enough studying if I'd been at Walker Street – my brothers would've been at me. I think I did OK – although Noreen's been having trouble sleeping these last few weeks, so she was always trying to talk to me at night. And some of the teachers steered us wrong in the mock exams—'

Father Mac suddenly took his hand off the gear stick and patted Fergal's shoulder. 'You did your best. Sure, that's all that counts as far as I'm concerned. I'm proud of you.'

Fergal shifted in his seat. He'd missed school the day they'd handed out the instructions on how to deal with compliments from anyone, never mind from a handsome priest.

~

After a lifetime in Belfast, Father Mac's parents had retreated to Derrygonnelly, a little town on the outskirts of Enniskillen. Their only other son, Seamus, had married a Derrygonnelly girl called Barbara and the moment she fell pregnant, she had convinced him to embrace the roads and fields of her childhood. Her parents were still young, and they were thrilled to get the chance to be hands-on grandparents, and it wasn't long before the MacManuses took the bait and followed their son.

Their eldest child, Dympna, had moved with them and commuted to and from Enniskillen, where she worked too hard and too long for the council. Her parents reminded her at every opportunity that she was lucky to have such a secure position. She'd started at seventeen and now, at almost forty, she was helping to pay the mortgage on her parents' large farmhouse where she had her own private floor.

Father Mac wasn't close to his brother, and that helped him understand Fergal's plight. Seamus had been cruel to him when they were growing up, and the thought of having to deal with more than one Seamus was enough to make him shudder. He had thought of trying to see his sister on her own, secretly, but the guilt had proved too much for him, and he had grudgingly dialled his parents' number to tell them he'd be passing through. He had also told them not to go to any trouble – his mother practically had to be prevented from ordering a marquee for the afternoon.

Mr and Mrs MacManus were quietly suspicious of Fergal, but Dympna went out of her way to be friendly, asking him about his recent exams and his family. Mrs MacManus, who had been studying his profile, asked him what his mother's maiden name was. When he said, 'Clooney. Angela Clooney from Mount Street', her mouth snapped shut and began grinding, as if she was chewing his answer to check whether it was a trustworthy flavour. She said that she'd known his mother, they had even worked together briefly. Their own mothers had brought them

140

into the linen factory for part-time shifts, swearing to the blind supervisor that they were old enough, when in fact they were only thirteen and skipping school.

Mr MacManus grilled Fergal about sport and asked him what teams he supported. When he mentioned that he didn't support any and that he thought the offside rule seemed like the work of a powerful bad loser, the old man couldn't hide his disgust. His expression said he understood why Fergal and his son were such good friends.

Seamus, even fatter than his heavily pregnant wife, arrived with their kids in tow. The two little boys turned out to be a glorious distraction from the undercurrent of disapproval and disappointment that no one seemed brave enough to voice. They stared at their uncle, who they'd never met before. Then Brendan, the older one, asked him, 'Do you know my daddy?' – which said more than all of the adult conversation put together.

Fergal and Father Mac dutifully ate a few sandwiches before employing the legitimate excuse that they were going to be late to the abbey. Their goodbyes were rushed and uncomfortable – frantic handshakes from Mr MacManus and Seamus, and a power cut of an embrace from Mrs MacManus. Only Dympna was brave enough to kiss them both.

As they drove on, unfamiliar radio stations announced local deaths and played traditional music that had them tapping the dashboard. When they got to the heavily guarded border, Fergal was stunned at how friendly the soldiers were to Father Mac – they weren't even searched. He wondered aloud whether it was his imagination, or whether the grass was suddenly greener, the sky bluer, the trees taller. Father Mac chuckled and blew smoke out the slit of his open window.

They pulled over at a garage to get tins of fizzy lemon and a family-size bag of sweets. As Fergal chewed, Father Mac said, 'Fergal, I'm sorry. I don't think it was such a good idea to visit my family. Apart from my sister, they weren't very friendly, were they? That's the last thing you need.'

'Ah, Father, I thought they were OK. Your da's just as sports-mad as mine and you're not like your brother at all, are you? His kids were funny, though, and your sister was lovely.'

Father Mac sighed. 'It took me right back to the time when I was entering the seminary at Maynooth. My parents spent weeks arguing about whether they should drive me there. My father thought it was a complete waste of time and petrol, but my mother sulked and prayed aloud till he agreed.'

'Father, how did you know you definitely wanted to be a priest? I mean, you hear all kinds of stories about visions and all... Was it like that?'

Father Mac's brow furrowed deeply. 'No. I struggled with my faith for a long time, and I made the mistake of sharing my doubts with my father... You know, Fergal, Brother Vincent was a tower of strength during those times. I hope you'll like him. He's a real larger-than-life character, with a wicked sense of humour, but he's very serious about his music. I know he's going to love your voice.'

~

As the afternoon sun played hide-and-seek, they saw the first weather-beaten signs for Sligo Abbey. They wound their way between hedges, along seemingly endless potholed roads – Fergal thought of Noreen's story about the broken-down bus – and then round a final corner that revealed the huge stone abbey set back from the road behind two colossal iron gates. Above them was a Latin inscription, which Father Mac translated: 'Brave are the men who answer God's call.' Fergal wondered about the women who had done the same.

The gates opened reluctantly and they drove around to the back of the abbey where there was a small collection of cars that belonged to the few employees who lived outside in the town. Inside, they were greeted by Mrs O'Carroll, the long-suffering secretary, who informed them that Brother Vincent was supervising an exam because old Brother Luke had been taken ill. She lowered her eyelashes every time she said the word 'Brother'.

Mrs O'Carroll found one of the sixth-form boarders – they were the only ones who were still at the school, taking their exams – to show Father Mac and Fergal to their rooms. His name was Eamonn, he was a barrister's son from Dublin and he was very friendly. The second he heard their accents, he started telling them about the time he had gone shopping in Belfast with his mother and they had ended up trapped in the chemist's for six hours because of a bomb scare.

As he talked, Eamonn led them towards their rooms. The abbey was a curious mix of old stone and relatively modern building work. They passed down a stone hallway, where four students nervously waited outside a panelled door for their turns to take their Irish oral exam; one boy was just coming out, greeted by a silent movie of panicked last-chance faces. Eamonn led them through deserted dormitories with stripped bunk beds, up a flight of stairs and through a room whose door held a plaque announcing 'Sixth Year Common Room – Smoking Permitted'. It housed a pool table and a couple of pinball machines and under a TV was a rack of videos with 'Property of Sligo Abbey' printed on their spines. Fergal was instantly jealous of anyone who had ever attended this extraordinary place.

Eamonn showed them their private rooms at the end of a corridor. To Fergal's quiet delight, his room was right next to Father Mac's. It held a single bed with a lamp, a sink with a small mirror, a writing desk and a wardrobe. A few posters of footballers he'd never heard of still adorned the walls, competing for space with invitations to parties and ripped pictures of nearly naked women.

Fergal lay down on the bed and thought about what kind of life the previous occupant might have led. It certainly hadn't been anybody from the Falls Road. He wondered if he was the first person from the Falls ever to visit the abbey. The room was a lot bigger than the one he'd shared with Ciaran, and the view was incredible. It was a shock to see trees and hills, instead of a too-close-for-comfort mirror image of his parents' two-up-two-down, with Mrs Black obsessively scouring her front step in every weather. Some young fella had been shot to pieces outside her house. He had staggered into her hall, pleading in a clotted voice, 'I want my mammy – please get my ma, will you?' before the last of the life ran out of him. Mrs Black didn't know who he was, and as her kids screamed the place down she had tried to shut her hall door, but he was too awkwardly slumped against it. An ambulance had finally relieved her of his riddled body, before the soldiers moved in and the missiles – bricks, six-inch nails, hatchets and broken hammers – started to fly in every direction. Hours later, when Mrs Black had finally reopened her door, her front step looked as though a tin of red paint had been knocked over it. She had bleached it and scrubbed it every morning since.

As the memory faded, a cloud moved away from the Sligo sun and Fergal's new room was momentarily filled with brilliant light. It was as if the sky had smiled approvingly at him. Two birds chased each other in circles that seemed perfectly choreographed, and Fergal was so relaxed and so glad to be somewhere else that he could have closed his eyes and slept for hours.

15

Fergal unpacked his tiny suitcase. His grandfather's name and address were written in green ink on a clean bit of the lid in under-confident, old-fashioned handwriting. It was strange, he thought, they'd never known each other, and yet here he was, all these years later, using his grandfather's name and his case. He thought about the blue velvet jacket he'd left in the car and laughed, remembering his mother pushing it through the back window.

'Are you going to let me in on whatever is making you so happy, Mr Fergal Flynn? Or am I just going to have to rely on divine inspiration?'

The unfamiliar voice startled Fergal. He hated being surprised.

He eyed the bulky frame in the doorway suspiciously, before realising this must be the Brother Vincent who Father Mac talked about so much.

When the monk saw Fergal's face, he said, 'Now, there's no need to look so worried, young man. I'm Brother Vincent McFarland, and we're all looking forward to hearing you sing later on. I've never heard Father MacManus so enthusiastic about anyone, ever, and he's a tough one to impress.'

'Oh, sorry, Brother – I didn't mean to stare. I was miles away. I'll do my best, of course.'

Father Mac had obviously heard his friend's voice from his room; he appeared silently behind him and put his hands over the monk's eyes. Brother Vincent knew instantly who it was. 'Well, by the smell of your hands I'd say you're still as addicted to cigarettes as you ever were, Father!'

They embraced warmly, laughing, and Father Mac stood back to look at his friend. 'I see they're feeding you well, Vincent. The size of you!'

Brother Vincent pretended to look hurt. He dropped his eyes and replied in a sad little boy's voice, 'Sure, I was only a wee slip of a thing in my youth, but all good things came to an end.' Then, in his normal voice, he boomed, 'Now there's more of me to love! Whoa!'

They all laughed this time. Brother Vincent regained his official composure and asked, 'Would you be ready to audition in about twenty minutes, before dinner?'

Fergal nodded and gulped all at once, trying not to look too panic-stricken, leaving Father Mac to answer, 'We're as ready as we can be.'

Brother Vincent looked pleased. 'I'll give you a little tour on the way,' he said, and led them downstairs and out into the vast grounds.

Fergal started to see a different side of Father Mac. He couldn't believe how the two grown men – although they addressed each other formally as 'Father' and 'Brother' – slagged each other playfully but mercilessly about their appearances and pretended to trip each other up, like excited schoolboys. Fergal knew only too well that there wasn't much to laugh about on the Falls Road, and that Father Mac had to maintain a certain level of profession-al distance around his parishioners, but he felt a little envious of Brother Vincent's ability to effortlessly transform Father Mac. He even seemed to look younger.

Fergal had fallen slightly behind the two men and Father Mac dropped his voice and asked Brother Vincent, 'How have the other auditions gone? Have you found anyone you really like the sound of?'

'We've had five hopefuls,' Brother Vincent said, equally quietly, 'and there were two – both from the choir in the abbey – who came close to the quality we're hoping for. So, if Fergal doesn't work out, all isn't lost.' Father Mac nodded, relieved in one sense and more nervous in another.

Fergal, watching them whispering, became a little paranoid. He badly wanted to be picked for the recording, especially after all the trouble Father Mac had gone to. He only hoped he was good enough… He took slow, deep breaths to try and calm the rising tide of nerves.

Outside the residence hall, they climbed a mound that looked out over the surrounding grounds. From this ancient vantage point, the abbey looked like a castle. Neat orchards and perfectly kept gardens ran all the way around it; beyond them was a cemetery and then thick, dark woods that seemed to stretch for miles. Brother Vincent gave a little running commentary about the history of the order, and how they pressed their own apple juice from the orchards and brewed their own beer, which always sold out at the local market. He said the graveyard was full of generations of Brothers, going as far back as the first monks known to have settled there around the twelfth century. He pointed out the beehives – most of them at the edge of the woods, but a few scattered around the greenhouses – where the famous honey was faithfully collected.

The abbey's main chapel was easily as big as St Bridget's Church, though it had no balcony. Row after row of enormous stained-glass windows depicted, in beautiful colours and intricate designs, a world that was long gone to outsiders but stubbornly maintained by the holy brothers. Fergal and the two men entered the vestry through a side door. About twenty purple satin robes hung neatly in a row on numbered pegs with their corresponding shoes and velvet-embossed prayer books on a bench below. Thick piles of music books were stacked against the walls and on some of the wooden seats. In a corner, a crowd of tall brass candlesticks were gathered, as if watching the visitors. Brother Vincent asked Father Mac and Fergal to remove their footwear and then opened another heavy door, placing a stubby finger solemnly against his lips as he motioned for them to follow.

Inside, the chapel was lit solely by winking candles and these, as Fergal and Father Mac soon discovered, were also the only source of heat. The floor was made of highly glazed mosaic tiles chronicling in minute detail the last days of Jesus' life. The fractured pattern reflected the candlelight in a million different directions, and it was breathtaking enough to make them forget about the drop in temperature.

They stood uncertainly at one side of the altar, not knowing where to go. Then, suddenly, the chapel came to life. In the darkened choir stalls on the far side of the altar, the waiting monks' bowed heads lifted one by one and they began their evening chant. It grew and grew in volume, to a continuous deep resonance that was hypnotic. Most of the Brothers were quite old, with a variety of long beards and glasses, and not one of them opened his eyes while they constructed the human wall of sound. Their mouths made the shape of perfect full moons as the notes undulated back and forth along the empty aisles.

When they came to the end of the piece, the monks stopped in the same mysterious way they had started: voice after voice dropped out, leaving just a single one to cradle the air into silence again. Fergal didn't know whether to cheer or cry.

Brother Vincent took him by the arm and placed him in front of the altar by a music stand, facing out towards the congregationless space. Father Mac took his seat at the organ beside the choir, its vast pipes running all the way up to the ceiling. As Fergal's eyes made their final adjustments, he almost stumbled in shock – the biggest crucifix he had ever seen was suspended right above the altar, the dying figure of Christ glowing marble-white with piercing, sorrowful, emerald eyes.

Fergal swallowed hard. Without warning, a chord rang out – the first chord of one of the hymns he had been rehearsing. He turned towards the organ to ask if he should sing. Father Mac shook his head to silence him until Brother Vincent counted him in with exaggerated swings of his arm.

Fergal had no time left to be nervous. He found the Latin

words on the manuscript in front of him and they rose from the pit of his stomach – a bit shakily at first, but once he felt the acoustics of the chapel supporting him, he relaxed enough to breathe properly. Then his high tenor voice was free to join the clouds of incense in the darkened reaches of the cloisters. The Brothers joined in, and Fergal kept his eyes glued to the music stand for fear that he'd lose his concentration. He had never sung with this kind of harmony before and it was hard not to let the strange beauty of it distract him. He focused on the organ and imagined he was back in Father Mac's sitting room.

The hymn came to an end. No one spoke.

When Fergal looked up, he saw that Brother Vincent's eyes were closed and he had a broad grin renting his face. The other monks kept their heads bowed. On cue from Brother Vincent, Father Mac played a single note on the lower register of the organ. With Vincent conducting, the monks launched into a light-hearted piece that Fergal definitely hadn't heard before. He threw a worried look at Father Mac – were they expecting him to join in? – but Father Mac shook his head, smiling, and placed a finger to his lips. As the monks reached the end of the piece, they rose to their feet and filed out one by one until there was no proof that they had ever been there.

Brother Vincent came towards the confused Fergal and said, 'Well, young man, please tell me you haven't made any plans for the weekend because we have a busy couple of days ahead. Your voice is perfect – just like you said it would be, Father Mac-Manus.'

Father Mac put an arm around Fergal's shaking shoulders. Fergal's heart was flying with the rush of excitement, not only from singing but from the relief of success. Until now, he'd never been singled out for anything in his life – not anything good, at least.

Father Mac led him back to the vestry where they'd left their shoes, then he hugged him and said in his ear, 'I knew you could do it!'

Fergal, overcome with the nearness of him, rested his head on his shoulder for a moment. Then he remembered. 'Could I use the phone?'

They were shown to Brother Vincent's little office. Fergal nervously dialled his Aunt Concepta's number – the Flynns didn't have a phone – and asked her to tell his ma that he had passed the audition and wouldn't be home till… He suddenly realised he didn't know when they'd be finished recording.

'Sunday,' mouthed Father Mac.

'Sunday,' Fergal told her.

Neither of them realised how hungry they were until a gong sounded and Brother Vincent explained it was the call for dinner. Fergal thought he wouldn't be able to eat he was so excited, but the food was delicious – much better than the endless tinned stuff he was used to. It was all grown in the gardens of the abbey and harvested by the monks with occasional help from a few willing pupils. For afters, they had fresh raspberries with thick cream and honey.

A memory started up like a little film in the cinema of Fergal's head. Tins of raspberries in the fridge and a turkey hanging upside down behind the kitchen door, which meant it was nearly time for Santa. Every Christmas Eve, the Flynns had a visit from one of their da's old hurling mates who'd married a woman from up the country. They had no kids of their own, so every year they drove up to the Flynns' house with a car full of giant cabbages, parsnips and the biggest, scariest, baldiest turkey ever seen. Angela hated the fact that it still had its head and the boys were all terrified of it in case it came back to life during the night and ran around the house trying to bite them. Once it had been wedged into their tiny oven and cooked till it was unrecognisable, though, nobody had any complaints about eating it.

Fergal and Father Mac insisted on helping out with the washing up – there were so many hands that it took about ten seconds. No one spoke unless they absolutely had to, and Fergal smiled at the thought that he was still being surrounded by Brothers who wouldn't speak to him.

It was coming up to half past nine, when the monks retired to the seclusion of their private quarters in the oldest part of the monastery – an area that was out of bounds even to some of the younger members of the order, not to mention the pupils. Brother Vincent accompanied his two guests through a maze of corridors and up another steep stairwell back to their rooms. He was very complimentary about Fergal's performance. 'Out of all the voices we've tried over the past month, you have the most appropriate tone – very pure, very natural. The fact that the other Brothers joined in with you tells me they feel the same way.' Fergal stared at the worn wooden floorboards, burning with embarrassment.

Brother Vincent said, 'Good night, my dears. If we didn't have such a busy day tomorrow, I would crack open the brandy I've been saving… but, sure, maybe tomorrow night – when the work is completed?'

'Of course, Vincent! You know how much I love a decent brandy. I hope it's none of that cooking muck, now?'

Brother Vincent giggled like a schoolgirl and padded off into the darkness. Fergal thought it was weird that such a big man should have such a little laugh.

He yawned before he could stop himself, and Father Mac laughed and ruffled his hair. 'Pleasant dreams.' The touch was like an electric current going straight through Fergal's body. He closed his bedroom door behind him, undressed as fast as he could and jumped under the cold bedcovers.

His thoughts turned to Father Mac in the next room. He pressed his ear to the wall that separated them, hoping he might at least hear Father Mac breathing, but he couldn't hear a thing. He whispered to the wall, 'Well, at least we're getting closer.'

He wanted to masturbate, but he had nothing to finish into. He laughed into his pillow, remembering something that had happened in Walker Street about two years previously.

Angela, sick and tired of finding odd socks when she was hanging up the washing, had decided to go where no mother had gone before – while the boys were at school, she went into the twins' room to look for the missing socks. She searched high and low and in the end she tried under the bunk beds. John, who slept on the bottom one, had found that his socks were perfect for his most private obsession. Almost every night, while Paddy Jr snored above him, he would impregnate whichever sock was to hand and throw it under the bed, amidst the dusty jungle of sports comics, shoes and the odd half-eaten plate of chips, then heave a satisfied sigh and fall asleep.

When the twins bounced in from school, Angela pounced. 'Right, you two! Which one of youse dirty bastards has been blowing his nose in his socks and then throwing them under the beds, eh? Jesus, didn't I have to snap them apart to get the washing powder in this morning – and the smell would've made you forget your own name!'

John went white in the face. Paddy said virtuously, 'It wasn't me, Mammy. I don't do that! I sleep on the top bunk. I'm a good shot, but not good enough to get a sock under the bottom bunk from the top one.'

Angela screwed her face up at John. 'John Flynn, what kind of dirty animal am I rearing that you would use your bloody good socks for something so disgusting? Sure, haven't we any amount of toilet roll that my mate Maureen risks life and limb to get past the hospital security? If I ever catch you again…'

She went for him but he sprinted out the back door into the yard shouting, 'It's not me who's the dirty animal – it's Fergal! It was him!'

Angela roared after him, 'Well, fuck me if our Fergal isn't the best shot in Ireland then – managing to get a slimy sock through the wall from his own fucking room all the way under your bed! Do you think I'm daft or something, you big lazy cunt? Stay out of my sight till dinner time – and if I find one more of them good socks stuck together, I'll kill you stone dead! Do you hear me, John? Stone dead!'

It was the only time Fergal could remember when he and his brother Paddy had laughed together. Ciaran had joined in uncertainly, not really knowing why he was laughing, but not wanting to be left out.

As Fergal drifted off to sleep, he wondered how many people, in all the decades of pupils who had passed through on their way to the adult world, had wanked in his new bed.

~

Father Mac was considering asking Brother Vincent for a sleeping tablet, or at least some of his private stash of brandy. He was convinced he was becoming an insomniac. He couldn't get comfortable no matter how hard he tried. He wondered if Vincent thought Fergal was attractive. Out of nowhere, he began to feel jealous. He got up wearily and opened the window to smoke, but after only a few annoyed puffs he stubbed out the cigarette and threw it into the darkness.

He tried to sleep with his back to the wall but, inevitably, he could only get comfortable if he was facing Fergal's room. Slowly he began to wonder what Fergal looked like as he lay sleeping. He reprimanded himself and closed his eyes but it was no use: Fergal's face floated in front of his mind's eye. *I just want to be with you, Father Mac. Why do we have to be lonely?*

Father Mac got out of bed and prayed silently. 'Dear Heavenly Father, thank you for the gift of my friendship with Fergal. To see him really beginning to shine is nothing short of a miracle. He's blossoming so profoundly, all he ever needed was to be exposed to the right kind of light. Did you hear him sing today? Wasn't he better than ever? Wasn't he... beautiful? Oh, Father, he's sleeping in the next room – so near, but so far – and it's all I can do not to go and tell him that I... that I...'

Even though no one could hear his thoughts, Father Mac could not finish the sentence.

16

Just before waking, Fergal had a disturbing dream.

He was a little girl on the back seat of a car travelling slowly along a dusty, winding road. There were two grown-up people in the front. The passenger was his mother, but she wasn't Angela. The driver was a man he didn't know. As the little girl, he noticed rice fields on one side of the car and a thick dark forest on the other. In the paddy field there was a man bent over picking rice plants; he looked exactly like the man driving the car. Then a voice rose up from the forest laughing hysterically. The little girl's parents acted as if they hadn't heard a thing, but she was terrified because she knew it meant the driver was about to be killed and the identical man in the rice field was going to take his place…

Fergal woke. For a second he didn't know where he was. He lay still wondering what the dream had meant. He had no idea what time it was, and through the window he could see that the sky didn't know either. He got out of the warm bed and pulled on his trousers and T-shirt. The dream had shaken him. He put his ear to the wall – if he could hear Father Mac breathing, he thought, it might make him feel better – but there wasn't a sound. He was beginning to feel a little scared. He crept out into the corridor but when he plucked up the courage to rap on Father Mac's door, there was no answer. He turned the handle slowly. If he opened it a crack and saw Father Mac sleeping, he decided, he'd go back to his own room.

He was surprised to find the room empty. There was a Bible by the lamp with a set of rosary beads coiled on top of it, and the bed showed signs of having been slept in. Fergal whispered to himself, 'Where could he be?' Maybe Father Mac had gone to the toilet somewhere, or downstairs for some water and had got lost? Or maybe he'd taken Brother Vincent up on his offer of a brandy, after all, and they were still drinking somewhere deep in the monastery. Fergal went back out, along the dark corridor and down the narrow stairs, listening all the while for hushed talking or muted laughing. He decided that, if he bumped into someone, he'd say he was looking for a toilet.

He came to the annex that led outside. A few stars had over-stayed their welcome in the slow morning sky. Fergal wandered towards the apple orchard. As he turned a corner, the sight of a fox stopped him in his tracks. It had something large in its mouth and carried on running, glancing sideways at him with the moon in its eyes. Fergal had never seen one before and was amazed at how small it was.

A cold breath of air brushed Fergal's neck. He was considering abandoning his walk for his warm bed when, out of the corner of his eye, he saw a red-orange glow floating amongst the branches of a flowering apple tree. He jumped in fear, thinking it was some strange one-eyed creature but his curiosity got the better of him and he moved closer – close enough to make out the silhouette of Father Mac inhaling a cigarette. Fergal didn't want to disturb him. He leaned against a wall, watching the priest smoke, as the birds started their first song of the day and the sun convinced the stars that it could be trusted to adopt the sky.

Father Mac got down a little stiffly from the branches, and was turning back towards the abbey when he saw Fergal.

'Fergal, is that you?' he whispered.

'Yes, Father Mac.'

'Is everything all right? What are you doing out of bed?'

'I had a bad dream and I went to your room to talk to you but you weren't there, so I came out here for a bit of air. I didn't want to call out in case I startled you and you fell into the muck.'

Father Mac put a hand on Fergal's hunched shoulder and they walked through the orchard towards the little cemetery. 'Tell me your dream,' Father Mac said.

It had already begun to evaporate from Fergal's memory. 'I can't remember.'

They walked the length of the graves and Father Mac lit another cigarette. 'Look, Fergal, it's natural to be nervous about new things. Sure, we all are. It's only human. Whatever your dream was, don't fret too much, my friend. I believe in your capabilities, and I'll be right beside you every step of the way – I promise.'

They embraced, awkwardly at first, then tightly. Father Mac wrapped the edges of his coat around Fergal's bare arms. Fergal realised he had grown in the past few months – they were almost the same height. He let his head rest against Father Mac's neck, and became aware of the secret tobacco sweetness that clung to his skin. Normally he couldn't stand the smell of smoke but this was intoxicating, mixing with the new perfume of the apple blossom that the waking breeze was carrying to tempt the sleepy bees.

They stayed in that position for a long while, neither wanting to be the first to unfurl from the moment. Father Mac hummed hoarsely, a soft familiar tune that soothed Fergal completely.

Then, instinctively, they slowly untangled themselves and moved back towards the abbey.

Brother Vincent had been watching the little scene from the arc of his window with great interest. The rest of the monks were beginning to surface from their unconscious state, for the chant that praised God for bringing light back into the world for another day. Father Mac and Fergal reached the door that would take them both upstairs, but the priest paused and let Fergal go on first, while he went in search of a toilet that he didn't really need to use.

When Fergal got to his room, he closed the door and sat on the edge of the bed, his head spinning. He lay flat in an effort to calm down but ended up planting tiny kisses on the pillow, pretending it was Father Mac's face.

His reverie was broken by Brother Vincent, who opened the door holding a tray with two cups of steaming tea. He said reproachfully, 'Now, Mr Flynn, you didn't sleep in those clothes, did you? Was it too cold in here? Don't tell me you've been up and out already!'

Fergal had no idea how to respond but Father Mac came to the rescue, whether he meant to or not. He appeared at the door behind his friend, saying, 'I don't suppose this would be a good time to tickle you, Vincent – what with your full tray and all?'

Brother Vincent giggled as Father Mac said, 'We set our alarms early, we didn't want to risk missing the first chant and we went for a walk in the orchards to wake ourselves up.'

Brother Vincent said coyly, with his tongue firmly in his cheek, 'Oh, there's no danger of sleeping in round here, my dears. We're all *very early risers*... Whoa!' He winked at them, put down the tray and floated off out the door. Fergal threw some cold water on his face and put on his jumper. He couldn't stop thinking about how easily Father Mac seemed to flirt with Brother Vincent.

Father Mac saw the serious look on his face. 'Are you OK?'

'Well, I suppose so.'

He closed the door. 'What is it, fella? Tell me.'

'It's just that... Brother Vincent – does he ever stop, you know, flirting with you?'

'Ah, Fergal, Vincent and I are old friends. He's theatrical, to say the least, but he's harmless. And he knows there's no way I—'

'What?'

'Well, I could never be interested in him, in that way. But he's a laugh – you have to admit he's funny – and underneath all the jokes is someone quite vulnerable.'

'Yeah, but... early risers? What's he like? Any excuse to get a double meaning going.'

'Pay no mind to him, Fergal – he's just starved of stimulating company like ours! Come on, now, we'd better get down there.'

As much as Fergal didn't want to admit it to himself, he knew in his heart of hearts that he was jealous of Brother Vincent's ability to make Father Mac so giddy. He wasn't sure he liked the way the two men morphed so easily into goofy, teasing boys before his eyes. Fergal didn't know how to do that – he'd never learned – and it made him feel left out again.

They caught up with Brother Vincent at the chapel door. Fergal didn't want to take off his shoes again – his socks were old with holes right at the heels, right where he needed protection from the arctic floor. This time, though, Brother Vincent offered them little sandals from a cupboard – 'I'm so sorry, I forgot to give you these yesterday!' – and Fergal was relieved. As they took their places at the altar and his eyes adjusted, he noticed that the Brothers were wearing an array of open-toed sandals and soft moccasins without any socks at all.

Brother Vincent started, issuing a low growl that grew thicker and darker with each added voice until it became a pulse. As the chanting pushed and pulled its ancient Latin cargo, it sounded like a swarm of bees, getting closer and closer, drawing them towards the centre of a giant hive. Then Vincent nodded for Fergal to begin and he sang, a full two octaves higher than the monks, like a sudden burst of sunlight beaming through the shimmering stained-glass windows.

The unfamiliar words were like a warning, calling over and over again to the world when it was a very different place. Fergal wondered what had inspired the monk all those centuries ago to compose such an unbelievable soundscape.

'*Nunc et domine et spiritus sanctus…*'

The words gathered more and more momentum and finally burst like a firework, up towards the roof of the chapel where the audience of painted angels waited, frozen, spellbound messengers of God, like mermaids of the deep sea foolishly venturing too close to the earth to hear the music that would trap them between worlds, free neither to walk nor to fly.

Brother Vincent looked Fergal straight in the eyes as the last chord spread its wings and flew homeward.

~

Over breakfast of surprisingly delicious porridge, honey and bread, Brother Vincent discussed the plan for the day. There would be more rehearsals after breakfast. The technical people were due to arrive, set up their recording equipment and have it all working before lunch. There would be a few obligatory run-throughs for sound balance, and then the programme of recording would start.

Fergal was nervous already. Brother Vincent smiled at him and said, 'Whenever I get anxious about anything, I go below to our little chapel and ask for strength from the icons. I always leave feeling much better.'

Fergal looked confused and the monk said, 'You mean to tell me you haven't heard about our Chapel of Icons?'

Fergal shook his head.

'Right, I'll take you there myself as soon as rehearsals are over. It's directly below the altar and is the most sacred place in all of the abbey.'

Father Mac seemed a bit distant and kept going out for cigarette after cigarette in the garden. One of the oldest Brothers was tending the beehives with no protection except for his robe, which was exactly the same colour as the newly turned soil. His hairless head ignored the strong rays of the sun. Father Mac was too far away to tell if he was praying or deep in conversation with the winged workers who mistook the old man's slow brown bulk for an unthreatening, walking tree. Whenever Father Mac watched Fergal sing, he witnessed a transformation that he found incredibly moving. Fergal's body seemed taller, less weighted down, his eyes shone so trustfully and that voice! All of the sadness was channelled into that voice... Father Mac was worried about the profound effect Fergal could have on him.

~

The rehearsals were long and intense. Fergal was relieved when he realised that he could have the Latin text in front of him. Brother Vincent enthused quietly and helped him with the odd bit of pronunciation but still none of the other Brothers spoke. Some of them stayed so still, you could have been forgiven for thinking they'd had some kind of stroke and died. Fergal wanted to ask Brother Vincent if it had ever happened but decided against it.

It was agreed that for two of Fergal's four pieces, Father Mac would accompany them on the organ. Fergal was greatly re-assured by this news. All it took was one gentle smile from the priest and his shoulders dropped from their tense position and he could find calm again.

Just as the last song came to a close, they heard the trucks arriving from the outside world with the equipment. The Brothers vanished out the side door, towards their quarters.

Fergal just managed to hear Father Mac say discreetly, 'Look, Vincent, I'm dying for a cigarette, but I'm trying not to smoke too much around our asthmatic soloist. Try and cheer him up and keep him from thinking about the recording too much, will you? Don't let his nerves get the better of him! I'm relying on you.'

Brother Vincent nodded and winked – seriously, this time. Then he took Fergal by the arm and said, 'Now then, Mr Flynn, I don't make promises I can't keep. Come this way and I'll show you our Chapel of Icons.' Relieved, Father Mac headed for the woods beyond the cemetery and disappeared from view, leaving behind a tiny trail of grey tobacco smoke.

Brother Vincent led Fergal around the main chapel until they came to an enormous holly bush, which framed a stairwell leading down into blackness. The steps that were visible had been worn down in the middle by centuries of careful, visiting feet. Their surfaces looked as smooth as skimming stones. Brother Vincent took them carefully explaining that he had once encountered a none-too-happy inquisitive badger at the bottom, so it was always wise to go slowly and make enough noise to announce your presence. By the bottom, Fergal could hardly see a thing.

Brother Vincent freed a large key ring from under the folds of his robe and selected the right key with myopic tenderness before beckoning his companion further into the nothingness. The mechanism turned reluctantly in the door and Fergal felt his way along the cold, moss-covered stonework. He touched the wooden frame of the door, and was just about to call out when a noise like a finger-snap triggered a tiny halogen light bulb.

It illuminated a gold-leafed Russian icon of Mary, Mother of Christ. The surrounding darkness gave the illusion that it was floating in mid-air. Fergal had never seen anything like it in his life. As he moved towards it, to take in its full glittering splendour, Vincent's voice told him that this was only one of many sacred icons brought as gifts from around the planet by visiting monks through the centuries.

'This one,' Brother Vincent said, 'was rescued centuries ago from the front of a tabernacle that had been very badly damaged in a fire. It's believed to be the work of a Brother Augustine. He was a famed womaniser and drunkard well into his adulthood – but then one morning he woke up not knowing where he was and he had a vision. An angel told him that he was wasting his God-given talent. He was so afraid that he gave up his wild ways that very day and entered a monastery. There he concentrated on carving icons that would survive long after him.'

Fergal's eyes had adjusted enough to make out the details of the room. The little wire trails connected to the lamps, the little alcove with a small kneeler to pray on, the dome-shaped ceiling. 'Yes, the ceiling is wonderful,' Brother Vincent said, following his eyes. 'It almost feels like you're in an Arabian tent, doesn't it? Come and feel the curve.'

As Fergal put his hand up to the ceiling, he said, 'It must be amazing to live here.'

Brother Vincent giggled. 'I love your accent – the way you say "amazing".'

Fergal smiled in surprise – no one had ever complimented his speaking voice before. He thought of John, who mimicked him all the time in an exaggerated 'girly' voice. 'Thank you, Brother. Where's your accent from?'

'Well, I'm from a wee town called Cootehill – do you know where that is?'

'No… It's a funny name.' They both giggled and the sound echoed in the darkness.

'It's not far from Monaghan. And it is indeed a privilege to live here at the monastery.'

'How did you end up being a Brother?'

Brother Vincent cocked an eyebrow. 'Do you really want to know?'

'I do, I do – if you don't mind me asking.'

'No, I'd be delighted to tell you – but first things first. I want you to take a seat over there in the middle of the little bench. Do you see it?'

'OK – yeah, I think so.'

Except for the single bulb illuminating the icon, there was no other source of light and Fergal had to squint to see the bench. He walked slowly towards the other end of the dim space and sat down. He was about to say something when, all of a sudden, another switch was thrown. Fergal gasped at the revealed gallery of bejewelled icons, each with its own individual birthmark, depicting the various stages of Jesus' life and those of the saints who had devoted their lives to him.

Brother Vincent came over to him and threw a final switch, above Fergal's stunned head. It illuminated the most ornament-ed and fragile golden icon of all. It was secluded from the rest of the collection – and, more importantly, from curious hands – by a protective grille. Fergal had never seen anything like it. 'Oh my God' was as much as he could manage.

Brother Vincent remained standing, as if he were about to recite a poem. He closed his eyes gathering his concentration, while Fergal and the audience of icons waited in anticipation. Then he spread his arms wide.

'Now, my children, say hello to our new friend, Mr Fergal Flynn from Belfast.'

For a second Fergal half-expected real children to crawl out from the darkest corners of the underground chapel, as if in some fairytale, but he soon realised what the monk meant.

The icons glistened a welcome. 'Fergal, on behalf of my glitter-ing children, welcome to our secret place.'

'Thank you, Brother Vincent. It's… it's like a dream or something. Ah, they're beautiful – I could look at them all day. No wonder you love living in this place so much.'

'I'm lucky to be alive at all, never mind living here.'

'What do you mean, Brother?'

'Now, I don't want to bore you to death – and I don't know how much time we'll have before they're ready for us upstairs – so I'll try and give you the edited highlights. You may have guessed that I love to talk as much as you love to sing.' He clapped his hands and they both laughed.

Brother Vincent looked around the room, making sure he had the full attention of his carved congregation. 'Now my children and our distinguished guest, are we all comfortable? Then I shall begin.'

He cleared his throat. 'Let me start at the beginning. My father was an only child and had inherited the family farm. He was wealthy, a bit of a catch, but he was also a very shy man and by his late forties he was a confirmed bachelor – the locals had written him off as "not the marrying kind". But the loneliness eventually got the better of him. So do you know what he did?'

'No, Brother – what?'

Brother Vincent giggled again and put his chubby hand to his mouth. In the soft light of the underground chapel, Fergal thought he looked about thirteen.

'Well, my boy, he secretly enlisted the services of a matchmaker! Can you imagine? Oh, the scandal of it all.' He inhaled dramatically again and put his hand to his head, his animation made Fergal laugh.

'It must have taken him years to come around to the idea. He was extremely religious and the Church frowned heavily on such

168

activities. But there was a lot of land at stake, and he didn't want to risk meeting just anybody. He was very specific about the kind of wife he had in mind.'

Fergal nodded, fascinated.

'Now, my mother had only just turned thirty. She was a schoolteacher from Dundalk and as smart as a whip, but in those days she was considered an old maid. Her family found her single status so embarrassing that they tried to encourage her to become a nun. She ended up taking a temporary headmistress post in – you'll never guess – Cootehill, and the scene was set. Well, after a bit of fancy footwork by the matchmaker, the hot gossip hit the streets – the old farmer and the young teacher were seen out and about together. As God or luck or Fate would have it, they got on famously. They were both mad about music, he played the fiddle and the accordion and she accompanied on the piano. They were married six months later. My father used to say that the moment he met her he knew she was a gift from God.'

Brother Vincent looked around at the icons. 'Well, my children, can you bear it if I go on? One wink for no, two winks for yes!'

Fergal laughed, then winked twice as Vincent rested his wide-eyed gaze on him for an answer.

'I'll continue, so. They'd all but given up on having children. My mother made trips to Lourdes and even put holy water in the bath – whoa! Can you imagine? But nothing seemed to work. The neighbours said it was because God disapproved of their union. Then, on her forty-third birthday, my mother found she was pregnant. It was regarded as nothing short of a miracle in the town. Suddenly the same neighbours were bringing her old family recipes and baptismal outfits – and I wasn't even born yet!

And a few months later, enter stage left, to rapturous applause, one Vincent McFarland. Hooray!'

Brother Vincent gave himself a round of applause. Fergal joined in, a little embarrassed but still fascinated. He thought Vincent seemed more childlike than ever.

'I was hardly what one would call a delicate child,' Brother Vincent said ruefully. 'God bless my poor wee mammy – sure, I was over ten pounds! Can you imagine it?' He pressed his hands to his own stomach, swollen for an entirely different reason, and a mischievous look came over his face as he groaned in mock labour.

Fergal roared laughing. Before he could stop himself, he said, 'I hope you weren't wearing that big robe when they delivered you! Sure, it must weigh a ton on its own!'

Brother Vincent gasped in pretend horror and for a split second Fergal thought he'd gone too far. There was something contagious about Vincent's humour that made him forget himself and feel at ease. A bell rang in the distance. Vincent bent over, hunching his back, and cried in an exaggerated lisp, 'The bellth, the bellth, Mathta!' He ran at Fergal with outstretched arms, swiping playfully at him. Realising that Vincent was messing with him in the same way that he did with Father Mac, Fergal laughed and pretended to swat him back. He was a bit unsure of himself, but he liked it.

Suddenly Brother Vincent straightened up again, as if his hunch had miraculously been cured by the audience of icons. 'Actually,' he said, grinning and a little out of breath, 'I'm sure I looked more like an overblown balloon with a full head of hair and a face painted on.' He puffed out his cheeks and widened his eyes to demonstrate.

Fergal dissolved into laughter again. Then he distorted his own features, sticking out his tongue at an angle and crossing his eyes. He was delighted when Brother Vincent's familiar giggle rippled around the tiny chapel. 'Now, Fergal, you should be careful – your face might stay like that!'

'Look who's talking, Brother!'

'I was an only child,' Brother Vincent resumed, 'and I was a bit of a loner at school – all of the other kids had loads of brothers and sisters. But I was lucky, you know. My parents had waited so long to have me that, when I came, they didn't want to let me out of their sight. We did everything we could together. I used to climb into their bed every morning. My mother taught me to play and sing and as soon as my legs would carry me I never left my father's side on the farm. You see, Fergal, they looked upon me as a kind of chosen child, sent to them by God to do his holy work someday. We went to mass every morning and I became an altar boy as soon as I was old enough. Just before my lovely daddy died – I was twelve years old – he made me promise that I would stay close to the Holy Father who would guide me now that he was about to leave for heaven, where we would be reunited someday.'

Brother Vincent's eyes filled up, so Fergal stood up and stretched out a hand to his shoulder.

'Oh, look at me, would you? Still a few tears for Daddy, after all these years.'

'And what about your mother?'

'Oh, she's up there with him. She passed away when I was in my twenties. I nursed her till the very last breath was out of her, and I'll tell you, it was one of the greatest privileges of my life. My goodness, that was more years ago than I care to admit… But they're together now and I love them today as I did then. Tell me, are you close to your parents?'

Fergal had known the question would come eventually and he brushed it off, 'Oh, they're like any family, really. Go on.' He wondered how much Father Mac had told Vincent.

'Well, I'd considered the priesthood a number of times, but I wasn't sure. Then I saw an ad in the paper, so I sold the farm and moved to your hometown of Belfast to train as a nurse at the Royal Victoria. I'd loved looking after my mother and I knew it was something I would be good at. Sure, that's how Father Mac-Manus and I met, you know – did he tell you? When I think of it, he was probably the age that you are now. It was at a classical concert in Queen's University – he was as cracked about music as I was... Fergal, you'll tell me if I'm boring you, won't you?'

'Far from it, Brother Vincent. Go on, keep talking.'

'After about a year, I got very restless. One day there was a notice up on the board advertising for nurses to go to London. I signed up one week and the next I was gone.

'Oh, Fergal, I can't tell you how exciting it was to be in London in the early 1970s! Walking down the King's Road, for me, was like walking on the moon, except the clothes were more ridiculous – whoa! The secret after-hours clubs on Frith Street put the wee lock-ins in Cootehill to shame. I kept hearing about free love and there was music everywhere. I saw some amazing people play in the West End when I was supposed to be studying for my nursing exams – Janis Joplin, Eric Clapton... Do you know, I once saw John Lennon get out of a paisley-painted limousine and dive into a shop followed by hundreds of girls? The screaming was deafening.'

Fergal and the icons hung on every word.

'But then, as I was coming up to my final exams – well, I don't have to tell you what happened in Belfast and Derry around that time, do I? Every night there was something awful on the news, and having an Irish accent in England became extremely danger-ous. The moment there was a bomb scare or a soldier killed, any-body Irish was a suspect and a terrorist until proven otherwise. Everyone stopped talking to me, I even got beaten up a few times – I reported it to the police but they did nothing, of course.'

'So what did you do?'

'Well, I kept my head down and finished my exams. I was going to go back home and work as a nurse. But when I was on my way home, I was stopped for questioning at the airport. I'd forgotten my identification, so I was arrested and held for two days. It was the last straw.'

'Brother, that's terrible.'

'I went through a bout of depression – I think it was a delayed reaction to my mother's death really… Afterwards I noticed an advertisement for a religious house in America that needed quali-fied nursing staff. A few months later I was living in Boston.'

Brother Vincent paced up and down, gesturing to illustrate his story as it unfolded further. He told Fergal that over the next year, during which he'd become desperately homesick, he and Father Mac had corresponded and one of Father Mac's letters had mentioned a book called *Let Your Heart Answer the Call*. Vincent had tried to find a copy but it was out of print – there wasn't even a second-hand one to be had anywhere. In the meantime, Vincent had become very close to a Boston minister and his family. They shared a passion for music, especially old hymns, and when the ageing reverend fell ill, Vincent offered to help nurse him. When the old man died, his grieving family gave Vincent an old suitcase full of some of the minister's favourite music and a few other books to remember him by. Vincent untied the string and pulled back the lid only to find a copy of *Let Your Heart Answer the Call* looking back at him from amongst the sheet music and prayer books. He was sure this was a sign from God that he should go home and join a religious order. He had heard about the chanting in Sligo Abbey for years and he had arrived there one overcast day more than ten years previously, and had never left. 'And that, my boy, is more or less how I ended up here.'

'Wow – that's a story and a half, Brother.'

'Truth is always stranger than fiction. Everybody's got a story. What about you?'

'Well – ah… there's not much to tell really, compared to you. I mean, this is the first time I've even been away from my family.'

Brother Vincent looked at him with kind eyes. Behind him the icons shimmered. 'Fergal, I know I've only just met you, but you seem much older than your years. What are you – nineteen?

'No – I'm seventeen now.'

'My goodness, as young as that? That's even more extraordinary. You see, the first thing I noticed about you was the sadness in your voice – a sadness that I can only guess you've been carrying for a very long time. It's in your eyes, too – something that tells me you had to grow up very quickly, so you didn't have much time to be a child. Would I be right?'

It was as if he had looked right into the centre of Fergal's being. Fergal suddenly shivered and his eyes leaked tears before he could catch them.

Brother Vincent put a gentle hand on Fergal's shoulder. 'I'm sorry – I didn't mean to pry… But, Fergal Flynn, whatever has happened on your journey so far has brought you to where you are now. It has contributed to the sound you make when you sing – and I have no doubt that that sound will take you to the far corners of the world and back. It's a God-given talent and you mustn't ever waste it or take it for granted. There is a beauty in your sadness, too.'

A thousand questions took flight in Fergal's head, like birds startled by gunshot.

Brother Vincent looked at him knowingly. 'But don't forget to be a child too sometimes. Make as many mistakes as you need to. Father MacManus is an incredibly kind and loyal person and he cares about you very deeply.'

That made Fergal a little panicky; he wondered how much Brother Vincent knew about them. He also wondered if Father Mac had been telling the truth about him and Brother Vincent being nothing but friends. But, as he looked into the monk's calm face, he could see no trace of anything other than kindness.

'Fergal, I want you to know you can come and visit me and my glittering children any time.'

Some of the recording crew passed by the top of the steps, laughing and Father Mac's voice called, 'Brother Vincent!' The spell was broken. They hurried back up the steps into the bright sunshine – Brother Vincent still talking a mile a minute, praising Fergal's singing and telling him there was no need to be nervous about the recording.

Father Mac called, 'Brother Vincent! How much longer do you think the sound crew will be?'

'I'll go and find out,' the monk shouted. He patted Fergal on the shoulder and hurried away. Fergal quickly wiped his eyes on the sleeve of his jacket, pretending the sun was too bright after the underground chapel.

'What did you think of the icons?' Father Mac asked. He surprised himself when he realised that he was a bit jealous of the fact that Vincent had been alone with Fergal.

Fergal walked slightly ahead of him to hide his face. Finally he said, 'Well, it was a bit spooky at first. The icons looked like a collection of souls or something, just floating there in the dark – like purgatory or something out of a dream… Brother Vincent's a bit weird, too, isn't he?'

'What do you mean?'

'Well, I only met him for the first time last night, and today he was telling me all these private things about himself. One minute he's all serious and the next he's like a wee girl. And he calls the icons his "glittering children". He's funny, though.'

'Look, I'm sorry I left youse. I should've come back sooner, but I got distracted in the woods – there are so many wild flowers in there. Is everything OK?'

It suddenly dawned on Fergal that Brother Vincent had done exactly what Father Mac had wanted. He had kept Fergal's mind off the recording. He had been so distracted by Vincent's stories and the messing and the icons, he hadn't had time to remember to be nervous.

At that moment they heard Brother Vincent calling to all concerned that their presence was required on the altar immediately. Fergal grinned at Father Mac and said, 'Everything's fine. We're here, and I'm dying to sing.'

17

Fergal, Father Mac and the monks took their places around the grand altar. The Brothers were wearing their purple robes, hand-embroidered with golden symbols. Microphones had been discreetly placed on boom stands and on the sides of some of the tree-sized candles so as not to inhibit any of the performances. Thick ropes of cable connected these to the mobile recording unit parked just outside the chapel.

After an initial run-through where levels and positions were adjusted, they were ready to record. The first few familiar chords marked their territory and Fergal gave it everything he had. He thought of Noreen and how much he wanted her to hear him sing. He pictured her sitting in the empty pews wearing her best coat, which was now too big for her shrinking frame and had to stay hanging on the back of her bedroom door. Even Father Mac turned around on his bench to acknowledge the startling combination of sureness and melancholy in Fergal's voice, supported by wave after glorious wave of harmony from the Brothers.

They recorded two versions of the first piece and three of the second, which was much harder to pace. They couldn't decide whether it should be fast or slow, so they recorded it at different paces to choose from at a later date. Then there was a short break. Brother Vincent made a point of being especially friendly to Fergal, as if they were meeting for the very first time. Fergal found it incredible that he could seem like a little child one minute and then in the next breath conduct and direct an important recording session. Then he remembered his own mother's vast collection of personalities that she'd obviously been accumulating since childhood.

The recording was off to a good start, although there was still a lot of work to be done. The next few pieces were simpler chants that did not include Fergal or Father Mac, so they sat mutely at the back of the chapel in complete darkness and let the music wash over them. Their eyes were closed as they inhaled the chant, but Fergal opened his when he felt Father Mac's kind hand take hold of his and attempt to rub some warmth back into his cold fingers. His touch excavated such a deep well of feeling that he couldn't stop his eyes from filling with unexpected tears. They sat there, hand in hand, staring at the altar, unable to speak for reasons beyond the restrictions of recording.

Brother Vincent searched the unlit back of the chapel with his hand up shielding his eyes from the light and signalled to Father Mac and Fergal to come back to the altar.

The next few songs went so smoothly that, while the master

tapes were being changed, they were treated to a playback of the first two songs, which Fergal had almost forgotten he'd sung. He listened to the sound of his recorded voice for the first time, and he couldn't look at anybody properly while it flowed from the speakers and hovered in the room.

Brother Vincent exhaled with satisfaction and moved everyone back to the altar to resume recording. Even though Fergal didn't understand any of the ancient words, the chants were mesmerising in their ability to conjure up images – one made him feel like he was trapped in the eye of a tornado, the next as though he was floating in space.

When the recording was finished and Brother Vincent had had a listen, everyone helped to pack up the recording equipment. The lorry pulled out of the gates and, as soon as it was out of sight, there was no trace of the twentieth century left. 'How do you feel now you've made your first recording for the Pope?' Father Mac asked and they had to stifle their laughter in case the Brothers were offended.

~

Dinner was in the main hall and was accompanied by glass jugs full to the brim with the beer that the Brothers lovingly brewed and kept in the cellars for special occasions. Proceedings livened up considerably with each refill, and a few strange-looking monks approached Fergal to say that they had people in Belfast and they thought it was a friendly enough place. Fergal, who was unused to the sly potency of alcohol, just giggled that he wouldn't mind swapping his house for theirs. After the meal, a huge honey cake was pushed in on a trolley to celebrate the end of a very hard day. Brother Vincent asked the monks to show their appreciation and raise a glass of darkness to Fergal Flynn's beautiful contribution, and they presented him with a miniature icon of St Christopher, the patron saint of all travellers. Fergal didn't know where to look, but Father Mac nudged him in the ribs and he managed a few respectful but mortified words of thanks before slumping back into his seat, somewhat light-headed.

As they cleared away the dishes, Father Mac said, 'You coped with the whole recording process wonderfully, even though it was all new to you. You must be tired after all that concentration and hard work.'

'Actually,' Fergal said, 'I thought I would be knackered after such an early start this morning, but I'm not. I feel much better after the food.' The beer had relaxed him and given the evening a bit of extra energy. 'Father, how near are we to the coast?'

'It's strange you should ask me that. We're not too far from a beautiful stretch of sandy coastline called Strandhill. I was there as a child one summer and all day I've been wishing I could go back for a look.'

'Can I come too?'

'Of course, but I'm not sure we'll have time tomorrow – we'll need to get back home.'

'I don't mean tomorrow. Why don't we go now? I'm not tired at all, are you?'

'No, I'm not, no – but… Well, I suppose if we were quick we could get there before it's too dark to enjoy it, if you like.'

Fergal didn't have to be asked twice.

The Brothers filed past them and bowed good night. Brother Vincent lingered for a moment, massaging his palm with the thumb of his other hand as he watched Father Mac and Fergal closely. His intake of beer had increased his giddiness and he wondered just how close his friend and Fergal were. Then a yawn overtook him. He went bright red as it ended in a burp, and said, 'I think I'll retire to bed, if you don't need me.'

'Thanks, Brother Vincent,' Father Mac said, 'but we're fine. We're just going to go for a quick walk before bed.'

The car was waiting to take them to the nearby coastline. As they drove, Father Mac commented on how different the landscape looked now that there were so many new houses and how he hoped he would recognise the turn to the beach. Luckily, one road sign had survived the changes and they turned on a steep bend and found themselves at the entrance to the beach's empty car park. They stepped out of the car just as the evening announced its arrival in broad technicolor.

Fergal noticed that Father Mac wasn't wearing his collar. He had on a blue sweatshirt and was carrying his coat under his arm, which made Fergal suddenly remember that he'd left his brother's blue velvet jacket on the back seat of the car, but he left it there.

The tide was going out and the strand was deserted. They walked where the sea should have been, listening to the waves lulling the sand to sleep in the privacy of the distant horizon.

'Will we climb one of the sand dunes and have a look at the view?' Father Mac suggested. Fergal's shoes sank into the powdery sand as they scaled the side of the dune, and Father Mac grabbed his wrist and pulled him to the top, both of them laughing and out of breath. Father Mac spread out his coat as neatly as he could and they sat on it together looking out at the sea. The only other time Fergal had been to the coast was on a compulsory school trip to Helen's Bay, when Big Sean Boyle, the coalman's son, had ducked him under the water – he shivered, his skin remembering. Now, though, he thought it would be nice to at least paddle in the ever-distant dark water.

'Father, do you want to go for a—'

'You don't need to keep calling me "Father", you know, Fergal. Call me by my first name.'

'Oh OK – sorry… but I don't think I know what it is. I know your initial is D – I saw a letter in the hall at St Bridget's, addressed to "Father D. MacManus", and I always wondered, Declan? David? Dominic? D'Artagnan?'

'What?' he laughed. 'My goodness, Fergal… It's Dermot, Dermot MacManus. I was named after my mother's father.'

'So was I, Fa— I mean, Dermot!'

'I can't believe I haven't told you before. Sorry, fella.'

Fergal felt closer to Father Mac than he ever had before. He loved being allowed to call him by his first name, it made him feel more like an equal.

The breeze coming in off the water was getting bolder and they leaned against each other instinctively. Two dogs ran like shadows in the shallow water far away, barking, shaking and chasing each other, but their owners, if they had any, were nowhere to be seen.

'Imagine being that free Dermot – nobody to tell you what to do, no soldiers stopping you all the time… Wouldn't it be great?'

Father Mac looked very serious for a second. Then he jumped up, grabbed Fergal by the arm and grinned wildly. 'Come on, then, Mr Flynn! What are we waiting for?'

They charged down the sand dune towards the silver-green water. The tide was much further out than it had looked from the top of the dune, so they were out of breath again when they eventually caught up with it. They took their shoes and socks off, and Fergal copied Father Mac as he tied his shoes together by their laces, pushed the socks into them and hung them around his neck like bunches of onions. Then they rolled up their trouser legs as far as they would go and held their breath as they waded into the freezing water. The waves, curious about their after-hours visitors, came sneaking up to meet them, pretending to be little but then soaking them both waist high before they could jump back. They protested out loud and decided to turn back. The sand clung to their wet clothes as they slowly braved the sand dune again and fell onto the top, laughing about who was the wettest.

Fergal looked straight into Father Mac's eyes. 'Fa— sorry, Dermot… this is the best thing that has ever happened to me.'

'We worked hard to get here, Fergal. But there's only so much I can do. You're the one with the voice – and already you've come on so much. You don't seem to be afraid to work hard.'

'Afraid? But I love it!'

'Ah, you've really earned this little trip, fella. You've been through so much. And… well… I'd do anything for you. You must know that.'

Fergal leaned against Father Mac again, at once weakened and strengthened by his words. Not far above their heads, a bird that looked like an albino raven mourned in slow circles and cried like a car alarm. It was only an ancient, nosy seagull patrolling, too old to sleep and always on the prowl for food.

Fergal was feeling brave. He turned his face to the side of Father Mac's neck and felt him tremble.

'Are you warm enough there, Fergal?'

'I could be warmer.'

'I know – me too. I wish we had a blanket or—'

'Will you put your arms around me, Dermot? Just for a while, till we get warm? Sure there's nobody around.'

They exhaled together, in relief more than anything else, and huddled closer. Fergal inhaled the cigarette smell from Father Mac's close breath as his forehead nested under the priest's chin.

The Sligo sky was quiet now, the last star finding its seat as the cinema torch of the moon shone imperiously. Father Mac stretched his wet legs, one and then the other. 'Should we go back?'

Fergal rolled over on the coat. 'Ah, no. Let's stay. Sure, it can't be that late.'

They lay on their backs side by side looking at the evening sky. 'What are you thinking about?' Father Mac asked.

'Well, I'm thinking about you.'

'Are you familiar with the constellations?' Father Mac asked, a bit too quickly.

'Not really. That programme *The Sky at Night* could never compete with the late-night football in our house.'

So, one by one, Father Mac picked out the Plough and the Bear and the other groups of stars and gradually Fergal was able to see what he was talking about. 'It's so clear tonight… There – look, right there. That's the North Star.'

Fergal's trousers were still sticking to him and he pulled at the wrinkled material clinging to his legs. 'We might as well have gone for a swim!'

They laughed, but the wind was picking up a little. 'We'll have to be careful or we'll catch cold,' Father Mac said, twisting the bottoms of his own trousers to get as much of the sea out of them as he could. Fergal did the same, and it was surprising how much water came out.

'It's no good,' Father Mac said. 'We'll have to take them off and wring them out or my car seats will be drenched on the way back otherwise.'

'Hey, we could lay them flat on the grass to dry,' Fergal suggested. The sky was well into its slow rejection of light, but they didn't want the evening to end. In their heart of hearts, neither of them wanted to be anywhere else.

As they spread their trousers on the grass, the full moon showed them a little hollow in the side of one of the dunes.

'Dermot, do you think it might be warmer in there? Come on – we'll have a look, eh?' Fergal didn't wait for a reply.

Father Mac gathered up their things and looked around at the empty beach, then followed him. The wind suddenly stopped as they sat facing each other in the shelter of the hollow.

Fergal's whole body suddenly shook violently for a second. 'Someone must have walked over my grave – isn't that what they say?'

'Ah, now, don't say such things.'

They could just see the moon from where they sat. Fergal was still shivering and he rubbed his arms to get warm. The sea sounded like someone shushing a child to sleep. Father Mac closed his eyes for a moment.

'Dermot, will you rub my shoulders?'

'Are you sure?'

'Yeah.'

He began to rub Fergal's cold shoulder blades with his big hands, and Fergal rested his hand on Father Mac's stomach.

'Fergal, you're freezing.'

'I know. Will you… come closer?'

Father Mac shifted in the sand until they were right beside

each other. Fergal had never felt anything like it in his life. It was like someone had plugged him into a mains socket. Father Mac's touch was so loving and strong. Gradually it got deeper, becoming more of a massage, making Fergal call softly in appreciation. Father Mac stroked his hair and began to massage his neck and shoulders. For some reason Fergal thought of his Granny Noreen for a brief second. He raised his head. Father Mac was lost in concentration, but he sensed a change in the atmosphere and opened his eyes – just in time to receive a tender, nervous kiss on the cheek.

It was as if the world stopped turning for a few seconds.

Father Mac stopped rubbing Fergal's shoulders and his fingers went to the spot where his lips had landed. A smile, a mixture of surprise and pleasure, rippled the surface of his face. Finally he said, 'Thank you, Fergal… thank you.' Then he took a deep breath and returned the kiss on Fergal's closed eyelids.

There was just enough room for them in the hollow as their lips found the courage they'd been lacking and each other. Fergal thought his heart would burst. He could feel the beginnings of Father Mac's beard and smell his skin. His hand gently began to make circular movements against Father Mac's belly. Father Mac took this as a sign to remove his sweatshirt, and Fergal followed his lead. The feeling of having Father Mac's bare chest pressed against his was beyond all Fergal's imaginings. They continued to kiss, carefully at first and then eagerly, their tongues darting playfully in and out of each other's mouth.

Suddenly Father Mac stopped and tried to pull away. 'Oh, Fergal, what am I doing? I'm sorry – I just…'

'Please don't be sorry. I'm not.'

Father Mac looked at him incredulously. 'Are you sure?'

'Look, Dermot – I've wanted to kiss you from the minute I saw you.' Fergal's heart knocked deafeningly on his rib cage.

'I hope you don't think—'

Fergal cut him off by kissing him even more passionately, surprising himself, tasting the mixture of sweet beer and tobacco on his nervous breath. He began to take off their final pieces of clothing and they lay side by side in the coolness of the grassy hollow on the driest parts of their clothes. Their arousals pressed against each other, making their kisses deeper and their breathing louder. Fergal had never experienced passion like it and he began to feel tears burn his eyes.

Father Mac felt them and panicked. 'Oh, Fergal, I'm sorry. This is too much for you… forgive me—'

Fergal wiped the fastest tear away. 'I'm crying because I'm so, so happy. Please, Dermot, whatever you do, don't let me go.'

'Are you su—'

Fergal clamped his lips to Father Mac's again before he got a chance to protest, and their hands moved lower. Fergal played with the thick hair on Father Mac's chest and brushed his nipples with the tip of his fingers, hearing him moan quietly. He moved his lips to Father Mac's neck and kissed his way gently towards his nipple. Father Mac massaged the back of his head, gently guiding it south.

Fergal was slightly nervous of going near his hardness, but he couldn't stop himself. He kept moving downwards, until he felt its length brush against his cheek. They both gasped a little, but Fergal was in too deep to stop now. He kissed and explored and finally opened his lips and took the smooth head into his mouth. It tasted like nothing he had ever known.

Father Mac lost his breath and then groaned deeply. Fergal

began sucking more confidently, enjoying the new sensation. The rhythm picked up as they grew braver with each other, until Father Mac pulled Fergal up by the shoulders full of the confidence that only intimacy can bring, and kissed him full on the mouth. Then he began to explore Fergal's body. He kissed his face and playfully bit his chapped lips, before dropping down to smell his chest with deep, slow inhalations. He kissed the damp hair under his arms and then turned him around. He ran his tongue down Fergal's spine, stopping to kiss the cheeks of his backside.

Fergal had never been touched in such a loving way, and he was speechless. He could only gasp, 'Yes – yes…' Father Mac turned him around again with his hands on his waist, he wet his fingers to brush a bit of sand from Fergal's erection, then locked eyes with his new lover as he took its length down into the depths of his throat.

Fergal groaned out loud, thinking he would burst that very second. He pulled Father Mac back up, explaining shyly, 'I'm – getting near…' They kissed more wildly than ever and Fergal pulled Father Mac on top of him in a sudden fit of excitement. He spread his legs, aching to receive the full weight of this man on top of him. Father Mac moved slowly against his body and Fergal held him tight, locking his legs around his arching back. His arms clamped Father Mac's shoulders, gripping him till they were both past the point of no return. Instinctively they searched for each other's hardness, and together they held their final breath eyes wide open to watch their own private waves erupting and crashing against each other's shore.

They stayed in the same spent position till they got their breath back. Father Mac kissed Fergal lovingly on the lips and then on the forehead, murmuring, 'You're so lovely – what a treasure you are… I'm so glad you're here.' Fergal could only groan through a cloud of exhausted ecstasy. They drifted in and out of a drug-like sleep.

When their shyness returned, they checked the dark beach for unwanted company and found none – their union's only witness was the Atlantic Ocean. They took it in turns to go to the edge of the returning tide and wash the evidence away.

Fergal's trousers were still very damp, as were Father Mac's, but they neither noticed nor cared as they got dressed and headed back to the car. The short journey back was warm, silent bliss. They had no conversation left; their bodies had done all the talking.

18

Fergal didn't even remember falling asleep. He woke up early again amid the remnants of a distant but powerful dream. He'd been walking around Ormeau Park in Belfast admiring the flowers when he came to a playground full of empty swings. In the corner there was a man sitting alone. When Fergal got nearer he realised that it was Jesus Christ in a wheelchair. He went closer, but as soon as Jesus saw him he put his arm out and said, 'Come no further! I don't forgive you, for you do know what you do!'

Fergal was confused for a second. He looked at the wall that separated him from Father Mac and retraced their lovemaking. His eyes rested on the tiny crucifix with the almost-naked saviour hanging there for all the so-called sinners of the world, but he was too happy and tired to let guilt get the better of him. A wide yawn stretched his face, and he pulled the blankets back over his head.

The next thing he heard was the neighbouring sound of Father Mac shaking out his razor in the water-filled sink. Fergal felt his own chin, it was as rough as a cat's tongue. He jumped out of bed, pulled on his trousers from the radiator where they'd been hanging to dry, and shouted through the wall, 'Father, can I borrow one of your razors?'

'I'll bring you one in when I'm finished,' Father Mac shouted back.

'But, Father, I'm not great at using them yet – I was hoping you might… well…'

'What's that? What are you saying?'

Fergal left his room and knocked on Father Mac's door.

'Come on in, if you're coming.'

Father Mac was standing at the sink in his socks with his shirt untucked, straining to see himself in the tiny mirror.

'Morning, Father.'

'Morning, Fergal.' Father Mac closed a few buttons.

They broke the silence in unison, 'Did you sleep all right?'

They both laughed, and Fergal answered, 'Ah, not bad.'

'You look taller today.'

'Well, I have my shoes on and you don't. Maybe you're shrinking?'

'Maybe I am. Look – we're the same height now or thereabouts. You're going to be taller than me soon.'

'I had a funny dream.'

Father Mac closed the door. 'What about?'

When Fergal finished telling him, Father Mac looked a little worried. Fergal thought he seemed almost angry. 'Look, Mr

Flynn, you mustn't worry your head about dreams too much. Sometimes they don't make any sense at all.' He finished shaving the hard-to-reach terrain under his nose in an uncomfortable silence.

Fergal mentally retraced the steps of his desire along Father Mac's chest. When the sink was free, he lathered up and brushed the soap into his patchy beard. Father Mac, patting his own face dry, saw Fergal struggling with his disposable razor. He opened a new one and said, 'Here, look – let me show you.'

In his hand the razor dragged a smooth path along the contours of Fergal's trusting face, like a snowplough removing winter from the roads. Fergal had never imagined shaving could be so sensual. He kept his eyes closed until Father Mac was almost finished, then he reached up, pushing the razor to one side, and tried to reward him with a kiss.

Father Mac pulled away. 'Don't, Fergal, please.'

'What? Dermot, what's the matter?'

He put his head in his hands and lowered his voice. 'Oh, Fergal... What's the matter? The matter is that I'm a priest, for a start – and you're ten years younger than me. I'm so sorry about last night. I lied when I said I slept OK, I couldn't sleep a wink and I must've smoked a hundred cigarettes. Oh, Fergal, I'm so sorry.'

'But what for? I don't understand.'

'I didn't plan on what happened last night. I know I should have said no, but I couldn't... All I want is for you to be happy. I don't want to hurt you or reject you, but... but this can't happen again.'

Fergal's eyes filled up, and that made Father Mac's join them in sympathy. Suddenly they heard the complaining wooden floors announce Brother Vincent's arrival. Father Mac quickly wiped his eyes on the sleeve of his black shirt, tucked the tails into his trousers and motioned for Fergal to continue shaving by himself, whereupon Fergal cut a lump out of his nostril and bled like a pig.

Brother Vincent went into Fergal's room first, just as Fergal called, 'I'm in here, Brother, borrowing a razor.'

Father Mac shouted, 'Come and join us!'

Brother Vincent informed them that the morning chant was about to begin and that the previous day's tapes were good enough to be sent off for a final mix. Father Mac – who was standing at the window, fully dressed and pretending to read a book – looked up to say, 'We'd love to join in the chant. We'll meet you down there in a second.' Brother Vincent left humming the theme tune to *Mission Impossible* and wondering why Father Mac seemed so distant.

When the burly monk was gone, Father Mac put his book down and straightened his jacket. 'Look, we'd better get downstairs or they'll be wondering where we are. We can't talk about this now. Dry your eyes on the towel there, and put a bloody shirt on.'

Fergal nodded his head, and they gathered themselves up and headed towards the church, looking like any other priest and his soloist going for the first sing of the morning.

The monks sang as beautifully and as movingly as ever. Fergal was sorry to be leaving, but he knew there was a price to be paid for everything. Breakfast was slow. Fergal didn't have much of an appetite but Father Mac reminded him of their journey, so he managed some porridge before they went to pack their things.

Brother Vincent came up to Fergal's room to give him some headed notepaper with his details on it. 'Fergal, I'm so glad that we met and I would like it if we kept in touch. I'm sorry you weren't able to stay longer.'

Fergal didn't know where to look.

'Never forget you have a God-given talent that you must protect at all costs, my boy.'

It was all Fergal could do not to shout, 'I'm not your fucking boy!' but he knew it wasn't Brother Vincent's fault that Father Mac had done a complete U-turn.

Brother Vincent lowered his voice. 'I want you to know I have the feeling that great things are ahead for you.'

Then he handed Fergal some carefully wrapped portions of the previous night's rich honey cake, to bring home to his family. 'You'll be doing me a big favour, my glands are playing up more every year.' He patted his considerable bulk regretfully. 'A moment on the lips, a lifetime on the hips!'

The monks lined the steps, waving, as Father Mac's car dug into the gravel and propelled him and Fergal away from a weekend they would never forget.

~

The weather wasn't great and they got stuck behind a load of sheep being herded from field to field. Every once in a while Father Mac would ask Fergal if he was OK. All Fergal could do was shake his head up and down. Once they were safely past the farms and over the border, Father Mac was able to cruise in fifth gear on the motorway. They listened to the radio and talked about anything but the beach. But as the number of miles to Belfast shrank before their eyes, so did their ability to avoid the inevitable. Father Mac turned off the radio.

He glanced at the hopeful green eyes and said firmly, 'Fergal, I shouldn't have let last night happen. There's danger every-where. The last thing I want is for anyone, especially you, to get hurt. Do you understand what I mean?'

'But it's not like you… you know… forced yourself on me.'

'That's not the point. I could never, ever do that to you, because I care about you far too much – and that's exactly why we can't… you know… repeat last night.' Father Mac had begun to sweat badly.

Fergal had gone very pale. 'No – I don't believe you… Dermot, last night meant everything to me. Please don't take it away.'

'Ah, Jesus, do you not think I feel the same? But we just can't… Oh, God, what have I done?' Father Mac stared out the window, unable to look at Fergal's sad face. He thought of how long he'd spent ironing the worry out of it with touch after tender touch.

'Why can't we?' Fergal demanded.

'Fergal, I'm a priest—'

'I know! Why do you keep saying that? Don't you think I know?'

'—and you're only sixteen.'

There was a pause. 'I'm not sixteen any more. I was seventeen yesterday.'

'What? Oh, my God… Why on earth didn't you tell me?'

'I meant to. I was going to tell you on the beach, but then…'

Father Mac couldn't look at Fergal for a very long minute.

'Well, look – happy birthday. Seventeen, eh? I can't believe you didn't tell me.'

'Yeah, well, birthdays aren't really a big deal in our house. Da made a fuss when the twins turned eighteen but that's about it.'

'Do you think they'll have presents for you when we get back?'

Fergal looked at Father Mac as if he was mad. 'Well, if I was a betting man I'd say no, but... never say never, I suppose.'

'But your mother must have realised before you went that it was your birthday...?'

Another silence fell like a fog. After a few miles Fergal said, 'Dermot, it'll be legal in a couple of years.'

Father Mac blinked in semi-shock. 'Look, Fergal, what we did was... well, it was illegal as you've pointed out.'

'Sure, loads of things are illegal. I buy drink for Noreen every week and no one says a word.'

'That's not the same thing!' Father Mac shouted. He exhaled in frustration and lowered his voice. 'Promise me you'll never tell anyone what happened, will you?'

'Dermot, who would I tell?' Fergal's wet eyes gave him away again.

'Fergal, the last thing I wanted to do was upset you like this. You know I didn't plan it. I hate that I've made you cry. You've done enough of that already.'

They met a sharp corner too fast and Fergal rolled sideways against him as Father Mac turned the steering wheel hard. He suddenly stole a kiss from Father Mac's lips, then straightened up and looked out the window as if nothing had happened.

'Fergal!' Father Mac cleared his throat uncomfortably and steadied the car.

'What? It's a belated birthday kiss.'

~

Father Mac turned up the radio, and Fergal eventually dozed on the front seat, his mind crowded with visions of all the awful things that could have happened to Noreen. Finally they pulled off the motorway and drove along the Grosvenor Road, past Dunville Park. Someone had actually gone to the trouble of stealing a car, ramming the park railings and crashing it into the fountain before torching it. Father Mac wondered where the local kids were going to play now – that had been one of their last little havens.

'Fergal, do you want to go to your granny's or to Walker Street?'

He had to ask twice before Fergal finally woke up. 'I want to see Noreen more than anyone out of that line-up.'

They pulled up outside her house and Fergal was about to say goodbye when Father Mac got out of the car. Fergal had known the day would come when he and Noreen would meet, so he took a deep breath and put his key in the door. Father Mac smiled at her neighbours and ducked through the low door frame.

The fire was out and the room was freezing. Noreen barked a 'Who's that?' when she heard them come in. Fergal ran upstairs to see her and Father Mac followed, crashing into a load of damp sheets and huge knickers hanging on a pulley suspended not far enough above the landing.

Noreen was sitting up in bed with a little girl's slide in her old lady's hair, clutching her portable chemist to her chest ready for battle with whoever it was. She was glad to see Fergal and even more delighted to see the handsome priest who followed him in.

She wasted no time. 'Fergal, son, have you been away that long that you've got taller?'

'Ah, Granny, I have not.'

'See, I told you, Fergal! That's what I said too, Noreen – is it all right if I call you Noreen?'

'Jesus, love, you can call me anything you like.' She turned her attention back to her grandson. 'Will you go and get a wee message for your oul' granny while the lovely young Father here gives me confession in case I don't last the night? Sure, then my soul will be nice and clean for Our Lord. Isn't that right, Father?' She coughed roughly and pulled a crumpled tenner from the sleeve of her cardigan, upsetting about a month's supply of revolting snuff-stained hankies.

Fergal looked at Father Mac, who nodded agreement. 'I'll be back as soon as I can.' He pulled over the commode – which, with its brown plastic cover on, doubled as a chair – so Father Mac could sit nearer Noreen's bed. He prayed it had been emptied.

While Fergal darted through the Sunday streets towards the back of Maguire's pub, which sold anything at any time including large bottles of gin, Father Mac began hearing Noreen's confession. He found it hard not to be distracted by the state of the tiny room that Fergal had obviously been sharing, and that made him feel even worse.

Noreen grabbed his hand. 'Father, I'm nearly at the end of my time, but our Fergal is only at the start of his. I want you to promise me one thing, will you?'

'I will if I can, Noreen. What is it?'

'Our Fergal's not like the rest of them, Father. They're all as hard as nails and as thick as planks. Promise me you'll look out for him, will you? Don't let him waste his wee life. Sure, you go to bed young and happy one day and wake up old and sick the next. You regret not being braver about the things that mattered and more careless about the things that didn't. Do you understand me, Father? Will you do that for me? Will you?'

She began to sob and looked for a clean bit on one of her hideous tissues. Father Mac gave her a new packet from his pocket, swallowed hard and promised that of course he would look out for Fergal. He told her how well her grandson had sung in Sligo, that she would be able to hear the record for herself, that even the Vatican might have a copy of it. This calmed her a bit.

'Noreen, did you know Fergal was seventeen yesterday?'

'Jesus, Mary and Joseph, he was not, was he? That means my Fergal is dead nearly eighteen years...' Her eyes flooded as she talked about her dead husband and how he'd loved singing too, at mass every Sunday, when he was a young fella. Father Mac wanted to ask her more about it, but she dried her eyes and lay back, suddenly distracted by the seclusion of some private film that was starting up in the cinema of her head.

While her eyes were closed, Father Mac took a good look at the neglected room. Fergal's little bed, which must have been far too small for him, stood in the other corner. His uniform was on a hanger hooked onto a nail in the wall, with his schoolbag and books under it. Father Mac suddenly understood why Fergal had never accepted a lift home before. Noreen began to snore lightly. He decided to make his way silently downstairs, to wait for Fergal to return.

~

The Flynn brothers were coming back from a hurling match, which they had lost badly to their rival school, when they spotted Fergal nervously weaving in and out of the church-goers with something hidden up his jumper.

'I bet that's my velvet jacket!' hissed John. 'Let's get the fucker!'

Paddy Jr and Ciaran, however, were starving and wanted to get home and eat themselves into a coma. They split up when they reached their turning and John broke into a sprint towards the school pitches that he knew Fergal would cross as a shortcut to Noreen's.

All weekend, while his hated brother was gone, John had been the rear end of jokes about what Fergal was getting up to in his prized jacket. That, mixed with the crushing defeat of that morning's match, was too much. He leapt on his unsuspecting brother from behind with such uncontrollable violence that Fergal hardly knew what had hit him.

'Where's my fucking good coat, queer boy? Where the fuck is it? Up your jumper? What the fuck have you done to it?'

Fergal didn't have a chance to answer. John winded him with a boot to the stomach and then grabbed him by the hair, dragged him to the ground and kicked him again and again, ignoring any protests.

'You're a queer cunt – a dirty queer fucking freak – what are you? Say it! You're a fucking twisted queer cunt!'

He ran out of breath and stopped for a second, panting like a wild animal. Fergal tried to crawl away from him, big drops of blood falling from his mouth.

~

Noreen woke up and started confessing to the empty room, 'Bless me, Father, for I have sinned… I was cruel to my children. I drove every one of them away. My nerves were at me and I couldn't stop them from crying, so I gave them something to cry about.'

She broke down and screamed into her sleeve. Father Mac heard her from downstairs and went to console her.

~

For a split second Fergal wondered if what had happened between him and Father Mac was written in the sky. He tried to tell John that it was Noreen's gin that he was hiding up his jumper but suddenly he felt his brother's full weight on his back – he had got his breath back and jumped on top of Fergal like the wrestlers did on the TV. Fergal's rib cage scraped against the concrete. The blows to his head felt like explosions. He was crying loudly now, but that only made it worse. John pulled his head up by the hair and punched him in the throat. 'Let's hear you sing now, queer boy! You won't even know your own fucking name when I've finished with you. Why did you bother coming back at all from your poofy holy-joe weekend?'

He dragged Fergal along the ground by the hair and planted a fist right in his mouth. His lip split against his teeth. There was blood everywhere. Fergal wondered, ridiculously, whether Noreen's gin bottle had survived. John was holding his fist in his opposite armpit shouting, 'Look what you made me do, you buck-toothed fairy! How am I going to play handball later, you fucking girl?'

He grabbed Fergal again but a woman with a dog screamed at him to stop. He shouted, 'Mind your own fucking business or you'll get the same!', but her dog wasn't easily threatened, it snapped at John as he aimed kicks at its mouth. The woman began yelling for help.

John turned back to Fergal and kicked him one more time, as hard as his hurling shoes would allow. 'Get up, you queer fucking cunt, before I really do you some damage. And if you think I'm ever going to wear that jacket after it's been near your queer body then you're dead fucking wrong. Oh, and another thing – if you tell anybody about this, I won't go as easy on you next time!' He cleared his throat and nose and spat the contents in Fergal's face. Then he headed back towards Walker Street with his chest puffed out and his reputation restored, in his own mind anyway.

Fergal spat out more blood. His jaw felt like it was on fire. The woman approached him carefully. Her dog wouldn't stop barking. 'Shut the fuck up, Columbo, will you? Let me try and see if this fella's all right. Columbo, *fuck up*!' She leaned over Fergal. 'Are you all right, love?'

His ears were ringing, but he dimly heard her say something about how she didn't want to worry him, but his head was badly swollen and he should get to a hospital in case he had brain damage. 'Although the other fella must've been brain-damaged to do that to you in the first place. Would you be able to recognise that animal, love? My eyesight isn't what it was.'

'Yeah, I hope so,' Fergal said weakly. 'He's my brother.'

The woman took a sharp intake of breath. 'He should be locked up and brought before God. It's beyond me how anyone could even do that to a stranger, let alone their own flesh and blood. I'm sorry for you, love.' Fergal spat out a clotted lump of blood and Columbo promptly swallowed it with a swipe of his big tongue. 'Oh, Jesus, Columbo, you're boggin', so you are! I'm sorry, son, that dog's a dirty bastard. Sure, he'd eat anything – birds' turds and all.'

She helped Fergal to his feet and offered to take him to the hospital but he told her he wasn't far from where he was going.

and that there would be someone there to help him. Miraculously, the gin bottle was a lot sturdier than it looked and had only suffered a few scrapes to the cheap label. As Fergal began to walk, his entire body protested and he yelped in agony. He stumbled on through the shortcut, ignoring the scared reactions of the kids playing in the road until he fell through the door of Noreen's house and onto the floor.

Father Mac was just coming down the stairs after calming Noreen back to sleep. He was convinced that Fergal had been shot, there was so much blood on his face.

'Oh my God, Fergal – what – how... Oh, Jesus help us—'

Fergal began to shake violently with tears and shock. Father Mac put an arm around him as gently as he could. 'Were you hit by a car or something?'

Fergal finally caught enough breath. 'It– it– it was our John. It was our fucking John, out of nowhere... I was running to get back with Granny's gin and he came out of nowhere, shouting about his oul' velvet jacket that Ma made me take – sure, I never wore it, even... Oh, God, my head...'

'OK – OK, Fergal... Look, stay there for a second and don't try and talk any more.'

Father Mac leaned him gently against a chair, went into the tiny kitchen and found a facecloth, but when he smelled it to check if it was clean, he nearly keeled over. He found toilet paper instead. He dipped wads of it into a bowl of water and began the slow process of cleaning the drying blood from Fergal's eyes and broken mouth. 'Oh, Fergal, what has he done to you... Look, I'm taking you to the hospital. Don't move for a second.'

Father Mac ran up to check on Noreen, taking the gin with him. She was out for the count, with some pharmaceutical help, so he left the bottle by her bed. Then he bundled Fergal into the car and headed for the hospital. Fergal was too weak to argue.

Because Fergal was being carried by a man of the cloth, they were rushed through the Casualty department reception and straight to a cubicle. A doctor examined him and his head was X-rayed to see how bad the damage was. Father Mac stayed with him the whole time.

An English nurse bandaged his bruised ribs and asked him what had happened. Fergal told her everything except the identity of the attacker.

'Do you remember what kind of shoes the man was wearing?'

Fergal mumbled painfully, 'His guddies – hurling ones, I think.'

'Guddies? Oh, you mean trainers. Sorry, you probably don't want to talk with your jaw being in such a bad way. Do you want to report the incident to the police?'

It hadn't even occurred to Fergal that he could. 'I'm not sure,' he mumbled.

'It's up to you,' she said, 'but bear in mind that, if he'd been wearing harder shoes, you probably wouldn't have survived – not without serious brain damage anyway.' Fergal retched up the last of the contents of his stomach.

The X-ray results confirmed that he had no serious head injuries and they gave him something for the swelling. They clipped the hair away from the cuts on his head, cleaned them and decided they didn't need stitches – the inside of his bottom lip needed two though. The doctors wanted to keep him in for observation but there were no available beds, all they could offer was a trolley in one of the corridors. Once Father Mac told them that he was trained in first aid and that Fergal would be staying with him, they gave him a prescription for painkillers and agreed to let him out.

As they arrived at St Bridget's, Fergal mumbled through a mouthful of gauze, 'I'm sorry for getting you involved in all this.' One of his ribs had a crack, and his jawbone was chipped, even breathing was almost unbearable.

'Don't be ridiculous,' Father Mac told him. He helped Fergal in the side door and up to his own room, where he knew the double bed would be waiting with freshly laundered sheets. Then he told Mrs Mooney to lock the door behind him and keep it locked until he returned, and went in search of a chemist who was open on Sunday.

As he was driving back, he suddenly noticed John's deep-blue velvet jacket, lying unworn on the back seat. Father Mac almost had a crash as he spun the car around and headed towards Walker Street.

19

Sunday was never any different in the Flynn house. The main concern was how many potatoes the twins could fit into their mouths at once. Paddy Jr was eating his whole with an avalanche of salt, John was mashing butter vindictively into his with a fork, while Ciaran was breaking his in half with his hands and stuffing them in noisily. The TV was blaring an argument about the match and Angela was busy draining the last of the spuds over the sink.

Father Mac knuckled the front door angrily, holding the velvet coat in a death grip. Through an open window he could hear the sports commentator telling most of the nation that Kerry had the ball, to the sound of synchronised groaning from the sofa. Father Mac moved over to the window just as Angela came out of the kitchen holding the steaming pot of potatoes. She stopped in her tracks.

'Jesus Christ on the cross, either there's a priest in our window or I'm going to have to change these tablets.'

She put the potatoes down on the arm of the sofa and went to the door, unclipping an enormous single roller from the front of her hair. She expected to see Fergal but Father Mac said, 'I'm alone. And I'd better come in, unless you want the whole street to hear what I have to say.'

'What's our Fergal been up to, Father? And where is he?'

Father Mac moved past her into the living room. Paddy and the boys were all wearing the same sports kit. Paddy looked up, and John's head dropped. The crowd cheered from the TV.

'What do you want?' Paddy asked.

Father Mac walked over to the television and switched the semi-final off. Paddy stood up, dropping a bit of his dinner on the floor.

'Nobody but me touches that TV while I'm watching the match. I don't care who you are!'

'Where's Fergal?' Angela asked nervously.

'I think you should ask John,' Father Mac said. 'He was the last person to see him before I had to rush him to the Casualty Department.'

All eyes went to John, who had gone white as a sheet. 'I don't know what the Father's talking about,' he mumbled.

Father Mac took a deep breath. 'John, is this your velvet jacket? Did you not beat Fergal to a pulp because you thought he'd been wearing it?'

Angela took the wrinkled jacket from Father Mac and began smoothing it with her hands.

'Well, John? Here's your chance to tell the truth, in front of your family and God himself and admit the awful thing you did to your own flesh and blood.'

John shook his head and stared at his dinner.

'I'll refresh your memory for you,' Father Mac said. He told them about Fergal's injuries and about how he had only been allowed to leave the hospital because he would be at St Bridget's House under the careful eye of Mrs Mooney. In the silence that followed, Angela put her coat on.

'What are you going to do?' Father Mac asked Paddy.

Paddy didn't take his eyes off the blank TV screen. 'If our John says he didn't do anything, then he didn't do anything.'

'What? I just told you, in detail, what he did.'

Paddy stabbed a potato and wedged it whole into his mouth, chewing it momentarily before swallowing it in one go. 'You see, Father Whatever-your-name-is, our Fergal's an awful fucking exaggerator. He's always running home crying for his mammy like a wee girl.'

Father Mac realised he was talking to a brick wall. In John's case, he thought, the apple hadn't fallen far from the tree.

'God forgive you, Mr Flynn.'

As he left in disgust, Paddy switched on the TV again and turned up the sound. None of the boys dared move.

Angela pulled on her stilettos and made it to the car door in time to see Father Mac punching the steering wheel. As she opened the passenger door, he shouted, 'I'm amazed that Fergal survived at all – not just today, but his whole life! What is *wrong* with your husband?'

She looked at him for a moment and then shrugged. 'Paddy had a very hard upbringing himself, Father.'

~

Fergal was sitting up in bed, under strict instructions not to fall asleep even though he was exhausted. Slowly, he began to take in the details of Father Mac's room. His head periodically felt like it was attached to a washing machine on a rinse cycle, vibrating with pain and throwing his brain against the walls of his skull. He was convinced that, if he looked in the mirror, his head would be as big as a beach ball.

There was another crucified Christ on the wall – Fergal tried to decide whether they were following him or he was following them. The wounds that the centurion had made in Jesus' side made him look at his own battered ribs. An announcement from a distant, guilty pulpit somewhere in his head told him this was God's punishment for unnatural acts. Another, quieter voice asked, *What's unnatural about loving someone?*

He thought about where he was lying and about the night, months before, when he had stood in the darkness watching this very window from the other side. Now here he was, under the covers.

Father Mac didn't say a word to Angela as they pulled in behind the chapel. Mrs Mooney nearly had a fit at the footwear that ascended her polished stairs, but in the circumstances she decided to say nothing.

Father Mac knocked on his own bedroom door and opened it slowly. The room was full of shadows. 'Could you bear a lamp on, Fergal?' he asked softly.

When the light flicked on and Angela saw her wounded child, she dropped her handbag. 'Oh, Fergal... who did that to you, son?'

209

Fergal stared. 'Our John!' he spluttered. 'Our John did it, when I was coming back from Maguire's with Granny's gin. He just came out of nowhere, shouting about his coat, the coat you made me take – and I didn't even wear it once, did I, Father?'

Father Mac shook his head.

Angela took a breath. 'Oh, Fergal… I feel awful, son. I was just trying to make sure you had a good coat with you – I didn't want them monks thinking you came from a bad home…'

'Does Da know?'

Angela reached towards him, her licked fingers ready to wipe what she thought was dirt from his cheek. He flinched and cried out, and she realised the smudge was one in a series of dark bruises. She dropped her head as if she was about to pray. After a moment she asked, 'Fergal, did you say anything to… to upset John?'

Father Mac didn't waste a second. 'Mrs Flynn, Fergal obviously didn't even have a chance to defend himself, never mind say anything,' he snapped. 'And no one deserves that kind of beating, no matter what they said.' He felt sicker still when he saw Fergal's unsurprised expression – he had obviously met this kind of reaction a million times over.

Thankfully, Mrs Mooney's timing was every bit as good as the tea she delivered. Angela was so unused to anyone making her anything that she stared at her cup as if it might be a trap, as Mrs Mooney asked her if she took sugar. She held the china cup in both hands and drank the sweet tea in a couple of gulps.

'You make a quare brew, missus, I'll give you that.' Then she asked, 'Fergal, wouldn't you be more comfortable back at Granny Noreen's?'

Father Mac took her empty cup. 'I gave the doctor my word

that Fergal would get as much rest as possible,' he reminded her, in a steely, calm voice. 'The only reason he's here and not in a hospital bed is because there wasn't one available. He needs twenty-four-hour care. He'll be staying at St Bridget's House for the foreseeable future. When the doctor thinks he's well enough, we'll make further plans.'

'Father, I don't want you to think you have to go to any trouble looking after our wee Fergal—'

'Your son is not a baby, Mrs Flynn. He's a young man who's just turned seventeen.'

'Seventeen? Oh, Jesus – sure, I knew that – Jesus, I'm sorry, son. Happy birthday, for the other day.' She leaned in to kiss Fergal, but he shifted out of her way and yelped as his whole body protested.

'Don't you worry yourself, Mrs Flynn, we'll look after Fergal,' said Mrs Mooney, and she led Angela out of the room.

Father Mac walked her to the front door. 'I'm sorry I can't offer you a lift back.'

Angela shook her head quickly, 'Ah, no, Father, I'll be glad of the walk. It'll clear my head.'

When the hall door was closed, he slipped up into his room again and sat on the chair beside the bed.

'I just can't believe your family, Fergal. I hadn't meant to, but I went over to Walker Street on my way back from the chemist.'

Fergal's face was wretched. 'I never want to see them again, Dermot. I don't.' He had known such extreme forms of hate and love in the space of only twenty-four hours that he couldn't take it all in.

Father Mac was lost for words. He reached over and held Fergal as carefully as possible, and they sat in silence in the low light. The very fact that Father Mac was there helped Fergal to calm down. He thought about Brother Vincent and began to understand how the abbey could offer at least some sort of shelter from things like this.

Father Mac took his shoes off and put his feet up on the bed. He felt even worse about what had happened between them on the Sligo strand. Was this God's way of punishing him for not remaining celibate – hurting the one he... loved?

Mrs Mooney knocked on the door, as quietly as she could, reminding Father Mac that it was time for the evening mass. She assured him that she'd keep a watchful eye over their patient until he came back.

No sooner had Father Mac left than Patrick Flynn arrived at St Bridget's House. Wee Mrs Mooney, against her better judgement, let him in and he stamped up the stairs behind her.

Fergal was as instinctively afraid of him as ever, and Paddy knew it. He stayed standing as the housekeeper left. 'Have you any idea how much you've upset your mother, bringing all this trouble home? And after us letting you go to Sligo and all... What the fuck were you thinking, getting the priest involved and the whole street in on it? We're fucking ashamed of you, so we are.'

'I didn't ask John to attack me,' Fergal managed to offer.

His da's lip curled in disgust. 'You needn't use them words that some doctor or the fucking priest put in your mouth. A few hard knocks is what makes a man – something you'll never be if you keep up this big girl's-blouse act!'

The tears tripped Fergal, confirming everything his father accused him of. But then, out of nowhere, he began to boil with rage.

'Da, if this is what you have to do to another person to be able to call yourself a man, then I want no part of it.' Fergal felt the pain in his mouth get worse but he kept talking. 'Why do you think there's only one way to be a man? And what's so manly about coming up behind your own brother, knowing that he hasn't a hope of defending himself and nearly killing him?'

'Jesus, there you go again, exaggerating like an oul' woman. Just like I told Father What's-his-face.'

'Father MacManus! It's MacManus for God's sake!' Fergal was far too angry to stop. 'And when he was over in Walker Street, John couldn't even admit he'd done this. Is that manly, Da?'

'Listen to me. Our John is twice the man you'll ever fucking be. At least he can fucking handle himself.'

'You mean he's like you, Da, quick with the fists. So scary that none of his kids will ever really know him. What is so manly about lying around and letting your wife do about three times as much work as anybody else? You know what, I'm glad I'll never be what you call a man. I want to be something better than that!'

It was the longest father-and-son conversation they'd ever had in their lives.

Paddy Flynn's piercing blue eyes gave the impression that he was permanently staring into flames. His arguments were never fought with words and Fergal saw him lift his hand only to drop it again. 'I wouldn't waste my fucking energy. You can stay wherever they'll have you, for you'll not darken my door again. You're no son of mine. You're a fucking nancy-boy disgrace.'

He slammed the polished door in its frame and nearly knocked over Mrs Mooney and her tea tray on his way out.

~

Father Mac could hardly concentrate on the service. As he hurried out of the church afterwards, he was stopped by a group of disappointed pensioners who wanted to know where 'that fella with the lovely voice' was. Father Mac had a sudden mental picture of exactly where he was – recovering under his own sheets, only a few feet away – but he decided not to share that information. He said he'd missed Fergal's singing during the service too but they needn't worry, Fergal would be back as soon as he was over his cold.

When the last parishioner finally released his hand from a bony grip, surprisingly strong for someone so old and frail, he raced back to the house. 'Your fan club was asking for you!' he called as he took the stairs two at a time. When he came through the bedroom door and saw Fergal's face, he knew something else had happened.

The details of Fergal's ex-da's visit trickled out a bit at a time. Father Mac was furious with himself for leaving Fergal when he was at his most vulnerable. 'I won't do that again. I promise.'

'Sure, you've better things to do than sit around looking after...' Fergal suddenly had a coughing fit and spat into a wad of tissue paper that Mrs Mooney had wisely thought to leave.

'For goodness' sake, Fergal. Why do you say things like that?'

'Because you'll be so busy. I know I won't be able to stay here forever. Sure, the phone's always ringing with people who need you more.' Fergal put his head in his hands. 'And what am I going to do about Granny Noreen?'

Father Mac came closer. 'Fergal, it's time to concentrate on yourself for once and on getting better. You have to stop worrying about Noreen all the time. Look at you – you were so happy in – in Sligo... Look, for now, you just rest. I'll be here – and when

I'm not, Mrs Mooney won't even open the front door. Wait and see. We'll get through this. We will.'

Fergal liked the sound of 'we'.

'After all,' Father Mac said, 'you have a fan club to satisfy next door – and they don't all have bus passes.'

Fergal tried to laugh for the first time that day, but it hurt too much.

Mrs Mooney was hovering in the doorway. For a second Father Mac thought someone had called to the door, but she only wanted to remind him it was nine o'clock, two hours later than her normal leaving time. 'But I really don't mind staying longer if you want me to, Father.'

Father Mac walked her back down the stairs and helped her into her coat. He thanked her again and again and assured her they'd be fine. As she was closing the front door behind her, she mentioned, 'I've made up the spare room for you, so you won't need to worry about moving that poor young man.'

Father Mac went back upstairs to see if Fergal wanted to try to eat something – he admitted he was hungry, which was a good sign. Father Mac left him propped up on about six pillows and went back down to the kitchen. After a quick look in the over-stocked fridge, he decided the safest thing would be soft-boiled eggs, toast and a bit of cooked ham, along with a pot of tea. He carried the whole thing upstairs on the famous wooden tray and Fergal sat up when he saw the feast.

Although it hurt like hell, he managed to open his mouth wide enough when Father Mac gave him his medicine and then started to feed him. It made him think of Granny Noreen becoming more and more like a needy child every week, so he took the fork and fed himself.

'Do you want to watch the TV?' Father Mac asked. 'Sometimes I bring it up from the living room at night, if I can't sleep.'

'No thanks, Dermot, my head's too sore.' He automatically called him Dermot, now that they were alone.

'Of course – how stupid of me. I'm sorry, fella. Is there anything I can do?'

Fergal looked at him longer than he meant to.

'Will you stay beside me? Look, I know you said we had to be careful and all that other stuff, but look at me. It's not like I'll be able to… well, you know.'

'Fergal, I don't know…'

'Please, Dermot – I'd feel safer if you did. Please?'

Father Mac took the tray downstairs. He looked at the Sacred Heart picture that eyed him from the hallway and thought, *What can I do?* He washed the dishes slowly and put them away. Then he switched off the lights as he climbed the stairs.

Fergal had turned onto his side to make room for him. Father Mac climbed onto the bed, fully clothed, and lay beside him on top of the blankets. He kicked off his shoes and exhaled loudly. 'It's been quite a day.'

Fergal moved closer. 'I'm glad you're here.'

'I won't leave you. Just rest your jaw – try not to talk.'

They lay there, together but apart, as the soundtrack of the city played outside the window. Cars screeched by and a group of girls sang in unison, too many streets away to be understood. Father Mac was exhausted and the room was warm and dark. His eyelids finally gave in, and he slept.

Fergal shifted onto his other side to try and ease the pain, and Father Mac woke up with a start.

'Are you OK?'

'What? Ah, yeah... It's just that my back hurts and I'm too warm.'

'Do you want me to do anything? More pillows, maybe? Or should I go?'

'No – no, don't go. Will you... will you blow against my skin? I'm hot... it might cool me down. Please?'

It was the way Fergal said the last word that made Father Mac forget himself. He took a deep breath, leaned over and blew softly against Fergal's hair.

Fergal was transported back to the breeze and the blissful hollow on the Sligo strand. 'Oh, that's lovely – keep doing that. God, my back is so sore.'

'Where, fella? Show me where.'

Fergal turned on his side and very gently pulled the blanket down. Father Mac wanted to burst into tears when he saw up close just how badly bruised he was, but he continued blowing air against his skin. With one finger he tentatively traced patterns along Fergal's back, being careful only to touch the skin between the bruises and the cuts.

'Oh, Fergal, I'm so sorry this happened to you. How can a human being even think of doing that to another human being? I don't understand. Actually, now I think of it, I did feel like punching your da in Walker Street. You deserve so much better...'

Father Mac remembered a passage in the Bible about the washing of the wounds, and before he could stop himself he planted a single kiss on Fergal's aching shoulders. It was better than any medicine.

It hurt Fergal to breathe and his asthma made it worse, but after a burst of his inhaler he settled down to rest. 'Thank you, Dermot. I don't know what I'd do without you.'

Father Mac stood up. 'Mrs Mooney has the spare room all ready and, seeing that you're so settled, I should sleep there. You need as much rest as you can get. My God, it's almost four o'clock in the morning.'

Fergal's bruised face stared at him from the mass of pillows and the enormous duvet. Father Mac had never seen him look so helpless.

'Look, I'm only along the landing if you need me. Please don't even think twice about calling out if the pain gets worse – and, sure, we're seconds from the hospital.'

Fergal was too exhausted to argue. He tried to say something, but another agonising coughing fit took hold of him.

Father Mac didn't have the heart to go. He went back to the vacant side of the bed and lay down on top of the covers. 'Look, I'll stay for another while. Let's just get this day behind us. I promise you, things will only get better from here on in.'

'I hope so…'

'Forget about your family for now and concentrate on getting mended. Then we can just take each day as it comes. You know you can stay here for as long as you need to.'

He sensed that Fergal was too far gone to answer, so he gave him one last tender reminder on his swollen face that at least one person in the world loved him.

20

The next morning Father Mac woke with a jump when he heard Mrs Mooney's key in the door. He was glad that he'd kept his clothes on. He stood up, straightened them and forced his feet into his shoes, even though the laces were still tied. He looked over at Fergal, who was still asleep. As quietly as he could, he slipped out of his room and along the landing to the spare room, where he ruffled the sheets to make it seem as if he'd slept there. Knowing no one else had a key, he felt a bit ridiculous as he called out, 'Is that you, Mrs Mooney?'

'It is, Father MacManus. I didn't wake you, did I? I thought I'd come a wee bit earlier this morning on account of poor Fergal.'

Father Mac came downstairs. 'I've just been in to check on him and he seems fine, all things considered.'

Mrs Mooney whispered, 'Oh, he's a strong one, all right, to have survived that crowd at all.'

'A truer word was never spoken, Mrs Mooney.'

Mrs Mooney was delighted with that. She rubbed her bony hands and set about waking the house up, bit by bit, as if each room were a different child needing a particular approach to get the best out of it. She talked away to the fireplace in the parlour, 'Did you have a good sleep? Sure, it won't be long before I'll get you going – the summer hasn't kept its promise this morning…' Father Mac wondered if they really needed the fire lit, but when he stepped outside to go and buy a newspaper he could see what she meant. The sky was blue enough over towards the mountain, but there was a protest of grey clouds directly overhead, brewing about something.

~

After a few days, when Fergal was able to walk without wobbling too much, Mrs Mooney helped him move into the spare room. The more time went by, the less he thought about his family – but, even though he was on the mend, he didn't want to see any of them. Gradually he grew strong enough to face the fact that the arrangement at St Bridget's House could never be permanent. He'd have to think about either moving back to Noreen's or finding somewhere else to live.

As Fergal had predicted, there were more and more demands on Father Mac's time. When he had a house call on Noreen's street, he called in to get some of Fergal's belongings. He wanted to tell her what had happened without giving her too much of a shock but, for all her failings, she certainly wasn't stupid. She already knew the bones of the story – Angela had been round to take over again and she'd had to explain why Fergal wasn't there – and she had guessed the rest.

When she saw Father Mac, Noreen burst into tears. 'If I had the energy I'd kill that fella John with my bare hands, Father, so I would!'

She made Father Mac promise to bring Fergal to visit her, she needed to see for herself that he was all right. He kept his promise and drove Fergal over in the hope that it would make him worry a little less about her too, but it had the opposite effect. Noreen was drinking even more than usual and eating nothing, so she had failed considerably since the last time he'd seen her. It was as if she had sunk even further inside herself. She barely said a word, and her nightdress hung on her little body like a tarpaulin badly attached to a scaffold, collapsing slowly but surely.

Paddy Flynn came to Sunday mass as stubbornly as ever but always left just as Communion started. Along with many of the men of his generation, he'd slip out the back door in the confusion as parishioners jostled for position in the queue to receive the host. Then he'd walk the length of the Falls Road all the way to Casement Park, refusing to take a taxi even in the heaviest of rain. In his mind this meant that going to the hurling wasn't a sin at all – pain before pleasure, always.

Angela came by St Bridget's House one afternoon bringing an already opened letter from the school. It said that Fergal would have to present himself in person if he wanted to know the result of his O-levels – countless post-office deliveries had been destroyed by rioting that month and a number of the vans had been burnt to shells.

Mrs Mooney answered the door and nervously looked over

Angela's shoulder for any sign of Paddy Flynn before she allowed her into the front room. Fergal only agreed to see her as long
as she was on her own, which he knew she would be. It was an
uncomfortable meeting.

Angela searched in her bag for the letter, avoiding Fergal's
eyes. 'Did you know that John and Paddy started work last
week?' He didn't respond. 'Aye, their dole was going to be
stopped if they didn't go for interviews and now the two of them
are out working. Paddy's in a glazing firm up the Glen Road –
and, sure, Jesus only knows with the amount of broken windows
round here he'll never be idle. Our John's got a start in the brewery, delivering all over the place. Sure, I don't know what to do
with myself.'

She located the crumpled letter and handed it to him, asking
in a lowered voice – she was convinced that Mrs Mooney was listening on the other side of the door – 'When are you going to
stop all this, Fergal? You've made your point now and you're
needed back at your Granny Noreen's.'

He closed his eyes. 'My point, Mammy? You know I feel awful
about Granny Noreen, and I try and see her when I can, but I
don't want to stay there now. I'm sorry – I wouldn't feel safe. I
just… can't.'

Angela loaded up her bag much faster than she had unloaded
it. 'You mean you won't!'

'Ma, you saw what he did to me, for nothing. You pushed that
jacket into the car. I didn't ask for it, I never even had it on my
back – and look what I got!'

Still she didn't look at him. Her hand found its way down the
back of her jumper and clawed at her skin.

'He's a lunatic, Mammy. And Da told me never to come near Walker Street again anyway.'

The silence was unbearable. Father Mac arrived back from a home visit to frantic sign language from Mrs Mooney. He entered the front room and tried to lighten the atmosphere.

'Mrs Flynn – what a surprise! The summer looks to be staying around this time. Isn't Dunville Park looking well, if only they could get the fountain working again?'

'My husband thinks I'm only at the shops,' Angela said uneasily. 'He'd go mad if he knew I was here.' Then she blessed herself and backed out the door.

Father Mac took the cup of untouched tea out of Fergal's hand and rubbed his shoulder until they heard Mrs Mooney coming to collect the tray. When she was gone again, Father Mac asked, 'What happened?'

'Ah, she brought me a letter from the school. I have to pick up my O-level results because the last lot of school post was burned in a hijacked van. Our Paddy and John were forced off the dole and now they've got jobs. And she wants me to go back to Noreen's – but I can't… What am I going to do? I can't stay here forever.'

'Fergal, you don't have to go anywhere for the time being.'

'For the time being? What does that mean? You've been so good to me already, and I feel like – like I'm bringing all this trouble to your door. You must be sick of me.'

Father Mac closed the door with his foot. Fergal had never heard such anger spoken so quietly. 'Fergal Flynn, I am most certainly not sick of you. What I am sick of is the way that, any time either of your parents comes here, you end up feeling like you're useless. I know you're feeling very vulnerable at the moment, but you mustn't let them get to you like this. I will keep saying it until it sinks in. I love having you here. I love that you're… that you're in my life.' He stared at Fergal intensely, searching his face.

'Why are you looking at me like that?'

'Fergal, please don't tell me that you've been thinking of running away again?'

'What? No! No, I haven't. Where would I go? My mother's sisters might be worse than her!'

They both laughed a little, but Father Mac was more worried than ever.

~

Father Mac drove Fergal back to his old school to pick up his O-level results from the secretary's office. He had passed almost every exam. The tiny strip of paper told him he had earned Ds in maths and physics, Cs in geography and English language, and Bs in religion, art, and craft design technology, which was basically metalwork with too much theory. There were even two As, in English literature and Irish. Fergal was more than surprised – the exams seemed like a faraway blur but the results made the volume of the approaching future a bit louder.

'Are you considering A-levels?' Father Mac asked him.

'They don't offer them here,' Fergal said.

'St Bridget's doesn't offer any exams beyond O-level,' the secretary confirmed. 'There wasn't enough interest from the pupils.' She handed Fergal a leaflet about an adult education course at the local girls' school.

He shuddered as they drove out of the gates with the school in the rear-view mirror but not far enough in the past.

That night Father Mac produced a secret bottle of champagne from the depths of the fridge and raised a toast in the front room. 'Fergal Flynn, it is no small miracle that you've done so well in your O-levels. So here's to the future whatever it brings. The only way is up, my friend.'

Once Fergal's smile got settled, it borrowed his face for the rest of the evening. Father Mac ended the night by sneaking out the back door with the empty champagne bottle and pushing it to the bottom of the bin.

Slowly but surely, they had started working on the music again. When the swelling in Fergal's head subsided and he had had two check-ups at the hospital, he started singing at the evening services. He loved being in the candlelit atmosphere, with the sounds of the chapel for company and, as terrifying as it always was initially, there was nothing that compared to singing in front of people. Sometimes he sang unaccompanied on the altar, if there was a song that was appropriate to the Gospel. This was when he was at his most nervous because he could see the faces of the whole congregation. He always kept a lookout for his brothers, but even when they weren't there, the congregation included fellas who'd made his life hell at school. Whenever he sang, they tried to muffle their laughter as their mortified girl-friends elbowed them in the ribs to shut them up. After Fergal's experience of humiliation at St Bridget's Secondary School, though, this was easily enough ignored.

The living arrangements at St Bridget's House stayed the same. Father Mac moved back into his room as soon as Fergal was settled in the spare one. When night came and darkness enveloped the house, Father Mac tried to distract himself by reading or doing crosswords but, in the end, he could never help rolling over to the side of his bed where Fergal had recuperated. Only then could he sleep.

~

One night there was a car bomb not far from St Bridget's and then a riot. A local child took a plastic bullet to the head and died in the arms of Father Mac, who had arrived only seconds before to administer the last rites on the side of the road. He closed the little boy's eyes and carried the limp body less than a hundred yards to the hospital where it was too late to do anything but sedate his poor mother.

When he got back to the parish house, Father Mac sent Mrs Mooney home, locked the front door behind her and cried his eyes out. All Fergal could do was stand in the living-room doorway watching him pile too much coal on the fire until it collapsed. When he stood up, dusting his hands, he broke down again because he'd made such a mess. Fergal came closer to try and comfort him, but Father Mac turned away, putting his dirty hands over his face. 'I'm OK – I'm OK…'

Fergal thought it might help if he went and got a box of tissues that he knew Mrs Mooney kept in the kitchen cupboard. While he was there he spotted a bottle of wine, so he found a couple of glasses and carried everything into the living room.

Father Mac went up to the bathroom and washed the dirt from his hands and his tear-stained face. He looked at himself in the mirror, but all he could see was the dead little boy's face staring blankly at him. He threw some cold water on his eyes and scrubbed under his fingernails.

When he saw the wine, he exhaled in appreciation. 'That's an inspired idea, Fergal. I never thought the day would come when I'd be so glad to see a drink. Pour me a large one – and I don't like drinking on my own.'

The riot startled up again, as news of the little boy's death spread like a forest fire. Outside, on the main road, they heard the army patrol cars pushing their gearboxes to the limit as they careered around corners from the nearby barracks.

Father Mac and Fergal cautiously went up to the spare room, where they had a better view of the road. They turned the light off – the street lamp had been shot out and the road was dark – and stood at one of the sash windows trying to see what was happening. A helicopter searchlight passed right over St Bridget's, and they were blinded for a split second. Suddenly a stray bullet whistled through the other window and there were shattered splinters of glass everywhere.

They flung themselves to the floor. Father Mac panicked. 'Fergal – oh, fuck – Fergal! Are you all right?'

'I'm fine. Jesus, that was close, though.'

'We should get out of here,' Father Mac whispered. 'Crawl.' They slid along the carpet like snipers until they reached the landing and Father Mac could kick the bedroom door shut.

He knew they would have to wait until the trouble was well over before they could even board up the broken window temporarily with a sheet of cardboard – it would be the next morning at the earliest before a glazier could come to the rescue. As they got back to the parlour, he looked at Fergal. 'Well, you can't sleep in there tonight, that's for certain. It'll be too cold – and there's no telling what will happen later.'

'Well, where then? The sofa in here?'

'You can do that, I suppose. You're so tall, though – I hope you don't end up with a sore back.'

'Where then? I can't go back to Noreen's, Dermot.' The old panic had returned to his voice.

'Fergal, do you think I would let you go out the door on a night like this, never mind to Noreen's? Calm down for goodness' sake. I wasn't thinking that at all. We'll figure something out.'

They sat in the front room, drinking the wine and watching the news on the TV. Fergal loved how the alcohol calmed him. There was a special news report about the incident – there had been 'unrest' in West Belfast and the army had been forced to 'retaliate' with anti-riot gear, tear gas and plastic bullets. There was no mention of the dead boy. Father Mac was furious, thinking about the tiny body that lay punctured and lifeless in the morgue only a short walk away. He looked at Fergal and thought how easily it could have been him, at any stage in his childhood.

He poured the last of the bottle into the glasses. 'Fergal, when I carried that wee boy tonight, I was thinking about you.'

'You were? Why?'

'Well, his eyes were like yours… before I had to close them.'

He began to cry again, and when Fergal came towards him he didn't turn away. It was the first time Fergal had seen Father Mac really upset. He was glad of the role reversal, glad that he was able to comfort him. He knew only too well how much he'd come to rely on Father Mac as the months had passed, but it was the first time it had occurred to him that Father Mac might need him just as much. The red wine softened the room and made his breath feel warm.

'It's all right, Dermot. It's all right.'

Fergal ran his hand through Father Mac's hair and down onto his back, rubbing in slow circles. Without meaning to, he blew against Father Mac's ear, as if trying to cool him.

Father Mac looked up at him, and they stared deep into each other. The wine made Fergal brave; he was determined not to look away, not even to blink.

Father Mac's eyes were full of tears. Fergal brought a finger up and collected them, then he put the wet tip of his finger in his mouth, drinking away his grief. Father Mac was startled for a moment, but he didn't get a chance to say anything. Fergal dropped two kisses on his eyelids and then one on his mouth. Father Mac exhaled and kept his eyes shut. He pictured himself taking control of the situation, telling Fergal to stop, but he knew he couldn't. He could only kiss him back, slowly at first, almost as if he was expecting to stop, but neither of them did. Outside the gunfire ripped through the sky, there was no telling how close or how far away it really was. A shop alarm bawled like a frightened ghost as Fergal began pulling at Father Mac's shirt, ripping one of the buttons off, and dropped down to smell his chest.

Still devouring each other, they moved out of the front parlour and attempted the stairs, but they had to give up when Fergal tripped and they fell awkwardly on top of each other.

'Fergal, are you—' Father Mac never got a chance to voice his worry. Fergal grabbed him between the legs for a second and then ran away up the stairs laughing, as if they were playing a game of tag. As he ran, Brother Vincent's playful voice resounded in the back of his mind, reminding him not to be afraid to be childish if he felt like it. There was no doubt in his mind where he was going to be spending the night. The broken spare-room window had been the shove they had needed.

Father Mac checked that the front door was double-locked, looked up at the landing and then followed. When he reached his room humming nervously, Fergal was already half undressed.

Father Mac searched his record collection nervously, buying time. 'Do you mind if I put some music on? I always fall asleep with music on, turned down low so I can still hear the phone or the doorbell—'

'Sure. What've you got?' Fergal moved over to him and began kissing the back of his neck.

'I don't know – let me see – Ella, Billy, Frank... Oh, I know, let's have some Joni Mitchell. Do you like Joni?'

'I don't really know. I've never heard of her.'

'What? Well, you're in for the biggest treat of your life, and hopefully the start of a love affair that will only get better as you get older.' Father Mac blushed as he realised what he'd said. 'Ah, no – no, I meant with Joni's music, a love affair with her music.'

The room wasn't the warmest. Father Mac looked at Fergal in his shorts and T-shirt and told him, 'Get into the bed, I won't be long.' Even though they'd been so intimate in Sligo, he suddenly felt self-conscious enough to go to the bathroom and undress there. He came back after about ten minutes, teeth freshly cleaned, wearing blue striped pyjamas.

'I thought you were never coming back!'

'Sorry, fella. I'm just a bit... you know.'

Once they were under the covers, the lights were out and the record had started, they naturally turned towards each other as Joni sang like a beautiful lonely blackbird. Father Mac had a habit of singing along when he was on his own. He forgot himself and joined in huskily, humming at first, then finding the words.

'You're not a bad singer at all, Dermot! And I love this song.'

'Ah, when I didn't smoke I could just about hold a tune, but I can't even do that any more.'

Fergal shifted closer and kissed Father Mac again and he responded enthusiastically. They were both unused to sharing a bed and, although they'd started out feeling cold, it wasn't long before they were both too warm.

'I'm roasting,' Fergal mumbled, sitting up to take off his T-shirt.

'I'm boiling too,' Father Mac agreed. He tried to unbutton his pyjama top under the duvet, but Fergal pulled it off roughly.

Under the cover of that riotous night, they tasted, smelled, kissed, nuzzled, licked, stroked and sucked every inch of each other with all the tenderness and recklessness they possessed, feeling more alive than ever. Outside, death was a hair's breadth away. Father Mac took Fergal in his mouth and wouldn't let go until he'd emptied every last drop of himself. Fergal had never felt anything like it in his life. Seconds later, Father Mac trembled as Fergal's hands drained him onto his waiting stomach.

They surrendered to damp exhaustion.

'Dermot, I don't know what I would've done if you hadn't looked after me.'

'Fergal, sure, what else would I have done?'

The music had finished, and the only sound left was their breathing.

231

They'd only been asleep for a few hours when another bomb ripped through a shop in the centre of town, shaking them both awake. The room was cold now. Their fingers investigated each other, their hands intertwining like sea creatures in the darkest depth of the ocean.

Father Mac was the more nervous of the two. He had promised himself and God time and time again that they would never repeat that night at the beach in Sligo. If Fergal hadn't been attacked, Father Mac might have had time to plant those promises a bit further down in the soil of his convictions, and their roots might have taken a stronger hold. But when Fergal had moved into St Bridget's House, he also had moved even further into Father Mac's heart. Father Mac had thought he had built those promises in steel. Now, with each tender, nervous kiss, they shattered as though erected from the thinnest film of ice.

The phone rang just before six o'clock, and Father Mac had to disentangle himself to answer it. He dressed quickly and went out to give the last rites to a ninety-six-year-old man, who died about an hour later. His family were grateful to Father Mac. It was at those times that he felt most useful to the community. When he got back home, he was wracked with guilt again. He hadn't the heart to disturb Fergal, who was sleeping peacefully under the duvet, so he went into the parlour and lay on the sofa under a spare blanket still fully clothed.

As he slipped into a deep sleep, he finally decided that he wasn't going to reject Fergal a third time – he couldn't have done it even if he'd wanted to. He blew a kiss towards the ceiling and didn't wake until he heard Mrs Mooney's key in the door.

'Ah, Father MacManus, I heard you were called out to poor old

Mr Harrison. You do too much, you look like you haven't slept at all.'

'Well, the window in Fergal's room got shot out last night, so I gave him my room and I stayed down here. Sure, I had loads of letters to get through – and, after last night's shenanigans, I knew I'd be called out for something.'

She picked up the empty bottle of wine and looked disapprovingly at the ceiling, as if she had X-ray vision. Then she cleared away her suspicions with the half-empty glasses.

~

They settled into a routine of sorts. Fergal helped Mrs Mooney a bit around the house – he loved living somewhere so clean. When he and Father Mac were left alone, they listened to music constantly, and Fergal even started to brave the piano on his own if Father Mac was called out. Fergal had started to wear some of Father Mac's old dark clothes that no longer fitted the priest's expanding waistline – Mrs Mooney's cooking was the culprit – but were too good to throw out. It had happened first by accident. One morning Fergal had woken up in Father Mac's bed with a start thinking Mrs Mooney was at the door, and pulled on the wrong trousers on his way to hide in the toilet. When Father Mac came back to tell him it was only the coal man delivering, he had realised – 'My goodness, Fergal, they fit you perfectly.'

They didn't sleep together every single night, nor were they intimate every time they did, but they were always loving, and Fergal adored waking up with Father Mac whenever he got the chance.

233

Father Mac was worried, though, and he constantly reminded Fergal that they had to be careful. Mrs Mooney hadn't failed to notice, over the passing weeks, the way that Father Mac and Fergal sometimes looked at each other. She'd even caught Fergal lying on Father Mac's bed one day, when he was out saying mass. He'd mumbled that he was borrowing a book, but in fact he'd gone in there to see if he could smell Father Mac off the pillows.

Mrs Mooney chose her moment. 'Father, forgive me for saying so, but do you think some people in the parish might think that it's… well… strange that Fergal lives here?'

Father Mac swallowed and tried not to look taken aback. 'Why, Mrs Mooney? Has someone said something to you?'

'No, no – it's just… Well, you know what people are like, especially around here. Some people might think it's… unusual for him to be here for so long without any friends of his own age, you know?'

Father Mac stared past her head out into the yard. 'Well, there's no accounting for people, is there, Mrs Mooney? I suppose some people might think that it's normal to beat their kids till they need to go to the emergency unit. Would those be the same people, I wonder, Mrs Mooney?'

'Well, it's not for me to say, Father.'

She got out the Hoover and they said no more about it, but Father Mac was shaking. That night he told Fergal what had happened and insisted that they should sleep apart. Fergal understood, but he couldn't hide his disappointment. It was the first time he had resented Mrs Mooney.

~

One morning, a package addressed to 'Father D. MacManus' arrived. Father Mac was out on a visit, leaving Fergal to stare at the Sligo postmark until he got home for lunch.

Inside there was a note from Brother Vincent and two copies of the monks' album, one on cassette and one on vinyl. The cover was a likeness of the most fragile icon that Fergal had seen illuminated in the dark chapel under the altar. They stared in wonder at their names highlighted in gold lettering under the chants they had performed.

Father Mac put the record on the turntable, and they sat silent and breathless as the speakers hummed and the dark grooves crackled. They revisited every note and phrase, until the final cadence brought Side 1 to a close. Neither of them could speak as Father Mac picked up the vinyl circle and flipped it over.

They listened again and again, more thrilled with each play, until Father Mac looked at the clock and realised he had to get back to his visits. As he was leaving, he turned to Fergal and said, 'I'm so proud to share this moment, Fergal Flynn. Mark my words, this is only the beginning.'

21

For Noreen, the beginning of the end had started a long time ago. Every time Fergal visited her – usually with Father Mac beside him – he couldn't believe how much she had deteriorated in the short time since his last visit. She couldn't get out of bed any more, so the doctor had recommended incontinence pads, which was just a polite name for adult-sized nappies. The dreaded commode was now redundant and sat in the tiny yard, rusting in the rain. Angela still delivered the gin, Noreen cried non-stop without it, and the doctor said there was little point in refusing her now.

The last time Fergal visited his granny, he and Father Mac were bringing her a month's supply of incontinence pads – the black plastic bag was far too big for Angela to manage. Fergal still had his key and let himself in. Father Mac went out the back to the toilet, and Fergal ran upstairs calling, 'Granny, it's me!'

She didn't answer. This wasn't unusual – she slept most of the day – but when he got to the landing, the unmistakable smell of shit nearly made him sick.

He opened the bedroom door. Noreen's bed was empty and his first thought was that she was dead, but then, out of the corner of his eye, he saw something moving beside a pile of old blankets. It was her, squatting by the wall like a filthy plucked turkey, totally naked. As he got closer, Fergal realised the awful smell was due to the fact she had ripped off her nappy and covered herself and the wall with the rank contents. He gagged and vomited into his hand. Noreen didn't seem to notice him. She stared blankly as he got behind her, lifted her up and carried her towards the bed. At least that wasn't too bad, only the top blanket was soiled.

Father Mac came bounding up the stairs, calling, 'How's my favourite girl?' – that usually got a cackle out of Noreen – but the smell nearly knocked him back down them. When he realised what was happening, he hurried to help Fergal and together they did the best they could.

She had reverted back to infancy. Fergal tried not to notice while he was wiping her clean that she had no pubic hair. Her skin was as thin as a baby bird's, he could see her veins through it. Father Mac brought basin after basin of water. They stripped the bed, taking it in turns to hold her, although she weighed nothing. When they pulled the bed away from the wall to free some of the sheets, gin bottles rolled everywhere. They found a clean nightdress and managed to settle her back under the covers.

Then they turned their attention to cleaning the wall. Fergal scraped around the window of her world with a blunt knife, removing the crusted paint so it would open for the first time in decades and let some air in.

The tears streamed down Noreen's face. Fergal, trying not to vomit again or cry, automatically sang, 'I'll take you home again, Noreen…' He knew she had given up completely.

Father Mac went next door, rang the doctor and told him what had happened. The doctor wasted no time. He arrived, examined Noreen and then called an ambulance to bring her to the Royal Hospital. 'Her kidneys have been weakened over the years,' he explained to Father Mac and Fergal, 'and it was only a matter of time before they would give out completely.' He bent his head. 'I'm sorry there isn't more I can do.'

Even though he didn't really want to, Father Mac jumped in his car and drove the short distance to Walker Street to find Angela. They got back just in time to see the ambulance men carrying her mother out on a stretcher. Angela screamed, 'Where are youse fucking taking her? Is she dead? Mammy! Mammy, don't die!' The whole street was watching as she jumped into the back of the ambulance, slapping one of the ambulance men for giving her a dirty look.

Father Mac and Fergal followed in the car. Fergal said, over and over, 'I shouldn't have left her… I should never have left her.'

For the first time, Father Mac lost his temper with him. 'For God's sake, Fergal! What more could you have done? You're not a doctor or a health visitor. How many times do I have to remind you that she is not your responsibility? Quit beating yourself up about it!'

'I know, I know, I know… but…'

'But nothing, Fergal. But nothing.'

~

At three o'clock the following morning, Father Mac was called to the hospital to administer the last rites to Noreen. Fergal went with him, and he held her tiny hand as she took her last breath.

Angela arrived only minutes too late, with her hair still in rollers. The night nurse gave her a little transparent bag that held her mother's diamondless engagement ring – the precious stone had been lost down a drain years previously in the dirty water of a million scrubbing buckets – and the thread-thin wedding band that Noreen had never taken off from the moment her husband pushed it onto her tiny finger. Angela cried like the lost child she was and Fergal put his arm around her, like the ghost of her father.

She looked at him through the clouds in her eyes. Then she made him take Noreen's wedding ring. 'She would've wanted you to have it.'

Fergal studied the fragile circle of old gold. It wouldn't even fit his little finger.

~

The wake was held in Walker Street, where Noreen's coffin was laid out in front of the unlit fireplace. The wreath on the front door attracted unwanted attention from nosy people who hadn't even known Noreen, but who knew they'd get a sandwich, a cup of tea – if not a nip of whiskey – and a good look at Angela's house.

Fergal almost talked himself out of going. His brothers would be there and his da hadn't lifted his banishment. Finally Father Mac offered to go with him, and assured him that they would leave at the first hint of trouble. 'But you know they won't misbehave in front of other people – especially not if I'm there.'

The front door was ajar and they could see the gathering through the bubbled glass. Fergal took a deep breath and they walked in. Most of the mourners bowed their heads when they saw that the Church had arrived, but Fergal could feel his brothers and his father staring at him.

He went straight to the coffin. He was startled by how peaceful Noreen looked. Her body was almost entirely covered in mass cards, and her shiny face floated like a little island in its rough ocean of folded paper. He thought of the icons in the Sligo chapel. Her hands made the shape of a prayer and her fingers, threaded with rosary beads, looked like they were carved from wax. Fergal bent forward and kissed the side of her face, but the coldness of her skin only reminded him that she had long abandoned her exhausted body.

'Where is Mrs Flynn?' Father Mac asked the room.

After a moment, a neighbour answered, 'She's round at her sister Concepta's lying down. She hasn't slept since the death.'

Father Mac looked at Fergal. 'Let's go,' Fergal said.

They drove to Concepta's, but she said she had given Angela something to make her sleep – it was the only way she could stop crying – and she wasn't going to wake her. As they were leaving, she said, 'God save us, Fergal, but haven't you got tall all of a sudden? You're like a big man, so you are.'

Fergal didn't know how to take that. 'Don't forget, will you?' he said. 'Tell Ma we called to the wake.' They left Concepta with a hallway full of oblivious children pulling at her skirt for more jam sandwiches.

St Bridget's House was quiet when they got back and Fergal went to sit in the chapel. The cleaners all knew him by now, some of them had even known Noreen when she was a girl and they came over to tell him they were sorry for his trouble. They rambled and rubbed his shoulders, and Fergal stared numbly at the altar, wondering if Noreen was watching him.

When Father Mac came to tell him dinner was ready, he followed mutely to the carefully laid table. His appetite had vanished and he picked distractedly at the plate, hearing Father Mac's voice talking away somewhere in the distance. He headed upstairs to the spare room early, defeated by grief.

He undressed and lay under the covers in the dark, but it was impossible to get comfortable. Finally he got up, turned the light back on and looked through the bookshelf for something to read. He took down a big book about films but as he opened it up, a tiny book fell out of the jacket. It was a volume of poems called *Secret Love*. Inside, there was an inscription: 'To Dermot, with love and understanding, from your sister Dympna x.'

In the table of contents, the same hand had drawn a star next to a poem called, 'I'm in Love with a Man'. Fergal turned the pages and read the lines half a loud.

I'm in love with a man –
I've tried to deny it as much as I can,
But I woke to find him cleaning my windows and
I'm in love with a man.

I'm in love with a voice –
It's the way that he talks that really leaves me no choice.
You won't find him trying to impress me with Wilde or Joyce;
I'm in love with his voice.

I'm in love with a look,
The one that he gave me when I offered to cook;
I've checked in my diary, I'd considered no plan –
I'm in love with a man – I am!
I'm in love with a man.

The door opened softly and Father Mac peeped in. Fergal jumped.

'Oh, sorry, fella – I didn't mean to startle you, I just saw your
light on and wondered if you were all right.' Then he noticed the
book of poems in Fergal's hand. 'Where did you find this? I
haven't seen it for years – I thought I'd lost it in Africa.'

'It was here.' Fergal showed him where he'd found it.

'I wonder how it ended up there.' Father Mac sat on the edge
of the bed. 'My sister gave that to me, the day I was ordained,
and warned me not to open it until I was on my own. It's a collection of love poems written by men for men, from as far back
as two hundred years ago right up to recent times. Most of the
authors' names are unknown.'

Fergal said nothing. Father Mac's heart nearly cracked as he
looked at him. He knew that no one and nothing but time could
bring Fergal any comfort so he stood up and leaned over to kiss
him. 'Good night, fella. Do you need anything?'

'Will you hold me for a while, Dermot? You don't have to if
you don't want to.'

Father Mac kicked off his polished brogues and lay down on top of the blankets. He reached for Fergal, pulling him as close as he could, and held Fergal's back against his chest.

They must have slipped into a deep sleep, because the next thing Fergal remembered was waking up in an asthmatic sweat, coiled around Father Mac, who was snoring lightly. He carefully released himself to go and find his inhaler.

Once out of the bed, he was suddenly cold. He pulled on his clothes and went downstairs. When he found Noreen's key in his coat pocket, along with his blue inhaler, he put the coat on and sneaked out the front door.

It was pitch-dark – not many of the street lamps had survived the most recent riot. He sucked a few puffs from his inhaler and felt his lungs open. As he passed the off-licence he thought that, if anyone was mourning Noreen more than he was, it would be the owner of that fucking place. Now who would buy all that liquid grief?

He found himself walking up Walker Street, and he stopped outside the house where he'd grown up. An uncontrollable urge to smash every one of its windows rose inside him, so he moved on before it got the better of him. The streets' silence was almost more frightening than any noise.

Suddenly, a woman's voice pleaded, 'Freedom! Freedom! Where are you?' She was wearing her dressing gown, slippers and a full head of rollers. She continued calling, seemingly to the clouds coming home late across the sky, until a little mongrel dog appeared out of a dark entry and ran towards her, wagging the tail off itself.

She bent down to kiss its nose. 'Freedom, love, where in the name of God were you? You know I can't go to my bed till you're

243

in. Now come on with me – them there oul' soldiers are creeping about.' She scooped the animal up into her arms as if it were a tired child and hummed to it as she headed back to her house.

An army patrol up the next entry stopped Fergal, asking him where he was headed so late at night. He told them that his granny had died and he was on his way to her house, but they made him wait while they radioed in his details. Then all of a sudden someone's headset spat a distorted message and they ran off, leaving him without another word.

Outside Noreen's house, he looked up at the little dark window that had provided her entire world view for so long. When he put the key in the lock, he half-expected to hear her calling him, but there wasn't a sound.

He closed the hall door and flicked on the light. From the look of things, the vultures had already started picking at the bones of her few possessions, and he was afraid that somebody might still be there, guarding the house. He called out, 'It's Fergal', but his name echoed in the empty mourning stillness that only a death can make. He climbed the stairs and stood at the bedroom door, listening for Noreen's familiar breathing, but the wind dancing around the back yard started to scare him, so he pushed open the door.

Her bed had been cleaned and roughly made, and Fergal suddenly felt that he would fall over from tiredness if he didn't lie down right there and then. He climbed in amongst her freezing blankets with all his clothes on and rolled into the middle of the bed where her bedridden shape had moulded itself into the old horsehair mattress.

He heard her voice in his head, saying his name over and over

again and telling him to go on a wee message for her. He remembered how she had loved weak milky tea with two sugars and
toast with piles of butter when she was well enough to eat it. He
remembered how her blue-tinted National Health glasses had
constantly slipped down her nose and how she had cursed them
to high heaven as she tried to read the paper, propped up in this
bed. Sometimes when he hadn't wanted to go to school, he had
thought it must be brilliant to be able to stay in bed all day, but
now he knew how miserable Noreen had been and how much
she would have given to be healthy and mobile. He thought
about Angela, growing up in this very house. He tried to picture
her as a little girl running around downstairs with all her brothers and sisters, his mystery aunts and uncles, driving Noreen and
her husband nuts with their noise and their nursery rhymes and
their fighting. He whispered questions to the cold, empty history in the room as if the answers might be written under the thick
layers of wallpaper. 'Why do people have to change? Why do
people have to get angry, or old and… and sick and lonely and
tired and… die?'

The smell of gin on the pillow suddenly brought tears to his
eyes. He lay there, shuddering with sobs, until he was too
exhausted to stay awake any longer.

~

Father Mac woke up with a start and was surprised to find Fergal gone. He dressed slowly, expecting to see him at any
moment, but when he descended the stairs and saw Fergal's coat
was missing, panic rose in him. He heard a key in the front door,

but it was only Mrs Mooney with an armful of fresh bread, giving out about the queue at the baker's. He ignored her questions about breakfast telling her he'd been called out and didn't know how long he'd be.

He drove to Noreen's house at top speed. He rapped on the door and Fergal eventually came to the window before staggering down the stairs, half asleep, to let him in. Father Mac could see that he'd been crying.

'Fergal, are you all right? I panicked a wee bit when I realised you were gone this morning. If you hadn't been here, I wouldn't have known where to look.'

'Sorry, Dermot. I just… I woke up and put my coat on and kept walking till I got here. I didn't plan it or anything.'

Father Mac put his chin on Fergal's head and hugged him hard.

'I want to make her bed before we leave,' Fergal said, so Father Mac followed him upstairs. As they were shaking the sheets, they found a holy medal of Saint Christopher on a silver chain. Fergal kissed it and put it around his neck.

As Fergal finished folding the last blanket, Father Mac said, 'What will happen to Noreen's house, now that she's gone?'

Fergal hadn't really thought much about it, but he knew only too well that she had been behind in her rent for years. 'I don't know. It's just so weird to think that I'll never see her again.'

Then he remembered the box of photos that she had shown him and he dropped to his knees to see if they were still under the bed. He pulled out plastic bags full of rubbish and bottle after empty gin bottle, but there was no sign of the box. Fergal realised his mother must have taken it.

Father Mac was amazed at how many bottles there were. 'What should we do with all these? We can't leave them here.'

They started carrying them, four each at a time, out to the yard, but Fergal stopped. 'We can't stack them out there. It's too dangerous.'

'What do you mean?'

Fergal suddenly remembered a game that the children on his road used to play when he was a tiny boy. As they carried the bottles to Noreen's dented old bin, he told Father Mac about it.

'When I was wee, there was this game called Colour Water Bottle Shop that everybody played. We all collected old milk bottles filled with water stained different colours – we kept them in our back yards. The challenge was to come up with the most unusual, beautiful colour. We used the maddest combinations of ingredients – markers we nicked from school, disinfectant, tea leaves, medicine, clay from the brick factory that had closed down... Then you stood at your back yard door and chanted, "Shop open, soon be closing, first here gets very good value!" and everyone went round the yard doors and bartered colours – there were all kinds of complicated, drawn-out deals. Everyone wanted the best collection, the one that everybody else would envy. Some kids even raided other people's colour water bottle shops during the night and then swore on their mothers' lives that they had discovered the colour themselves. Seeing as the ingredients were such a secret, you had to just bite your lip or steal it back the next night or pour the other kid's bottle down the drain and deny that.'

There were some scenes that Fergal had edited out. Angela had hated the game. She was sick of knocking over the treasured bottles in her panic to grab washing off the line before the rain ruined her efforts. She would yell, 'Fergal Flynn, I don't know why I even bother getting these sheets dry, when you soak them with pish every fucking week that God sends us! Come out here and pick up these fucking bottles before I kill you stone-dead, you wee cunt!'

Sadly, like a lot of innocent things, the game had come to a disastrous end. Without warning, a new colour filled bottles in the area – the dull, oily pink of petrol. Topped with lit rags, it flew through the air and struck the green-grey army tanks in mini-explosions of orange and blue flowered flames. Foot patrols descended like locusts, snatching anyone who looked like he might be over sixteen. If they had raided a house and found a collection of empty bottles, they would have assumed that they'd uncovered a petrol-bomb factory. The men of the house would have been arrested and taken away to an unknown location with no guarantee that they would return in the same condition, if at all.

Fergal could still see the twins and his da smashing every last one of his bottles with their hurling sticks. He'd watched through the back window heartbroken as all his hard-won colours of the rainbow were reunited down the drain. 'I was devastated. I thought they were the most beautiful colours in the world.'

Later that same distant day, one of his da's mates had come round. They had poured hot tar all along the top of the yard walls and shovelled the shards of his precious bottles into the thick black liquid as though they were planting seeds. 'They made sure the sharpest bits stuck up like sharks' teeth, ready to rip anybody to shreds if they were stupid enough to try and climb over.'

Father Mac, placing the last of the gin bottles in the bin, thought how incredible it was that children's imaginations managed to manufacture such beauty even in the ugliest of circumstances.

They turned off the lights in the house, and Fergal shut the door and turned the key on a part of his life that was closed forever.

22

When they got back to St Bridget's House, Mrs Mooney was on the phone, which she handed over to Father Mac. It was a call from Sligo Abbey. Brother Vincent was phoning to say that they'd just had a very interesting visitor, a globally renowned vocal tutor from Italy, who was exploring the possibility of including the monks' chants in his teaching. When Brother Vincent had played him their recent recording, he'd become very excited about Fergal's voice. He'd expressed an interest in meeting Fergal as soon as possible, as he wasn't staying in the country for much longer.

Fergal, distracted by thoughts of the coming funeral, didn't really take in the details as Father Mac recounted them aloud when he'd hung up.

'Apparently this man, Alfredo Moretti, is very influential, and he's prepared to extend his visit by a day if he can meet with you. He's prepared to travel to Belfast too. Brother Vincent says that we should definitely meet him. He also says that the other monks were asking after you, and they all hope we like the way the record turned out. Well, what do you think? You haven't got anything to lose, have you? I wonder what this Alfredo Moretti is like… Fergal?'

He realised that Fergal's mind was, understandably, elsewhere, so he said they could talk about it later.

~

The cortege was due to leave Walker Street at midday, and Fergal and Father Mac arrived just as the coffin was carried out of the house. Paddy Flynn, Concepta's husband and the twins, guided by two of the funeral men, carried Noreen the length of the road. At the gates of St Bridget's, she was transferred to a trolley piled with flowers and wheeled to the front of the altar.

Father Mac gave a beautiful mass in her honour. Fergal sang 'I'll Take You Home Again, Kathleen' from the balcony as the procession made its way back down the aisle. Various shoulders took it in turn to carry her coffin along the Falls Road. Fergal waited until his brothers' efforts were relieved by distant relatives before he moved in to take a corner. He was surprised at how heavy it was, seeing that she'd weighed so little towards the end. At the gates of Milltown Cemetery, his family came to the front of the funeral procession, and he moved towards Father Mac for safety.

At the deep, freshly dug hole in the ground, Father Mac said a few words, and Angela and Concepta threw handfuls of earth onto their mother's coffin as it was lowered down. Fergal moved to his mother and kissed her cheek, but she was too far gone to notice, courtesy of another instalment of Concepta's wee pills.

He could feel his brothers and his da nearby, but they didn't come near him and he didn't go near them. All eyes were closed for the final prayer, but Fergal was distracted by a flock of starlings high up against the greyest sky ever, like lost strokes of ink in search of a blank page to begin recording the story of someone else's brand new life. He wondered if at that very moment a little girl was being born somewhere in the city, and if her parents might call her Noreen.

Once they trudged out of the cemetery, most people went across the road to the Gravedigger's Arms for too much whiskey with a watertight excuse. Grief was thirsty work.

Fergal and Father Mac went for a drive up to the lookout point on the Black Mountain. They parked and sat in silence for a while, watching the whole city of Belfast through the windscreen. Then they got out and walked along a nearby path. Fergal wondered what it would be like to hold Father Mac's hand in broad daylight – they had only ever held hands under the cover of night-time blankets – but he knew not to ask.

They could make out Samson and Delilah, the giant cranes that stood over the city, and Fergal thought he could see the Divis Flats, but he wasn't sure. It was the first time he had been so high above his hometown and yet it had only taken them about fifteen minutes in the car to get here.

'Belfast is tiny from here, isn't it?' he said.

'Sure, all of Ireland is a wee drop in the ocean when you look at the map of the world.'

Fergal felt very small at that moment, and all he wanted was to be held. They went back to the car and drove home. Mrs Mooney had left a note on the hall table saying that lunch was in the oven and she'd gone into the town for the afternoon. Fergal wasn't hungry and went up to his room to lie down. Just as he'd started unbuttoning his shirt, Father Mac appeared and helped him pull it off. Together, they reminded themselves that they were very much alive.

Inevitably the phone rang and Father Mac had to leave to visit a needy parishioner. Fergal stayed in bed. He couldn't stop replaying the funeral in his head. It was real. Noreen was dead and buried. He felt cold all of a sudden, as question after un-answered question filled his mind. Where was he going to live? What was going to happen to Noreen's house? It didn't seem fair that she hadn't owned it, after all the decades of rent she'd paid to the council – she must have paid for it three times over. It wasn't right that some stranger would end up getting it.

Fergal got up and ran a bath to wash the sex off his body. As he lay stretched out in the warm water with only his face above the surface, he had a vision of Noreen lying in the same position under the damp soil, in the freezing dark, all alone. He ducked his head underwater and wondered what it would feel like to be dead. He knew he could open his mouth, suck the bath water into his lungs and find out. Maybe it would be a way to see Granny Noreen again. But he knew that, more than anything, he wanted to stay alive and do something with his life that would have made her proud.

~

Father Mac came back just before six o'clock and announced that they were going to have a special dinner that night – and he himself was going to cook it. Mrs Mooney, phoning her husband to come and take her home early for the first time she could remember, didn't like the idea at all. Even though she complained often enough about having too much to do, she was fiercely protective of her kitchen. The previous priests in her care had been completely dependent on her – left to themselves, they would have burnt water – and that was the way she liked things. At least that way she knew where she was. She reckoned it was her job to help keep the priests' lives clean, and they helped her keep her soul clean. As her husband drove her away, she looked at herself in the passenger mirror and wondered if she looked old. Although she felt sorry for Fergal, she was beginning to resent him being there so much.

Father Mac was cooking pasta. As he laid out his ingredients, he said with a smile, 'You'll have to get used to pasta if this tutor takes a shine to you and invites you to go to Rome!'

Fergal looked puzzled. 'What? What are you talking about?'

'Don't you remember the phone call from Brother Vincent this morning? Sure, I told you all about it.'

'No.'

'Well, I suppose it's only natural – your mind was on other things. Look, sit down here and I'll tell you.'

Fergal uncorked the wine as Father Mac filled him in about Alfredo Moretti.

'So? What do you think of that?' Father Mac asked as he finished stirring the pasta sauce. 'I mean, it sounds promising, don't you think? You should definitely meet him.'

'I suppose.'

'You suppose? Are you…? Ah, look, you've had a very hard day. Let's take it as it comes, eh, Fergal? There's no need to look so worried.'

Fergal managed a half-smile. 'It's just that it sounds a bit too good to be true.' It was the kind of thing that only happened to other people, he thought, not to him.

'Imagine it – Italy! Wouldn't that be something?'

'It would… God, I'm nervous even thinking about it. You're going to be with me, aren't you – when we meet him?'

'Of course, of course.'

They agreed that they would meet him in Belfast. Going back to Sligo wasn't feasible for Father Mac as he couldn't take any more time away from his parish. He phoned Brother Vincent with the news.

After they had talked for a while, the excitable monk put Alfredo Moretti on. His English was perfect, but he found it hard to understand Father Mac's Northern Irish accent, and Father Mac's Italian went no further than the correct pronunciation of 'lasagna'. But they managed to establish that Alfredo would come to Belfast the very next day and they would meet him at the bus station.

Fergal was more nervous about the sudden visit than he had been about the recording that had prompted Alfredo's interest, because now he had something to live up to. He convinced himself that he had a sore throat, but Father Mac massaged his shoulders till they relaxed and reminded him that he'd survived an awful lot worse.

~

Alfredo Moretti, vocal master and former opera singer, certainly knew how to make an entrance. He was the first passenger to step off the Sligo bus in Belfast's central station, leaning on a walking stick. He was a corpulent man with a well-fed smile and enough raven-black hair for at least three people. He was dressed immaculately in a linen three-piece suit the colour of uncooked oats, with a broad-brimmed hat to match, and the contrast made his olive skin glow. Half the station stared, and someone said under his breath, 'Jesus wept, I hope we get the weather he's expecting.'

Alfredo kissed Father Mac and Fergal on each cheek – they both blushed, but they were delighted. As they drove the short distance to St Bridget's House, he talked constantly and pointed out every wall mural, asking excitedly about the 'street artists'.

Mrs Mooney had cut a cake and boiled the tea just as they arrived. When Alfredo asked politely for coffee, she nearly impaled herself on the railings outside for not having thought of it. She blessed herself before lying from the kitchen, 'Found it, Father! I'll just be two ticks boiling that kettle.' Then she shuffled out the back door towards Magill's shop as fast as her short legs would allow. She almost got killed crossing the road on her way back, clutching two jars of coffee as though her life depended on it.

Alfredo Moretti had been a celebrated opera singer in Italy for many years, but his leg had been injured in a car accident and it had never healed properly because he refused to rest. He had been left reliant on his walking stick and when the constant treadmill of touring and recording had become too exhausting for him, he had decided to detour into teaching. Now in his late forties, he had taught some of the leading voices in the world of classical music.

After their tea and coffee, Alfredo asked to see the chapel, so they went up to the balcony, where the organ was waiting. Alfredo could tell Fergal was nervous. He sat down at the keyboard and played a little of the 'Ave Maria'. He hummed a bit of the melody and then said, 'Fergal, come here – help me with this, will you?'

Father Mac nodded and Fergal moved to the organ and began singing, his voice gradually gaining strength as he relaxed into the music. They were about halfway through when two drunks burst into the church arguing about whose turn it was to go and rob drink, screaming obscenities at each other. Father Mac hurried downstairs to break it up. He returned mortified and full of apologies, but Alfredo reminded him he was Italian and not unused to passionate exchanges of opinion. 'Father MacManus, that was like a little scene from an opera.' They all laughed.

'Shall we go back to the parlour?' Alfredo suggested. He found the acoustics of the church a little distracting and wanted to hear Fergal in a smaller space with a cleaner sound. Fergal was convinced that he hated his voice and felt miserable.

Back in St Bridget's House, Alfredo asked, 'May I use the piano?'

As he looked through the pile of music on the shelf, he came across a collection of arias. 'Ah, Father McManus, I see you are not only an opera fan but a Puccini fan too!'

Father Mac nodded. 'I love the sound of the Italian language – it's so melodic.'

'Well, then, open the book at any page you like and I will teach Fergal a little something!'

Fergal nodded nervously.

Without looking, Father Mac opened the book. When he put his selection on the piano, Alfredo's eyebrows leapt.

'"Recondita Armonia" from *Tosca*? Ah, I have not looked at this for a while. There is nothing like being thrown into deep water, is there, Mr Flynn? But we don't have to do it all now. It is for two voices, so I will join in.'

He began teaching Fergal the first passage of Italian, going through the notes and writing out the words phonetically for him. Over the next twenty minutes, Father Mac flushed with pride as Fergal rose to the challenge. The new language suited his voice – even though his accent still came through on every other word – and he sang beautifully.

They finished the piece and Alfredo sat quietly looking at the piano keys. Fergal shot a worried glance at Father Mac, who said nothing.

Then Alfredo carefully turned around on the stool, leaning on his cane. 'Fergal, your tone reminds me of one of my favourite singers in all the world. His name is Tito Schipa and he possessed one of the finest voices ever to be recorded. Have you ever heard him?'

'No, Mr Moretti.'

'You will, my boy – you must. There are notes that you don't yet know exist, but they are only sleeping because you haven't woken them – and I feel I could. You are using only about half of your range, but your tone, even at this stage, is naturally beautiful – and it will be much more beautiful in ten years, if you work hard enough. Are you prepared to work harder than you ever thought possible? It means singing and studying for hours every day – oh, yes, and you must learn Italian. You are young, so we have time. How young are you, by the way?'

Fergal was staring at him in disbelief, but he managed to say, 'I'm seventeen.'

'Ah, I thought you were a little older. Perfect.'

Father Mac couldn't help interrupting. 'Mr Moretti, what exactly are you saying?'

Alfredo cleared his throat and said, 'I want Fergal to come study with me in Rome, as soon as possible. This kind of voice is not found every day, and it would be a sin not to offer him the chance to explore its full potential.'

Fergal thought he was hearing things and wondered if he was going mad with delayed grief. He needed to be alone. He excused himself and went and sat on the toilet lid for a few minutes. He felt Noreen's St Christopher medal on his chest and pulled it out of his shirt. The patron saint of travellers was wading through water, carrying a child on his shoulders. Fergal kissed the medal then flushed the toilet and went back to the parlour.

Father Mac and Alfredo were deep in discussion about organising a fundraising concert to pay for Fergal's travel expenses. Alfredo said he was prepared to waive his usual fee. 'And my family owns several restaurants, so Fergal can have a job at one of these. This will also be an excellent way for him to learn Italian – he will be surrounded by it every day – but most of my family speak English, so it will not be too difficult for him to talk with them!'

Fergal watched them discussing his future. Finally he broke in, 'What if my parents won't let me go? I'm not eighteen yet.'

Father Mac looked at him and said, very seriously, 'Fergal, there are always ways of doing things. I promised your granny that I'd make sure you didn't waste your life – or let anyone waste it for you. Don't you worry about anything, my friend.'

Alfredo laughed. 'Bravo, Father MacManus! So, Fergal Flynn, do you want to come to Rome?'

Every question that had been weighing Fergal down, particularly since Noreen's death, suddenly flooded his mind. What was he going to do with his life? Would he ever escape Belfast? Where – and, indeed, how – was he going to live? As he looked at Alfredo Moretti's huge smile, the questions evaporated one by one.

'Yes – yes, of course I'd love to come to Rome. I want to be a singer more than anything in the world, Mr Moretti. Thank you – oh, thank you!'

Fergal's eyes filled up, and Alfredo hugged him. 'We singers are very emotional people. This is a good sign, my boy!'

That made them all laugh, but a sore patch of sadness was growing in the quietest corner of Father Mac's heart. Fergal didn't even dare think about the one remaining question in his mind – the most troubling one of all – how would he be able to leave Father Mac?

They talked for another hour or so and listened to some of the Sligo Abbey recording again, then Father Mac played a few of the songs he and Fergal had been working on. Alfredo asked if he could see a little of Belfast before he caught his train to Dublin Airport, so Father Mac drove them into town and they found a parking space not far from City Hall. The security presence was high as they walked around the town, and Alfredo asked, 'Why are there so many soldiers with guns? And half of the vehicles seem to belong to the army… Why is this?'

Father Mac said, 'I'll explain another time,' and Alfredo realised he should drop the subject. They stumbled on an Italian café and Alfredo, discovering the owner was from Northern Italy, chatted to him in Italian. Fergal thought the language sounded beautiful. Someday, he thought, someday I might be able to speak it…

Their espressos arrived and as Fergal drank down the dark warmth, Alfredo asked him about his family.

'Are there any other singers in your family, Fergal? What about your father – or, indeed, your mother?'

'God, I don't think so, Mr Moretti. My grandfather used to sing a wee bit, I think, but he died just before I was born, so I never heard him.'

'Ah, I see. And your brothers – you say you have three of them?'

Fergal didn't want to think about his brothers. At the funeral, the mere sight of John had made him shiver as his body remembered the beating. He couldn't stop his shoulders tightening. 'I... well, I don't think they care too much about singing. We're – we're not close... Well, they're mad about sport and I'm not.'

Alfredo laughed throatily, but it wasn't lost on him that Fergal's expression grew a little darker and his voice a little more strained with each question about his family.

When Fergal went to the toilet, Father Mac explained, 'Things with his family are a bit difficult to put it mildly. That's why he's been staying at St Bridget's. Well, if the worst comes to the worst and he can't go until he's eighteen, it'll give us more time to raise money.'

Fergal returned just as Alfredo pointed to his watch. As they said goodbye at the station, they were a bit more prepared for the two kisses that Alfredo automatically planted on each of them. Then he tapped his way down the platform with his walking stick, waved it in the air and boarded a first-class carriage on the southbound train.

~

That night, Fergal couldn't sleep. His head kept replaying the meeting with Alfredo, and he felt a sudden rush of excitement about leaving Belfast behind – living in a different country from his family, never having to worry about bumping into John again… Noreen's face floated in front of him, and he whispered to the quiet room, 'Granny, I miss you – I do. I wish I could tell you about Mr Moretti. He wants me to go to Rome – Rome! You always said you wanted to go there and visit the Pope, didn't you? I'll tell him you said hello… if Ma and Da let me get a passport.'

In his thoughts, his father's angry voice said again, *You're no son of mine!* Fergal wanted to shout back, *If I'd had the choice, I wouldn't have picked you for my father, either, so you can go and fuck yourself!* He was happy to be estranged from his family, but there was a part of him that still wanted to punish them – and another, more deeply buried part that wanted them to say they were sorry. He just wanted one of them to say that they'd made a mistake.

He rolled over, but sleep wouldn't come. The window had been fixed, but the frame was old, and there was a gap in one corner just big enough for a draught to slip into his room. He wondered if Father Mac was asleep. He got out from under the blankets, shivering, and tiptoed out onto the cold floorboards of the landing. When he saw that Father Mac's light was still on, he tapped the door gently.

'Dermot? Dermot, are you still up?'

Father Mac had been reading. He appeared at the door in his pyjama bottoms, with his hair sticking up at the back. The sight of his chest made Fergal's heart quicken.

'Are you all right?'

'I am, but I can't sleep. What time is it?'

'It's… my goodness, it's four o'clock.'

Fergal looked down at his bare feet. 'Dermot, can I… can I get in with you?'

Father Mac's heart raced too, and he paused for a second before opening the door wider. 'Well, just for a while. You can't stay the whole night. Remember what we said.'

They lay under the covers, more awake than ever.

'What a day, eh, Fergal? No wonder we can't sleep.'

'I know. I thought I was hearing things when Mr Moretti started talking about Rome and all.'

'He seems like a very genuine person.'

'Yeah. But he looks like a detective off the TV or something, doesn't he – with his walking stick and all?'

They laughed.

'So why can't you sleep, then? Are you worried about something in particular – like going away?'

There was a long silence. Then Fergal said, 'What's going to happen, Dermot?'

'What do you mean?'

'I mean, what's going to happen with… us?'

Fergal swallowed hard. Father Mac turned away and lay on his back, looking at the ceiling rose as if the answer might be written in its circle.

'Well, I think this is the kind of opportunity that doesn't come along every day. And you deserve everything it may bring. It's just the beginning for you. Me… well, my life here is just beginning too in its own way – the parish is just starting to accept me, and… well, my place is here. And you need to go where your voice takes you.'

263

Fergal closed his eyes and whispered, 'But maybe you could come with me?'

Father Mac turned around, and Fergal saw that his eyes were wet. 'Ah, Fergal, thank you for wanting me to. It means so much. If things were different, then who knows what would happen? But, at the end of the day, I'm a priest – if I weren't, we would never have met. Anyway, it's not up to me. The bishop decides where I go, and Rome is hardly starved of priests, now is it?'

He'd hoped to make Fergal laugh, but it didn't work.

'But—'

'Fergal, you haven't even left yet. There's so much that's good about what's happening. Let's just try and think about that.'

'You're right, I know you're right. But… I'll miss you.'

'Ah, fella, the thought of not seeing you is… hard to think about – I won't lie to you. But it's not as hard as the thought of seeing you waste your potential. Look, let's just take one day at a time and cross whatever bridges we come to, OK? Right now, there's a lot of work to be done to raise the money to even get you to Italy.'

'I know.'

'How do you feel about doing a solo concert here in Belfast?'

Fergal sat up. 'Really?'

Father Mac was glad that he'd been able to steer him away from the difficult conversation that he knew they would have to have eventually. 'Yes, really. We'll advertise everywhere – maybe we can get the local papers involved… Wait till you see, Fergal, it's going to be brilliant. And one day people will say, "Sure, I saw Fergal Flynn in the local hall before he was famous, you know!"'

This time Fergal did laugh, and they moved closer to each other. Father Mac switched off the bedside lamp and they kissed.

Fergal wanted more than anything to feel what it was like to have Father Mac inside him, wanting them to experience everything they possibly could together. He moved Father Mac's hand down between his legs and took hold of his erection. Fergal made him let go and pushed his hand further south. They kissed hungrily, and Fergal widened his legs and encouraged Father Mac's finger to start the careful journey into him. It was painful at first; he flinched and cried out. 'Jesus!'

'Oh, Fergal, sorry—'

'No, Dermot. Keep going.'

'Are you sure?'

'Definitely. Kiss me, Dermot. Keep kissing me.'

So, very slowly, he relaxed and began to move against Father Mac's finger, and gradually it grew more and more pleasurable. Fergal widened his legs further, pushed a pillow under his back and pulled Father Mac's full weight on top of him. Father Mac kissed his forehead, which was soaking with sweat. Fergal could feel his thick erection pressed against his belly.

'Dermot, I don't want to leave you without knowing what's it like to have… Will you… will you go inside me?'

Father Mac looked at him. 'Are you sure?'

Fergal nodded his head and pushed his erection further down.

'Look, the second you want me to stop, I will, OK?'

'OK.'

Father Mac took hold of his hardness and slowly guided the tip of himself into Fergal. Fergal held his breath, expecting it to be agony for a moment, then he exhaled as their bodies began to join, bit by bit. He knew they could never be closer than they were at that moment.

'I don't want to hurt you—'

'Dermot, aren't you supposed to… you know, spit or something?'

Father Mac remembered hearing about people doing that. He withdrew, spat on his fingers and rubbed them on himself, then on the place where he'd just been. Little by little, he slid inside Fergal again. Fergal loved the smell of him, the feel of his weight. He held on to the backs of Father Mac's thighs and breathed in time with his gentle motion. A deep calm surrounded him. He had never felt so close to another human being in his life.

'How does it feel, Fergal?'

'It… it's great. You can do it a wee bit… harder if you like.'

Father Mac began to move more firmly against him. He too had never felt so deeply connected to another person, and his heart had never felt so full. At that moment they both felt that their very souls had melted into each other.

The last thing Father Mac wanted to do was let Fergal go, but it felt so good that he knew he wouldn't be able to last. 'I have… I have to stop.'

Gradually their movements slowed again, and Father Mac carefully withdrew and lay on top of Fergal. Their kissing was like another language. Fergal wrapped his legs tightly around Father Mac's waist and felt as if he could stay that way forever.

Then Father Mac asked, 'Do you want to… to try?' and Fergal heard himself say, 'Yeah.'

Father Mac rolled over onto his stomach and Fergal climbed on top of him. It took a few giggly attempts before he succeeded in entering him, tentatively, knowing how tender it could be. Then, slowly but surely, they found a steady rhythm. Fergal had never felt pleasure like it.

'Oh, Fergal…that feels fantastic…'

Father Mac arched his back so he could touch himself. When they were near to finishing, their bodies parted and they rolled over, side by side and out of breath. They reached for each other's hardness, kissing slowly and lovingly before, simultaneously, their bodies stiffened in release. Their gasps subsided and they moved closer, their arms entangling in an effort to stay warm and in the moment. As they submitted to the calming waves of a brief, untroubled sleep, Fergal felt as though Father Mac had reached inside him and healed every wound that John had inflicted. He ached in a completely new way.

After about half an hour, Father Mac was the first to come back to the surface. He saw how peaceful Fergal looked as he slept. He didn't want to disturb him, but he knew he had to. Fergal would have to go back to his own room – Mrs Mooney had her own key, and she seemed to be arriving earlier every week.

Father Mac had been almost glad that Mrs Mooney suspected something more than friendship was blossoming between him and Fergal. He had always known their affair couldn't last and she had given him the excuse he needed to begin dismantling it. That night had been the most intimate they had ever spent together but, as soon as the heat was gone, he could feel his heart heading back to shore. Fergal would have to swim the rest of the way alone.

He leaned over and shook Fergal's arm gently.

'Five more minutes, Dermot – come on…'

Father Mac got up. He was craving a cigarette and his pack was in his coat pocket down in the hallway. While he was gone,

Fergal opened his eyes drowsily and looked at the empty space in the bed. The warm sense of love that he had felt was replaced by loss. Somewhere, a part of him started to see that what they had could never last.

He got up and went to his own room, before Father Mac could come back. He didn't want him to see his face.

23

The brightly coloured poster for the upcoming concert took pride of place in the frosted windows of Moore's family shop.

Saturday, 25th August

A very special concert with local singing sensation
FERGAL FLYNN!

Help send our local lad to the home of the Pope to study
with one of the world's greatest teachers!

Come and hear the voice of an angel as he prepares to take flight!

Concert starts at 7.30 p.m. sharp
Venue: St Bridget's Assembly Hall

All are welcome, so come and support your own!
(Tea and biscuits available.)

Underneath was a photo of Fergal, with his hair combed to attention and a half-smile, trying not to look mortified.

Moore's shop was the kind of place that sold anything and everything. You could buy a light bulb, a school blazer, three slices of bacon and a packet of custard, all from the same shelf, and pay them off in weekly instalments. Loaves of fresh bread dusted with flour sat in warm racks along the counter, but not for long. As soon as old Mr Moore opened the front door, the first flock of mothers snapped them up and buried them deep in their shopping bags, with maybe a slice of ham wrapped in grease-proof paper for the husband's lunch. Vinyl records, mostly by overdressed singers nobody had heard of, were hung on a line with clothes-pegs, like frozen washing. Underneath were glass jars of out-of-reach sweets and tins of stewed steak, which were bought for Sunday pies at the end of the month if mothers and fathers were feeling flush enough.

Fergal's poster campaign found its way onto every notice-board and telegraph pole in the tiny area and, in spite of the addition of the odd Hitler moustache or glasses, the signs were mostly greeted with interest. Inevitably, people stopped Angela in the street to remark on how proud she must feel, and for once she was lost for words. A few men made the mistake of bringing it up with Paddy – a poster had found its way onto a wall in the betting shop – but they quickly changed the subject when they saw his taut expression and felt the swift change of temperature in the smoky room. The Flynn brothers were struck dumb, especially John. On the bus to the brewery, the morning after the posters went up, he had to face the questions of old schoolmates who'd ended up in the same job – it was that or the dole, and they were all in a hurry to be men. He walked home that evening, disgusted and tore down three of the posters on the way.

~

On the afternoon of the concert, Fergal and Father Mac drove to the empty car park of St Bridget's Secondary School, where the caretaker let them into the deserted assembly hall to rehearse their repertoire – traditional songs, hymns that the audience would recognise and 'Annie's Song' by John Denver. Father Mac thought Fergal needed to rehearse at least once in the actual room where the concert was going to be held. They went to the music room and Baldy Turner helped them wheel the upright piano down the corridors, leaving a trail on the plastic tiles. Fergal was shivering from head to toe. He couldn't work out whether it was because the heating hadn't kicked in or because of pure nerves. Father Mac reminded him, 'I'll be right there beside you the whole time. You want to make Noreen proud, don't you?' That did the trick and he stopped shaking.

As Father Mac adjusted the height of the piano stool, Fergal looked out at the bare wooden floor and remembered the terror of lining up there in his ill-fitting blazer six years before, to be called into his class for the first time. How many thousands of times had he stood there, year after year, getting taller, broader, hairier, wishing that he could be somewhere else – only to wake up one morning with nothing but a few exam results to prove he'd been there at all? That frightened eleven-year-old could never have imagined that he'd end up doing what he was about to do that evening.

The concert was sold out. Almost everyone from the area turned up, more out of curiosity than anything else. The tea and biscuits did a roaring trade, there was something about eating them in a school hall that made them tastier somehow.

The nerves had returned, in neat bundles, in the middle of Fergal's stomach. He had been given one of the PE changing rooms as a dressing room – he laughed out loud at the irony. He'd already had a long, roasting bath at Father Mac's house and combed his hair until his head was sore. He could hear voices and footsteps as people were directed down the corridors to their wooden seats borrowed from the classrooms. One past pupil said reminiscently, 'The place hasn't changed much, has it? It's still boggin', so it is!'

Fergal waited backstage as the principal gave a monotonous speech and then introduced Father MacManus. He said some very embarrassing things about Fergal, who thought his heart was going to jump out of his mouth. Then, all of a sudden, he heard the wave of applause that meant it was time to face the music.

He felt like he was floating as he moved across the makeshift stage that was only used for the local slimmers' club and Christmas concerts. He was blinded by a single spotlight and deafened by the silence. He heard Father Mac play the first few chords of the opening hymn, 'Be Thou My Vision'.

His voice wobbled a bit at the start – he'd forgotten to breathe, but Father Mac reminded him with exaggerated swells of his chest. Frustrated with himself, Fergal stamped his foot on the floorboards in defiance, and the strength returned to his voice, to fill every corner of doubt in the hall. He closed his eyes and sent the words into the air like little hopeful balloons, waiting for the wind to carry the trapped breath to a different world.

At the end of the hymn, the applause rippled and then grew as thunderous as the waves on the Sligo strand. Father Mac, at the piano, turned the enormous manuscript pages of sheet music to a County Down song called 'The Flower of Magherally'. Fergal's eyes were getting used to the light, and he couldn't help looking for members of his family or people he knew. The only person he recognised was a friend of his mother's, who was smiling hugely and seemed to be having a great time. Behind her was the oldest man in the area, who had a plastic nose because his real one had been bitten off by a dog. No one usually sat beside him because if you looked closely you could see right into his skull.

As the night went on, Fergal felt more and more confident. Some of the older people in the audience joined in softly with the songs they knew. The whole concert seemed to go incredibly quickly and, in no time, Fergal found himself saying, 'This is the last song of the evening', which was greeted by friendly complaining from the back. When Father Mac played the introduction to 'Annie's Song', there was a murmur of delight, and someone squealed, 'Oh, Jesus, I love this one, so I do!' Fergal found himself laughing as he sang the first few lines:

You filled up my senses, like a night in a forest,
Like a mountain in springtime, like a walk in the rain,
Like a storm in a desert, like a sleepy blue ocean,
You filled up my senses – come fill me again...

Most of the room joined in, singing sweetly, with every chorus (although a few of the men sat with their arms folded, thinking that he sounded too much like a girl). Fergal had relaxed enough to enjoy the participation and swayed and stretched his arms out to encourage them. He shot a glance at Father Mac for approval, but the priest had his eyes shut, lost in the moment, and that made Fergal even happier.

When he left the stage, the applause was wild. The principal gave Fergal a push, and he inched reluctantly back on stage and pointed towards Father Mac at the piano. The crowd roared their appreciation. A few people were even standing up. The caretaker, who thought the concert was over, had turned the lights up, and Fergal saw his mother clapping nervously at the edge of the audience.

The clapping didn't stop and Fergal looked at Father Mac with widened eyes that said, *What now?* They suddenly realised they hadn't prepared an encore. Fergal was going to suggest doing 'Annie's Song' again, but Father Mac gestured for silence and asked the audience for requests. Someone at the back shouted, 'Here, Fergal, can you whistle?', and there was a roar of laughter, followed by a few older women waving their good handbags and warning the shouter to behave.

Under cover of the noise, Father Mac whispered, 'You see? They're fighting over you already!'

'What'll we do?'

'What about something unaccompanied?'

Fergal's eyes lit up and he said, 'I'll have a go at "Carrickfergus".' For a moment he had thought of singing 'I'll Take You Home Again, Kathleen', but he knew it would make him cry.

His sweet, high tenor delivered the first line, 'I wish I was in Carrickfergus…' and a ripple of recognition washed forward, leaving the rest of the hall silent, hanging on every word. It was one of those songs that nobody remembered learning but everybody knew. It was as if he'd said, 'Once upon a time…' to a room full of children.

When he came to the chorus, the women were the first to join in, but gradually even the manliest men could hold back no longer, though they stalled at the lines, 'I wish I could find a handsome boatman to ferry me over to my love and die.' Fergal tried not to look at Father Mac, but the song took him over, their eyes met for a split second and he was overcome with loss.

He began the last verse, 'And in Belfast, it is reported, there are marble stones as black as ink.' The audience giggled approval, noticing that he had changed the city from Kilkenny to Belfast. Then they grew quieter still. He could hear the blades of an army helicopter patrolling in the distance, and to him it was like the sound of leaving. Then the last chorus ambushed the sadness, and the whole audience sang their hearts out.

Sure, I'm drunk today, and I'm seldom sober,
A handsome rover from town to town.
Ah, but I'm sick now and my days are numbered.
So come, all ye young men, and lay me down...
So come, all ye young men, and lay me down.

The audience instinctively dropped out before the last line, and Fergal finished alone, as he had started. His solo voice owned the air again before finally coming to rest in the darkness.

The audience erupted, stamping their feet and cheering. Fergal bowed awkwardly and vanished off the stage. Father Mac followed him into the wings and hugged him till he thought he would stop breathing. The principal came onto the stage and called them back out to take a final bow together. All the lights were back on, and all the audience were on their feet. Fergal looked for his mother, but she was gone.

They went back to the changing room. Fergal was surprised at how much he'd sweated – his shirt was soaked through. He loosened it around the waist and tried to waft cool air up his back, and Father Mac gave him a towel.

'How do you feel, Fergal? How do you feel? Your first *sold-out* concert!'

Fergal looked into his eyes. 'I couldn't have done it without you.'

'Ah, now, somehow I don't think that's true. That encore took the roof off.'

They moved towards each other, but then remembered where they were and thought better of it.

There was a knock at the door. It was the principal saying that there were some people waiting to meet their local star. Fergal was still flushed from the spotlight, and he went even redder with embarrassment. He and Father Mac were greeted with smiles of appreciation, and the older women couldn't stop hugging Fergal. One of them had known Noreen, and she started to cry as she told Fergal how proud his granny would have been if she'd lived to see his first performance. It almost set him off, but Father Mac reminded them that Noreen had had the best seat in the house, at God's side, and she wouldn't have wanted anyone to feel sad on such a joyous night.

A reporter from the *Andersonstown News* was interested in doing a story on Fergal, if he and Father MacManus wouldn't mind answering a few questions. He asked them how the extraordinary opportunity had come about, how long they had known each other, when Fergal had realised he could sing... As he and Father Mac told the story together, it struck Fergal just how amazing the whole thing was. But it was real – he really was going to Rome to study singing.

The reporter's last questions were about his family. Surely they were going to miss him? Were they available for a photograph? Father Mac came to the rescue. 'Naturally they're proud of Fergal and excited about his good fortune, but they're very private people.' Luckily, that seemed to satisfy the reporter.

He took a few photographs of Fergal and Father Mac, standing side by side in front of the 'SOLD OUT' poster on the door of the assembly hall, smiling into the lens, embarrassed but happy. Between the concert and a donation from the school, they had raised the money for Fergal's trip to Rome.

By the time they got back to St Bridget's House, it was much later than they had expected. Father Mac made a pot of tea and they sat on the sofa, drinking it by the kinder light of a few candles. Fergal's head rested on the cushion by Father Mac's shoulder. They said nothing. They just listened to each other's breathing while the fire sang to itself in a high melancholy voice, sending the tune up the chimney to the answering wind.

They leaned closer to each other. Fergal rested his hand gently on Father Mac's face and traced a line around his lips with the tip of his finger, loving the roughness of his new stubble. Father Mac opened his mouth and took Fergal's finger into it. They kissed slowly, like lovers who hadn't tasted each other for a while and needed to remind themselves, silently and lovingly.

Father Mac peeled Fergal's shirt back to kiss his bare shoulders before Fergal pushed Father Mac's jumper over his head and stroked his breastbone. The hallway clock clacked in its case like an old horse moving carefully down a cobbled lane. They sought the floor and lay in each other's arms by the warmth of the fire. Fergal wanted to spend the whole night there, but it would have been quite a sight for Mrs Mooney when she arrived the next morning. He giggled to himself, picturing her face.

Father Mac was lost in thought too. He was remembering the look on Fergal's face as he sang. He had never seen him look as happy. Father Mac knew he was going to lose him, not only to Rome and Alfredo Moretti, but to another way of thinking. It was only natural, when someone as young and as curious and as hungry as Fergal went into the world. Fergal was literally about to learn another language, one that Father Mac wouldn't be able to understand, and was about to experience new places and people from which Father Mac would be excluded. Inevitably, new possibilities of love would present themselves, and a priest living far away in Belfast would never be able to compete. A cocktail of grief and joy made Father Mac's heart full and heavy, but when Fergal's eyes looked for the reason his lover was so distant, he pretended everything was fine.

They moved upstairs and continued their lovemaking under fresh white sheets, laundered to perfection as if for the altar. There was a desperation in the sex that was new and exciting, but as soon as they were spent they separated. Fergal went to his own room and fell asleep quickly.

~

Early the next morning, Father Mac got a phone call from Alfredo Moretti. 'How was the concert received, my friend?'

'It couldn't have gone any better,' Father Mac told him happily. 'We raised even more money than we expected.'

Alfredo was delighted. Then he asked delicately, 'The situation with Fergal's family... has it changed at all? Do you think they will give permission for him to get the passport?'

'That's my next priority,' Father Mac assured him. 'I think my best bet is his mother, if I can get her on her own. There's no talking to his father.'

'I wish you luck,' Alfredo said. 'I will await your news impatiently. There will be so much to organise, if he can indeed travel soon.'

When Father Mac put the phone down, he sighed heavily. Looking up, he saw a bleary-eyed Fergal sitting at the top of the stairs. Mrs Mooney, bustling in, took one look at Fergal and asked – she had, of course, been to the concert – 'Why are you looking so downhearted? You've every reason in the world to be the happiest fella in Belfast.'

'Sorry,' Fergal said. 'I'm just tired.'

'Ach, I'm not surprised, love. I don't know how you got up in front of all them people and sang like you did. I'd have been dying, so I would.' She turned on her foam-slippered heel and headed for the kitchen.

'That was Alfredo,' Father Mac said. 'He wanted to know about your passport. I told him it's next on my list.'

'There's no chance my parents will let me go,' Fergal said. 'What's the point in getting our hopes up?'

Father Mac tutted and raised his eyebrows in mock despair. 'Fergal Flynn, what are you like? Sitting at the top of the stairs feeling all sorry for yourself... Come down here a minute till I remind you of a few very important facts that you seem to have forgotten.'

Fergal exhaled heavily and descended the stairs one by one, as if his legs weighed a ton.

Father Mac brought him into the parlour and put a hand on his shoulder. 'Now, did you or did you not perform a sold-out show last night and get a standing ovation?'

'Well… yes, but—'

'Fergal, look at how your life has transformed completely in the last while. You did really well in your exams, you made your first recording, Alfredo wants you to move to Rome – and now, after the concert, we've raised enough money to send you there. How can you stand there and say there's no point in getting our hopes up? There's every point. Look, your mother may be a lot of things, but she's not the devil – it's not like she'll deliberately stand in your way. She just has to be very careful. She's married to your father, remember, and she's afraid of what he'll do if he finds out she's helped you. But I'll convince her that it's the right thing to do. If my plan works, he'll never even find out.'

'What plan, Der— I mean, Father?'

'Look, Mr Flynn of little faith, my plan is simple – and I have a promise to keep to your Granny Noreen, God rest her soul.'

They both blessed themselves.

'No one, but no one, is going to stop you doing what you were put on this earth to do. You were given this gift so you could share it with as many people as possible, and it's a huge responsibility. Look at how happy you made all those people last night. You transported them. I'm going to see your mother as soon as I can pick up the passport forms from the post office. The worst-case scenario is that you'll have to wait another few months, until you're eighteen – but I honestly don't think it'll come to that, fella. Look, let's just stop talking about all this for now.'

They ate their fried breakfast while listening to the morning news on the radio. Two young men, Fergal's age, had been shot dead during the night, in the playing fields not far from where John had attacked him. He recognised their names – they had been at St Bridget's with him and one of them had sometimes called to Walker Street to go to matches with his brothers. Fergal shuddered. They hadn't even been men yet, and now their lives were over.

Fergal and Father Mac went to the post office together, and Fergal was surprised at how many people stopped them to congratulate him on the concert. Even people who normally wouldn't have given him the time of day grabbed his hand and almost shook it off his arm, telling him he'd better remember them when he was famous. He was mortified, of course, but, in some small way, it confirmed everything that Father Mac had ever said to him.

They got the passport forms and went to Devine's chemist on Springfield Road, so Fergal could get passport pictures in the photo booth. He fixed his hair self-consciously in the booth's little mirror, while other customers spotted the priest and changed their minds about what they had come into the chemist's to buy. When the four pictures came out, he looked shy and slightly startled – except in the last one, where he had pulled in an unsuspecting Father Mac from behind the curtain and they had pushed their faces towards the lens, laughing hysterically. The flash had captured the moment beautifully, and the photo made them laugh all over again.

When they got home, Father Mac helped Fergal fill out the form that would change his life for good.

24

It was early in the afternoon by the time Father Mac got a chance to check the hurling championship timetable in the local paper. He drove along the Falls Road and stopped near the top of Walker Street, outside the Flynn house, just as the Flynn men were heading into Casement Park a few miles up the road. As usual, the eagle-eyed neighbours sprang into action, scrubbing their steps and shaking rugs out their front doors, to demonstrate that their homes – and therefore obviously their souls – were spotless. Father Mac nodded to them and blessed himself before knocking at the Flynns' door.

Angela came to the door wiping her flour-powdered hands on her skirt and chewing on an enormous lump of toasted soda bread. When she saw who it was, she panicked, tried to swallow the buttery mush too quickly and choked. Father Mac slapped her between the shoulder blades with his flattened hand, and the half-chewed lump of bread shot into the road and down the drain. A few concerned women ran over to see if they could become more heavily involved, but Father Mac thanked them politely but firmly and made his way behind the hall door.

'Oh, Jesus, Mary and St Joseph I'm disgraced, so I am, Father!' Angela was still gathering her breath. 'I could've choked there and then on the doorstep in front of the whole street, only for you. Will you take a cup of tea? I was just having one myself when I heard you at the door.'

She went out to the kitchen, talking all the while and not waiting for answers. 'Them there sodas is as hard as bricks – Jesus, you'd be better off throwing them at the… Well, just wait till I see that wee twisty-eyed man in the bakery. I'll bust his frigging hole! Oh, sorry, Father, but only for you I'd have been dead. Sure, God is good. It's a miracle, that's what it is.'

She reappeared with two cups of steaming tea and two currant squares – most kids hated them and called them 'flies' graveyards', but they were a national favourite because they were so sweet and cheap. 'My husband and the boys are all away to the hurling final' – Angela was off again, going at full speed from nerves – 'and it's pure luxury to have the place to myself for a change.'

'I'm sorry for calling with no warning,' Father Mac said, 'but it's important. I couldn't leave it any longer, especially after the success of the concert.'

'Oh, God, Father, I'm sorry I didn't stay and see youse after the show. But Fergal reminded me so much of my own father that… well, I started to cry, and I didn't want anyone to see. Daddy used to sing wee bits of "Carrickfergus" to the air in the morning, when I was only a girl. He'd be out in the yard, breaking up the coal to get the fire going – he thought nobody could hear him so early. Then he'd call us down when the room was warm. Oh, he was so kind...' Her voice trailed off for a second and she seemed to shiver, then she was off again at breakneck speed. 'Fergal's da couldn't come to the concert – he hasn't been feeling too great these past weeks, and he went to bed early that night.'

She looked away and dried her eyes on the corner of her sleeve. She knew rightly that Father Mac knew she was lying. On the night of the concert, she had told her husband that she was going to visit her sister Concepta. Paddy had sent Ciaran for a bottle of whiskey that she found empty on the table beside a cold fish supper when, later that evening, she had slipped back into their life again.

Suddenly she stopped. 'Is Fergal all right? Is something wrong again, Father?'

'No, no, he's never been better.' Father Mac leaned towards her and said softly, 'But he needs your help, Angela – if I may call you Angela?'

She looked puzzled. 'Listen, Father MacManus, if there's one boy out of my brood that never needed anybody, it's our Fergal.'

'Ah, Angela, that's not true.' He took the passport form out of his pocket and explained why they needed her to sign it, and the promise that he'd made to poor old Noreen.

She was instantly afraid of anything vaguely official. Father Mac remembered what Fergal had told him – she'd had to leave school when she was only thirteen to work in the linen factory, and her reading and writing had never got a chance to go beyond what she'd picked up from the other girls. Fergal had told him how he was her dictionary and her calculator. When it came to reading anything or writing notes to teachers, she would fly into a rage if he wasn't sure about a certain word and stab him with the broken end of the pen, which she'd crushed with her teeth in pure frustration. Sometimes, if she was in one of her dark, unreachable moods, Fergal wouldn't even bother showing her things, he'd just reply in her handwriting.

Angela took a pair of glasses out of her bag and held them at arm's length, just like Noreen used to do, scanning the passport form. 'When there's anything needing to be signed, I usually leave it to my husband. He went to the best grammar school, you know, Father, right up until his oul' da died.' She put the form down.

Father Mac put his hand over hers. 'Mrs Flynn – Angela – here's your chance to do one of the most important things you could ever do for Fergal's future.' He looked at the Sacred Heart above the TV where Noreen's mass card leaned by the red bulb. 'Angela, he needs you to do this, or he'll have to wait until he's eighteen. There's only so much I can teach him, you know, I'm not a proper vocal coach like Alfredo Moretti. He's offered Fergal the chance of a lifetime – and when you sign this consent form, you'll help send him on his way. There really isn't a second to waste. The sooner Fergal starts to have proper training, the quicker he'll reach his full potential. You want him to do that, don't you? I know your mother did. Look, Angela, all of you were so generous to give that money the other night at the concert – you wouldn't want to see it wasted, would you?'

She was turning her cup in her hands, like a child trying to read the tea leaves. The overfed fire was making both of them sweat. Angela glanced up at the framed picture of her mother and father, hanging on the opposite wall.

'So, Angela, will you sign his passport form? Will you?' Father Mac asked, as softly as he could.

At last she nodded. 'But I don't have a pen.'

He produced a silver one from his inside pocket and she placed her little-girl's signature in all the places he had highlighted. When she was done, he folded the paper precisely and put it next to his heart for safekeeping.

'You've done a great thing,' he reassured her. Then he read her quick upward glance and added, 'And don't worry – I promise your husband will never find out.'

As he turned out of Walker Street, Father Mac looked in his rear-view mirror and saw two of Angela's neighbours racing each other to her door, desperate for details. She took her time answering the door and, when she did, she refused them entry.

~

Father Mac arrived home wearing a grin the size of the Royal Victoria Hospital. He found Fergal upstairs in his room, lying on the bed, half dozing and half reading. He held up the signed form. Fergal leapt up and jumped up and down on the bed, waving his arms and narrowly missing the lampshade, then he trampolined right onto Father Mac, and they fell on the floor in a heap.'How did you do it? How did you do it? Let me see, let me see!'

They got their coats and drove to the main post office in the city centre. Once inside, Father Mac's collar was a kind of passport in itself. They managed to skip an enormous queue when he explained that Fergal was expected in Rome as soon as he could get there. That was all it took. The security man unhooked a velvet rope and they were shown to a special desk.

Father Mac witnessed the application, handed over twenty-five pounds from the fundraiser kitty, and made doubly sure the passport would be posted to St Bridget's House and not to Walker Street. That was it. Within ten minutes, they were back outside.

Fergal was still in shock. He had believed that neither of his parents would sign anything that would be of benefit to him, but his mother had proved him wrong. He would never forget it. He had to find a way to see her and thank her.

Mrs Mooney made a special celebratory dinner, and they shared a bottle of blood-red Italian wine. Afterwards, Father Mac telephoned Alfredo Moretti and told him the good news. Alfredo was very excited and congratulated Father Mac on his hard work, and reassured Fergal that everything would be ready for his arrival in a little over a month. Suddenly, their lives seemed to be on fast forward – and, as excited as Fergal was, he was also extremely nervous.

The wine had made them both sleepy so they said good night and retired to their separate rooms. Fergal's asthma woke him early; he was breathing as though a gale was blowing through his tight lungs. He sucked at his inhaler and began to breathe normally again, then he looked at himself in the bedroom mirror and said, 'Ah, Jesus, Flynn, don't tell me you're allergic to Italian wine?'

He got into the shower and let the water run over the top of his head like a warm waterfall. For a few precious moments, he was able to think about nothing and nobody.

As he stepped out to towel himself dry, Father Mac knocked at the door. 'Leave the water running for me, will you?' Fergal wrapped a towel around himself and opened the door. Father Mac shyly stepped out of his bathrobe and into the shower as quickly as he could. As the steam rose and the water collided with his waking body, he began singing to Fergal from behind the shower curtain about what a beautiful day it was going to be. Fergal thought about giving up on getting dry, dropping his towel and joining him, but his instinct told him not to.

'I can't believe that I'll have my own passport soon, Dermot. I can't wait!'

Father Mac turned off the water and reached for his bathrobe again. 'Oh, it's all real, Fergal – you're not about to wake up in Walker Street, late for school and exhausted from such a long dream!' That made Fergal smile.

Father Mac went about his duties, and Fergal headed off for a walk into town. People were being stopped and searched at the barrier by the police station and he had to wait in the queue. Prams were turned upside down while kids howled, red-faced and teething in their mothers' arms. Soldiers no older than nineteen searched and questioned men at least twice their age. Fergal passed the time by trying to figure out how best to approach his mother one final time before he left. He knew he couldn't risk going to Walker Street.

Then his heart jumped. Across the road was his brother John, arm in arm with a heavily made-up, bleached-blonde girl. They seemed to be in the middle of an argument and they both looked very unhappy, or very hungover. Fergal wondered whether his imagination was playing tricks, or whether John had gained a fair amount of weight around his belly since the last time they'd seen each other. Then he remembered, Angela had told him John was working in the brewery.

The woman stopped and slapped John hard across the face, shouting, 'John Flynn, you're nothing but a tight, drunken, nasty bastard. Go and fuck yourself!' Then she marched off in the opposite direction. John rose up on the balls of his feet, as if he was going to hit her, but then he realised that people were staring and he shrank back down again, red-faced.

Fergal hid behind a very fat couple who were excitedly telling anyone who would listen that they had saved up and were going into the town to buy a video recorder. 'We love films, so we do. Anything with Clint Eastwood or Paul Newman and you won't get us shifted from that sofa – not until the vodka runs out, anyway!' Fergal watched John from his safe distance and saw how vulnerable he looked, now that he wasn't in familiar territory. Suddenly he felt sorry for him. He wondered what kind of life John would make for himself. How much trouble he would create for himself and for any poor girl stupid enough to marry him and how precisely he would continue the awful Flynn cycle of violence.

Fergal knew he would never have a life like that – never, no matter what happened. He vowed to himself that he would rather die than end up in some dead-end existence, terrified and dulling the terror by getting drunk at every opportunity. As John shuffled off towards the taxi that would take him back home, all Fergal could think about was going forward.

Finally the queue started to move and Fergal was on his way into the city centre. He wandered around City Hall and looked into shop windows. *One day, Fergal Flynn, you're going to have your own money – you're going to be able to go into any shop and buy anything you want! Imagine that…* He thought of the docks, not far away, and remembered the last time he had been there. Father Mac had been right, he realised, in the short space of time since then, his whole life had turned around.

He bought a can of Coke and decided to walk home instead of getting a taxi. As he walked down the Falls Road, he realised he knew it so well that he could have travelled the length of it blind-folded, giving a running commentary on the details of every building. When he reached St Bridget's, he went into the church and lit a single candle. Kneeling in front of it, holding his St Christopher medal, he said a prayer for Noreen and one for his mother.

~

Exactly one week later, a little parcel addressed to Fergal arrived at St Bridget's. Father Mac propped it up against the teapot and Mrs Mooney called Fergal, who was still in a deep sleep. He untangled himself from some forgotten dream, struggled into his clothes and stumbled downstairs, still half asleep but, when Father Mac pointed to the package, his eyes lit up.

He could only stare, unblinking, at the little purple book that meant he could go anywhere in the world for the next ten years. He looked at his picture and wondered what his life would be like in ten years' time. He would be twenty-seven. He thought it sounded ancient until he remembered that Father Mac was about that age – but, sure, that didn't count. Each page of the passport was smooth and new, and he wanted to smell them over and over. Mrs Mooney thought his picture looked lovely – 'All grown up,' she said – and Father Mac made him promise to keep the passport safe in his dresser.

After breakfast, Fergal went straight back upstairs. He sat on the bed and studied his passport for a long time. As he finally put it in the top drawer of his dresser, under a Bible, he thought it was like a precious patch of purple cloth from the robes of the Sligo monks.

The next few weeks melted away. Father Mac arranged Fergal's plane tickets to Rome through the travel agency that the Church always used. Mrs Mooney, for all her resentment of Fergal, kept bursting into tears at very odd moments. She washed the few clothes he had three times over, and one day he caught her ironing his socks. Her efforts touched him and made him uncomfortable, all at once.

And suddenly it was Fergal's last week in Belfast.

Fergal knew that, on Wednesdays, his mother worked at one of her cleaning jobs on the Ormeau Road and finished early – he'd accompanied her there every now and again, if the load of laundry was too heavy for her to manage by herself. It was just after two o'clock when Angela started down the Ormeau Road, pulling her headscarf out of her bag, and heard, 'Mammy!'

She looked up with a start. 'Jesus, our Fergal! What are you doing here? Is something wrong?'

Fergal looked at her little frame. It was hard to think that someone so small could have caused him so much pain. 'Why does something always have to be wrong?'

She looked up at him like a scolded little girl.

'Do you have time to go for a cup of tea somewhere, Mammy? We're not far from town.'

Angela walked beside him towards the city centre. They found a table by the window in a wee café called Lundy's, on the Donegall Road. A waitress with the thinnest eyebrows Fergal had ever seen came over and gave them a menu.

Angela glanced around, keeping her handbag on her lap as if she was about to leave at any second. 'Your da would kill me if he knew I was here.'

Fergal wondered for a second what his mother would have been like if she had never met his father. He hated the fact that she couldn't even relax over a cup of tea with him in case someone she knew saw them and his da found out. As he looked into her little tired face, he realised she had risked life and limb by going to his concert. All of their neighbours had been there and Paddy could easily have heard that she had gone. Fergal had been convinced that Angela hated him – she had beaten him enough times – and he had thought she would refuse to sign the passport form out of pure spite. But she had taken the risk and helped him, when it would have been so easy for her to say no. If his da put two and two together, she would probably end up in hospital. She didn't have a passport herself – she'd only been outside Belfast a few times in her life – now he was off to Rome and she had played an important part in making it happen.

'I didn't want to cause any trouble by coming to Walker Street, Mammy. There's been too much of that already. I just wanted to say… well… thanks. Thanks for signing the form for my passport. I'll never forget it. Look, do you want to see it? Here it is.'

He pulled it out of its new permanent home in his pocket (it was supposed to be in his top drawer at St Bridget's, but he couldn't bear to let it out of his sight), and she unzipped her bag and fished out her National Health glasses to study it. Fergal couldn't believe how much they made her look like Noreen, and he told her before he could stop himself. 'My God, Mammy, you look so much like Granny with them glasses on.'

Angela's eyes flooded, and she found a paper napkin. 'Fergal, I miss her. I didn't think I would, not this much, but I really do. I mean, she was an oul' bitch at times – don't get me started – but I nearly made her dinner the other night. I miss her... I'm nobody's child now.'

'I never thought about it like that.'

She blew her nose and stared at his passport picture for a long time. 'She would've adored to see you at that concert, you know. So would my daddy.'

'What did you think of it? I saw you, you know – just for a second.'

'Fergal, you reminded me of my own daddy, God rest his soul. He sang a wee bit himself, when he thought we couldn't hear him. He was very shy, but he had a lovely voice.'

'I know. Granny told me about the lamppost and all.'

'Did she? Jesus, she probably told you more than she ever told me.'

They sat together in silence as the café filled up. Fergal caught sight of their reflections in the mirror tiles along the opposite wall. There they sat, mother and son. Fergal suddenly saw how much bigger he was than her. He had always thought she was huge, but she wasn't any more.

The waitress was none too pleased when they only ordered tea, but Angela kept her glasses on and started giving out about the prices on the menu. 'Jesus in high heaven, Fergal, do you see how much they want for a sandwich? For fuck's sake, you could buy a whole loaf and a quarter of ham from oul' Da Moore's for that, and still have taxi fare home.'

'Mammy, I leave at the weekend. Father Mac has it all

organised. I'm going to live with my voice teacher's sister, near the centre of Rome.'

'Is that right? Did I tell you Paddy and John are working, and they've steady girlfriends and all?'

Fergal thought of John and his steady girlfriend fighting near the police station, but he kept the memory to himself. 'Yes, Mammy, you told me.'

Fergal paid for the tea and walked Angela back to Castle Street. A black taxi, nearly full, was about to leave.

'See you, then, Mammy.'

'Aye, Fergal.'

All she could do was hug him and step up into the back seat of the taxi. Fergal watched the back of her head disappear and felt a shadow move across his heart. He was glad that he had been able to see her in a different light before he left, but he knew it would be a long time before he saw her again.

As he walked home through the back streets with the passport burning a hole in his pocket, Angela Flynn realised that no one had ever thanked her for anything in her life, until now.

25

The next day, Alfredo Moretti phoned to say that everything was ready at his end. He had arranged for Fergal to have a job at his sister's restaurant where he would start off by washing up in the kitchens until his Italian got good enough for him to work on the floor with the customers. Alfredo reminded Fergal that many great singers had started this way. He had also arranged for an old friend of his, who was a schoolteacher, to tutor him in the language. 'I know it sounds like a lot, Fergal, but you will get used to it. And, above all, it will be fun – I promise! What a singer we are going to help you become.'

Father Mac seemed busier than ever. The phone and the doorbell never stopped ringing, as one needy parishioner after another came looking for him, and in the final few days he and Fergal hardly saw each other. Even at night, which was their only private time, Father Mac would talk about anything but the imminent departure, then he would kiss Fergal on the forehead and head up to bed alone. In his own way, he was trying to let him go. One night Fergal went to his bedroom door, but Father Mac pretended to be in a deep sleep, so Fergal crept back to his own room, deflated.

But on their last night together, Father Mac ordered a Chinese takeaway, and they sat on cushions as he shared out the portions on their plates. He had bought some wine, and as they raised their glasses he made a toast, 'I wish you the very best and only the very best, Fergal, in all the days, weeks, months and years to come.'

Fergal leaned across to him, and all Father Mac could do was surrender his lips. They slept in the same bed that night. Their intimacy was slower and more intense than ever, as they whispered that they would miss each other, that they would always stay in touch. But it all felt very final.

Fergal made Father Mac promise him, over and over again, that he would do his best to visit him in Italy.

'Of course I want to – of course I'll try… But you know it's not my decision. This isn't a nine-to-five job, Fergal. You live here. You see how people ring or come to the door at every hour of the day and night. That's my job.'

Inevitably, lust drowned out logic. They climaxed together for the final time, then lay apart wordlessly, until sleep finally took over their bodies.

~

The next morning, Mrs Mooney was inconsolable. She burnt the toast for the first time in all her years working for the priests. When Fergal had put his packed bag into the boot of the car, she wouldn't come to the front door – she stood in the kitchen, wiping her hands on her apron over and over. Finally she threw her arms around Fergal and pushed a twenty-pound note into his hands.

'Mrs Mooney, I have enough money – I can't take it from you.'

'It's from me and my husband. Light a candle for us when you're passing the Vatican.'

'OK, I will, but I don't know if they're that big.'

She had to stand on tiptoes to reach his forehead with her maternal kiss.

It was early, and the air was bitterly cold. Father Mac had the car engine running to clear the windscreen. They drove through deserted streets towards the mountains and up over Hannaghstown Road, the scenic route to the airport. Father Mac suddenly reached over, took Fergal's hand in his and squeezed it, hard, for a long time.

After being waved on through the army checkpoint, they found a space in the airport car park. At the Departure Desk, Fergal brought out his ticket and his precious passport. He would be changing planes in London, but could check his one bag through all the way to Rome. Father Mac accompanied him as far as a sign that said 'Passengers only beyond this point'.

They looked at each other in silence. At that moment Fergal wanted to kiss Father Mac more than he ever had before, but they had to make do with a long hug and a flow of tears.

As they let go of each other, Father Mac said, 'Oh, I nearly forgot to give you this – just something to remember me by.' He handed him a neatly wrapped packet.

'Dermot, you've given me so much already—'

Father Mac winked. 'Don't open it till you're on your own.'

Then he gave Fergal an envelope with the rest of the money they'd raised. 'Don't forget to put your return ticket somewhere safe when you get there. It's valid for a year, remember. Alfredo and I will sort out the tuition fees, so you're not to worry about any of that. Just work hard, won't you? And mind yourself. Oh, yeah – and have fun too.'

For the fiftieth time that morning, they checked that he had his passport and his ticket and his emergency money and all the right contact numbers. Father Mac had bought him an address book and had insisted he write out all the numbers he might need in his own handwriting so he would definitely be able to read them. Father Mac stood by the security barrier as Fergal walked through the scanner. It squealed. An enormous uniformed man ran an infrared gun over his body, then asked him to take off his St Christopher medal and put it through separately. Once safely through, Fergal turned and waved a final goodbye, then he was gone.

Father Mac went back to the car park and sat in the car with his seatbelt on. He watched the planes taking off overhead. As each one became airborne, he wondered if Fergal was on it. Finally, he blew a kiss skywards, started the engine and drove back to the Belfast morning in a daze. He felt as if someone had died.

Fergal went into the toilet nearest his gate in the departure lounge and sat in one of the cubicles with his head in his hands, weeping in short, concentrated bursts. Then he opened the little package. It held the book of secret love poems that Father Mac's sister had given him when he was ordained. Fergal smiled through his tears as he read the card Father Mac had written: '*FF, these are yours now. Sing with all your heart and know that you have mine. All my love, D x.*'

When he heard his flight being called, he came out of the cubicle, washed his face and headed for the gate.

As the plane took off, he felt light-headed and a bit sick – he tipped his head back and closed his eyes. The nausea subsided, and he opened his eyes and watched through the circular window as Belfast fell further and further away and the clouds got closer and closer, massive pieces of cotton wool waiting to wipe the slate clean.

He thought about the year that had turned his life upside down. A thousand memories fought for his attention – his constant fights with his da, the schizophrenic way Angela had treated him, the way his brothers had tried to grind him down, the way he'd worried about Noreen till the bitter, helpless end – and he suddenly understood that these were what had brought him to this moment. The loss of Noreen still pulled at his heart, but he allowed himself to think that she was somewhere just beyond the clouds that enveloped him, having a blissful time. He thought of Father Mac, dear Father Mac, and wondered what would have become of him if he hadn't met the handsome priest that day, coming into the chapel out of the rain. He remembered how powerless he had felt back then, how he'd thought that his life would never get any better. But it had.

As they gained altitude, Fergal felt the weight of the world slipping away from his shoulders.

At Heathrow, Fergal was stopped by the security men. When they discovered that his previous address had been on Walker

Street just off the Falls Road, they took him to a grey room and made him wait for over an hour while they checked his story and went off with his treasured passport. Fergal began to panic. He told them he had a connecting flight to catch, but the security man just sneered at him. Finally, without explanation, they told him he could go. It was as if Belfast hadn't quite finished punishing him for leaving.

He was convinced that he'd missed his flight to Rome, but he made it to the check-in desk with ten minutes to spare. He nearly phoned Father Mac just to check that he'd got back to St Bridget's but the queues for the phone boxes were ridiculous.

On the plane, he was sandwiched in the middle row beside a young family with a screaming, teething, purple-cheeked baby. As the mother tried to quiet her baby, Fergal's thoughts returned to his own family. He wondered what they were doing and whether they knew he was gone yet. He knew Angela wouldn't have been able to tell any of them that she'd had a farewell cup of tea with him. But the *Andersonstown News* had run a story about the concert, with a glowing review and a photo of Fergal and Father Mac – Mrs Mooney had even pinned it to the cork noticeboard in the kitchen of St Bridget's House. Fergal knew his family must have read it – the *Andersonstown News*, with its large section on local sports, was the only paper that ever got through the door of Walker Street.

'Would you like some lunch?' asked an Italian stewardess.

'No – no, thanks.' Fergal assumed he would have to pay and he knew he should save as much money as possible.

'Are you sure?'

He got embarrassed – he didn't want her to think he was tight with money – and started to get his wallet out. She stopped him, smiling. 'No, no, it is included in the ticket.' Fergal, feeling more foolish, pulled down his tray from the seat in front of him.

The coffee was strong, and all around him he could hear the curious mixture of English and Italian being spoken at once. He thought about Father Mac, getting ready to hear confessions and say evening mass before retiring to the empty house. He tried to read the in-flight magazines, but they were all in Italian. He closed his eyes, thinking that he'd never be able to sleep, but the next thing he heard was the tannoy announcing bilingually that they were about to begin their descent into 'Roma'.

Fergal's stomach felt like he was smuggling a thousand butter-flies. He must have gone a funny colour because the stewardess came over and told him to breathe deeply and lean his head back. He stared out the window as the plane bounced off the tarmac and they were welcomed to Da Vinci Airport.

The weather outside looked incredible. The colours were so strong and bright. Fergal thought the sky was the same shade of powder blue as the carved robes gathering around the Virgin Mary's feet in the vestry of St Bridget's. The plane finally came to a standstill and they filed off down the aluminium stairs, to the sudden heat rising off the tarmac. Fergal squinted, took off his coat and undid the top two buttons of his shirt.

The handsomest security guards in the world directed them to the baggage halls. Fergal's bag was one of the last to appear on the overloaded carousel – he couldn't believe how many cases some people had – and then, just when he thought it was all over, he saw the queue for Customs. After forty-five frustrating min-utes, he reached the Customs official – only to be told he was missing a form and he would need to fill it in and start again at the back of the queue. He tried to explain that someone very important was waiting for him, but the guard didn't seem to know or care what he was saying, he was more interested in the contents of his own cigarette-stained fingernails.

Fergal thought about Alfredo waiting for him, and the panic rose in his chest. Between that and the thin air-conditioning, he had to pull out his inhaler. He made sure he joined a different queue this time and the Customs woman at the desk took pity on him and helped him to fill out the form.

'Why have you come to Rome?' she asked.

'To study to be a singer.'

'With whom?'

'Alfredo Moretti.'

She widened her eyes and laughed, thinking he was joking, then she stopped. 'You mean *the* Alfredo Moretti?'

When he nodded, she whistled and stamped his passport. 'You must be good! Best of luck with your singing!'

And finally, after two hours in Italy, Fergal reached the Arrivals Hall. Da Vinci Airport was as busy as Heathrow. There were hundreds of people waiting for the hundreds of people still stuck in Customs, and he prayed that Alfredo was among them. He walked up and down the hall. There were drivers holding up boards with names that he couldn't even pronounce, but there was no sign of Alfredo. Fergal was convinced he'd given up and gone home.

'Oh, Jesus, I can't do anything fucking right!'

He hadn't meant to say it so loud, and he realised he was standing right beside three nuns who gave him deeply disapproving looks.

He felt in his pocket for his address book. Just as he was about to find a phone and make a reverse-charge call to Alfredo – *like a pathetic idiot*, he thought – he saw a sign saying 'Information Desk'.

Five minutes later, the airport tannoy sounded two notes and a woman announced, first in Italian and then in English, 'Would Mr Moretti, awaiting the arrival of Fergal Flynn from Ireland – that's the arrival of Fergal Flynn – please come to the information desk immediately.'

Fergal waited by the desk. Slowly, out of the babbling jungle of endless human traffic, came a regular tapping sound, growing louder and louder. It was the slow and sure impact of a silver-tipped walking stick on the highly polished floor.

It drew closer and closer, until the final, cushioned tap of recognition fell on Fergal's shoulder. He'd been looking in the wrong direction for far too long. All of a sudden, his future was standing right beside him.

Acknowledgements

Thank Youse!

To all at the Tyrone Guthrie Centre, Annaghmakerrig, past (Bernard and Mary Loughlin) and present (Sheila Pratschke) for invaluable space and coal fires.

This wouldn't be a book without the careful and considered editing skills of Ciara Considine, Eilis French and Claire Rourke. Thank you Breda Purdue and all at Hodder Headline Ireland.

Eamonn McCann, Anita Gibney, Turlough McShane and all at Wonderland in Belfast. Pat McCabe, John Glennon and all at PKF Ryan Glennon & Co, Dublin.

Love
Brian Kennedy

Permission Acknowledgement